THE WOLF LEADER

THE WOLF LEADER

Foreword by Jonathan Maberry

ALEXANDRE DUMAS

Translated by
ALFRED ALLINSON

WFP
WordFire Press

THE WOLF LEADER
Originally published in 1904 in London by Methuen.
This work is in the Public Domain.
Foreword copyright © 2020 Jonathan Maberry

EBook ISBN: 978-1-68057-094-6
Trade Paperback ISBN: 978-1-68057-093-9
Hardcover ISBN: 978-1-68057-095-3

Edited by Tracy Leonard Nakatani
Cover design by Janet McDonald

Published by
WordFire Press, LLC
PO Box 1840
Monument CO 80132
Kevin J. Anderson & Rebecca Moesta, Publishers
WordFire Press eBook Edition 2019
WordFire Press Trade Paperback Edition 2019
WordFire Press Hardcover Edition 2019
Printed in the USA
Join our WordFire Press Readers Group for
sneak previews, updates, new projects, and giveaways.
Sign up at wordfirepress.com

CONTENTS

FOREWORD

JONATHAN MABERRY

Ask most readers about Alexandre Dumas and they'll smile and mention *The Three Musketeers* or *The Count of Monte Cristo*. A few deep divers will talk about *The Corsican Brothers* or *The Prince of Thieves*.

Ask me and now, as when I was a child, the answer will always be *The Wolf-Leader*.

Yes, I was a strange little boy and grew up to be, arguably, a strange adult. My writing bears this out. I write about the things that go bump in the night. Vampires, ghosts, demons, and, yes, werewolves. Been a fan of lycanthropes of all kinds since I was a kid. I blame my grandmother.

Short version is this: Maude Blanche Flavell was born in Alsace-Lorraine. She was forty when she had my mother, and my mom was 41 when I was born in 1958. That meant that my grandmother (we called her Nanny) was born in 1877. In the 19th century, and in rural France. She grew up in an age when spooky stories were much more likely to be believed. Nanny was very much like Luna Lovegood from the Harry Potter books, in that she believed in everything. Absolutely everything. That belief in what she called the "larger world" never went away, which made her both the coolest and the creepiest grandmother ever. When I was a kid, she taught me to read tarot cards, listen for voices on the night wind, search for power stones while on walks through the woods, and to keep a very open mind.

She also encouraged me to read. She sparked that by telling me stories … mostly unnerving, usually involving something weird and bitey. Later, after she began giving me books—novels and short stories—I discovered that some of her stories were her whisper-down-the-lane retellings of classic legends or works of supernatural fiction. This is how I discovered Henry James, Robert W. Chambers, Bram Stoker, Mary Shelley, William Henry Ireland, Sheridan Le Fanu, Edgar Allan Poe, Ambrose Bierce, and many others. Some were translations, such as works by Friedrich von Schiller and Heinrich Zschokke. Names I didn't know then but treasure now.

One of the books she gave me—and I remember well because it was my ninth birthday—was a book written by someone whose name I'd heard of, or at least *seen*—Alexandre Dumas. Less than two months ago the local ABC affiliate in my home-town of Philadelphia played the 1948 Gene Kelly version of *The Three Musketeers*. I was confused. If Dumas was writing books about swashbuckling swordsmen, why was my creepy grand-mother giving me something of his to read?

As it turned out, the book wasn't anything that would have made a vehicle for Gene Kelly. It was a novel about a werewolf.

The Wolf-Leader. Published in France in 1857 and translated for a 1904 British edition. The copy she had was the 1904 edition —long lost to time now, alas. It was not the 1950 American edition that was somewhat butchered by a writer who later became a friend and mentor of mine, L. Sprague de Camp. I read and re-read that novel a dozen times over the years, the last time was a few months prior to my grandmother's death in 1978 at the venerable age of 101. By then the copy was battered and threadbare, with pages held in place by tape. I have no idea what happened to it, or to any of Nanny's books, following her death.

And that's a great loss, because there were other wonderful works of classic horror in her library.

The Wolf-Leader is a remarkable book. Entertaining, thought provoking, and influential. The story itself is clearly influenced by Johann Georg Faust, a real-life alchemist and astrologer whose outrageous life and reputed sins have been famously fictionalized by Christopher Marlowe, Johann Wolfgang von Goethe, and Thomas Mann, among others. In each story a man discontented with what he can humanly achieve strikes an unholy deal with the Devil. In the case of Thibault, the wronged shoemaker of *The Wolf-Leader*, it is revenge rather than knowledge or financial gain that drives him.

I love me a good revenge story, but even more so I enjoy stories with twists, and Thibault's quest for vengeance is in no way a straight line. Things seldom go as planned and more often there are other forces at work in both the natural and supernatural fabric of the story's reality. This is what caught my attention the first time, and on repeated readings over the decades I've found fresh nuances to consider, allowing me to "rediscover" the essential elements of the tale anew.

I read it again before writing this introduction, and since my own life has changed since my last reading, the story was once more different to me. The last time I read it I was still writing nonfiction at night and teaching by day. I hadn't yet shifted gears to become a writer of fiction. Now I'm a full-time writer and, at this writing, working on my 37th novel. I've also written over 150 short stories and hundreds of issues of comic books. That process has changed me on many levels, including substantially deepening my appreciation for a good story well told. I've always loved this book, but I think I love it even more now that, as a novelist, I can see the carpentry of how it was constructed.

I can also see influences of this work on later pieces of fiction. The tragic elements of the werewolf story are vastly different from those of, say, the vampire. Bloodsuckers are more often than not, the true villains of the piece. Sure, there has been a wave of romanticized vampires, including sympathetic takes on Dracula, who was every bit an unredeemable monster in Bram Stoker's original novel. But, historically, vampires are predator creatures who lust but rarely love.

Werewolves, on the other hand, despite being more overtly monstrous and demonstrably violent, are often presented in fiction as cursed and deeply torn. These are characters in whose hearts and minds the human "better half" is at war with their beastly natures. We see that even in early werewolf films such as *The Werewolf of London* and *The Wolf Man*. The thematic homages to *The Wolf-Leader* are obvious to any scholar of the genre, even if in the 21st century Dumas' landmark book is often unfairly omitted from Best Of lists of werewolf literature.

This book echoes through most of the most important works of shapeshifters that followed. Even, dare I say it, *The Strange Case of Dr. Jekyll and Mr. Hyde*, which is a werewolf story in everything but length of hair.

There is a redemptive element of the book that has always touched my heart, and when I did the novelization of the 2010 reimagining of *The Wolfman*, I drew on the influence of this book when exploring the heart and soul of a creature as conflicted and complex as Thibault. That book was my first *New York Times* bestseller, and I owe a great debt of gratitude to Alexandre Dumas for writing a complex and nuanced novel that, upon repeated readings, yields more insight and entertainment even after more than one hundred and sixty years. The novel's themes are timeless and its ability to entertain endless.

Turn the page, then, and enjoy *The Wolf-Leader*. Go on … take a bite.

—Jonathan Maberry
January 2020

PROLOGUE

I

Why, I ask myself, during those first twenty years of my literary life, from 1827 to 1847, did I so rarely turn my eyes and thoughts towards the little town where I was born, towards the woods amid which it lies embowered, and the villages that cluster round it? How was it that during all that time the world of my youth seemed to me to have disappeared, as if hidden behind a cloud, whilst the future which lay before me shone clear and resplendent, like those magic islands which Columbus and his companions mistook for baskets of flowers floating on the sea?

Alas! Simply because during the first twenty years of our life, we have hope for our guide, and during the last twenty, reality.

From the hour when, weary with our journey, we ungird ourselves, and dropping the traveler's staff, sit down by the wayside, we begin to look back over the road that we have traversed; for it is the way ahead that now is dark and misty, and so we turn and gaze into the depths of the past.

Then with the wide desert awaiting us in front, we are astonished, as we look along the path which we have left behind, to catch sight of first one and then another of those delicious oases of verdure and shade, beside which we never thought of lingering for a moment, and which, indeed we had passed by almost without notice.

But, then, how quickly our feet carried us along in those days! We were in such a hurry to reach that goal of happiness, to which no road has ever yet brought any one of us.

It is at this point that we begin to see how blind and ungrateful we have been; it is now that we say to ourselves, if we could but once more come across such a green and wooded resting place, we would stay there for the rest of our lives, would pitch our tent there, and there end our days.

But the body cannot go back and renew its existence, and so memory has to make its pious pilgrimage alone; back to the early days and fresh beginnings of life it travels, like those light vessels that are borne upward by their white sails against the current of a river. Then the body once more pursues its journey; but the body without memory is as the night without stars, as the lamp without its flame ... And so body and memory go their several ways.

The body, with chance for its guide, moves towards the unknown.

Memory, that bright will-o'-the-wisp, hovers over the landmarks that are left behind; and memory, we may be sure, will not lose her way. Every oasis is revisited, every association recalled, and then with a rapid flight she returns to the body that grows ever more and more weary, and like the humming of a bee, like the song of a bird, like the murmur of a stream, tells the tale of all that she has seen.

And as the tired traveler listens, his eyes grow bright again, his mouth smiles, and a light steals over his face. For Providence in kindness, seeing that he cannot return to youth, allows youth to return to him. And ever after he loves to repeat aloud what Memory tells, him in her soft, low voice.

And is our life, then, bounded by a circle like the earth? Do we, unconsciously, continue to walk towards the spot from which we started? And as we travel nearer and nearer to the grave, do we again draw closer, ever closer, to the cradle?

II

I cannot say. But what happened to myself, that much at any rate I know. At my first halt along the road of life, my first glance backwards, I began by relating the tale of Bernard and his uncle Berthelin, then the story of Ange Pitou, his fair fiancé, and of Aunt Angélique; after that I told of Conscience and Mariette; and lastly of Catherine Blum and Father Vatrin.

I am now going to tell you the story of Thibault and his wolves, and of the Lord of Vez. And how, you will ask, did I become acquainted with the events which I am now about to bring before you? I will tell you.

Have you read my memoirs, and do you remember one, by name Mocquet, who was a friend of my father's?

If you have read them, you will have some vague recollection of this personage. If you have not read them, you will not remember anything about him at all.

In either case, then, it is of the first importance that I should bring Mocquet clearly before your mind's eye.

As far back as I can remember, that is when I was about three years of age, we lived, my father and mother and I, in a little Château called Les Fossés, situated on the boundary that separates the departments of Aisne and Oise, between Haramont and Longpré. The little house in question had doubtless been named Les Fossés on account of the deep and broad moat, filled with water, with which it was surrounded.

I do not mention my sister, for she was at school in Paris, and we only saw her once a year, when she was home for a month's holiday.

The household, apart from my father, mother, and myself, consisted—firstly: of a large black dog, called Truffe, who was a privileged animal and made welcome wherever he appeared, more especially as I regularly went about on his back; secondly: of a gardener, named Pierre, who kept me amply provided with frogs and snakes, two species of living creatures in which I was particularly interested; thirdly: of a negro, a valet of my father's, named Hippolyte, a sort of black merry-andrew, whom my father, I believe, only kept that he might be well primed with anecdotes wherewith to gain the advantage in his encounters with Brunel, and beat his wonderful stories; fourthly: of a keeper named Mocquet, for whom I had a great admiration, seeing that he had magnificent stories to tell of ghosts and werewolves, to which I listened every evening, and which were abruptly broken off the instant the General—as my father was usually called— appeared on the scene; fifthly: of a cook, who answered to the name of Marie, but this figure I can no longer recall, it is lost to me in the misty twilight of life; I remember only the name, as given to someone of whom but a shadowy outline remains in my memory, and about whom, as far as I recollect, there was nothing of a very poetic character.

Mocquet, however, is the only person that need occupy our attention for the present. Let me try to make him known to you, both as regards his personal appearance and his character.

III

Mocquet was a man of about forty years of age, short, thick-set, broad of shoulder, and sturdy of leg. His skin was burnt brown by the sun, his eyes were small and piercing, his hair grizzled, and his black whiskers met under his chin in a half circle.

As I look back, his figure rises before me, wearing a three-cornered hat, and clad in a green waistcoat with silver buttons, velveteen cord breeches, and high leathern gaiters, with a game bag over his shoulder, his gun in his hand, and a cutty pipe in his mouth.

Let us pause for a moment to consider this pipe, for this pipe grew to be, not merely an accessory, but an integral part of Mocquet. Nobody could remember ever having seen Mocquet without it. If by any chance Mocquet did not happen to have it in his mouth, he had it in his hand.

This pipe, having to accompany Mocquet into the heart of the thickest coverts, it was necessary that it should be of such a kind as to offer the least possible opportunity to any other solid body of bringing about its destruction; for the destruction of his old, well-colored cutty would have been to Mocquet a loss that years alone could not have repaired.

Therefore the stem of Mocquet's pipe was not more than half-an-inch long; moreover you might always wager that half that half inch at least was supplied by the quill of a feather.

This habit of never being without his pipe, which, by causing the almost entire disappearance of both canines, had hollowed out a sort of vice for itself on the left side of his mouth, between the fourth incisor and the first molar, had given rise to another of Mocquet's habits; this was to speak with his teeth clenched, whereby a certain impression of obstinacy was conveyed by all he said.

This became even more marked if Mocquet chanced at any moment to take his pipe out of his mouth, for there was nothing then to prevent the jaws closing and the teeth coming together in a way which prevented the words passing through them at all except in a sort of whistle, which was hardly intelligible.

Such was Mocquet with respect to outward appearance. In the following pages I will endeavor to give some idea of his intellectual capacity and moral qualities.

IV

Early one morning, before my father had risen, Mocquet walked into his room, and planted himself at the foot of the bed, stiff and upright as a signpost.

"Well, Mocquet," said my father, "what's the matter now?

What gives me the pleasure of seeing you here at this early hour?"

"The matter is, General," replied Mocquet with the utmost gravity, "the matter is that I am nightmared."

Mocquet had, quite unawares to himself, enriched the language with a double verb, both active and passive.

"You are nightmared?" responded my father, raising himself on his elbow. "Dear, dear, that's a serious matter, my poor Mocquet."

"You are right there, General."

And Mocquet took his pipe out of his mouth, a thing he did rarely, and only on the most important occasions.

"And how long have you been nightmared?" continued my father compassionately.

"For a whole week, General."

"And who by, Mocquet?"

"Ah! I know very well who by," answered Mocquet, through his teeth, which were so much the more tightly closed that his pipe was in his hand, and his hand behind his back.

"And may I also know by whom?"

"By Mother Durand, of Haramont, who, as you will have heard, is an old witch."

"No, indeed, I assure you I had no idea of such a thing."

"Ah! But I know it well enough; I've seen her riding past on her broomstick to her Witches' Sabbath."

"You have seen her go by on her broomstick?"

"As plainly as I see you, General; and more than that, she has an old black billy goat at home that she worships."

"And why should she come and nightmare you?"

"To revenge herself on me, because I came upon her once at midnight on the heath of Gondreville, when she was dancing round and round in her devil's circle."

"This is a most serious accusation which you bring against her, my friend; and before repeating to anyone what you have been telling me in private, I think it would be as well if you tried to collect some more proofs."

"Proofs! What more proofs do I want! Does not every soul in the village know that in her youth she was the Mistress of Thibault, the wolf leader?"

"Indeed! I must look carefully into this matter, Mocquet."

"I am looking very carefully into it myself, and she shall pay for it, the old mole!"

Old mole was an expression that Mocquet had borrowed from his friend Pierre, the gardener, who, as he had no worse enemies to deal with than moles, gave the name of mole to everything and everybody that he particularly detested.

V

"I must look carefully into this matter"—these words were not said by my father by reason of any belief he had in the truth of Mocquet's tale about his nightmare; and even the fact of the nightmare being admitted by him, he gave no credence to the idea that it was Mother Durand who had nightmared the keeper. Far from it; but my father was not ignorant of the superstitions of the people, and he knew that belief in spells was still widespread among the peasantry in the country districts.

He had heard of terrible acts of revenge carried out by the victims on some man or woman who they thought had bewitched them, in the belief that the charm would thus be broken; and Mocquet, while he stood denouncing Mother Durand to my father, had had such an accent of menace in his voice, and had given such a grip to his gun, that my father thought it wise to appear to agree with everything he said, in order to gain his confidence and so prevent him doing anything without first consulting him.

So, thinking that he had so far gained an influence over Mocquet, my father ventured to say, "But before you make her pay for it, my good Mocquet, you ought to be quite sure that no one can cure you of your nightmare."

"No one can cure me, General," replied Mocquet in a tone of conviction.

"How! No one able to cure you?"

"No one; I have tried the impossible."

"And how did you try?"

"First of all, I drank a large bowl of hot wine before going to bed."

"And who recommended that remedy? Was it Monsieur Lécosse?"

Monsieur Lécosse was the doctor in repute at Villers-Cotterets.

"Monsieur Lécosse?" exclaimed Mocquet. "No, indeed! What should he know about spells! By my faith, no! It was not Monsieur Lécosse."

"Who was it, then?"

"It was the shepherd of Longpré."

"But a bowl of wine, you dunderhead! Why, you must have been dead drunk."

"The shepherd drank half of it."

"I see; now I understand why he prescribed it. And did the bowl of wine have any effect?"

"Not any, General; she came trampling over my chest that night, just as if I had taken nothing."

"And what did you do next? You were not obliged, I suppose, to limit your efforts to your bowl of hot wine?"

"I did what I do when I want to catch a wily beast."

Mocquet made use of a phraseology which was all his own; no one had ever succeeded in inducing him to say a wild beast; every time my father said wild beast, Mocquet would answer, "Yes, General, I know, a wily beast."

"You still stick to your wily beast, then?" my father said to him on one occasion.

"Yes, General, but not out of obstinacy."

"And why then, may I ask?"

"Because, General, with all due respect to you, you are mistaken about it."

"Mistaken? I? How?"

"Because you ought not to say a wild beast, but a wily beast."

"And what is a wily beast, Mocquet?"

"It is an animal that only goes about at night; that is, an animal that creeps into the pigeon houses and kills the pigeons, like the polecat, or into the chicken houses, to kill the chickens, like the fox; or into the folds, to kill the sheep, like the wolf; it means an animal which is cunning and deceitful, in short, a wily beast."

It was impossible to find anything to say after such a logical definition as this. My father, therefore, remained silent, and Mocquet, feeling that he had gained a victory, continued to call wild beasts, wily beasts, utterly unable to understand my father's obstinacy in continuing to call wily beasts, wild beasts.

So now you understand why, when my father asked him what else he had done, Mocquet answered, "I did what I do when I want to catch a wily beast."

We have interrupted the conversation to give this explanation; but as there was no need of explanation between my father and Mocquet, they had gone on talking, you must understand, without any such break.

VI

"And what is it you do, Mocquet, when you want to catch this animal of yours?" asked my father.

"I set a trarp, General." Mocquet always called a trap a trarp.

"Do you mean to tell me you have set a trap to catch Mother Durand?"

My father had of course said trap; but Mocquet did not like anyone to pronounce words differently from himself, so he went on:

"Just so, General; I have set a trarp for Mother Durand."

"And where have you put your trarp? Outside your door?"

My father, you see, was willing to make concessions.

"Outside my door! Much good that would be! I only know she gets into my room, but I cannot even guess which way she comes."

"Down the chimney, perhaps?"

"There is no chimney, and besides, I never see her until I feel her."

"And you do see her, then?"

"As plainly I see you, General."

"And what does she do?"

"Nothing agreeable, you may be sure; she tramples all over my chest: thud, thud! thump, thump!"

"Well, where have you set your trap, then?"

"The trarp, why, I put it on my own stomach."

"And what kind of a trarp did you use?"

"Oh! A first-rate trarp!"

"What was it?"

"The one I made to catch the gray wolf with, that used to kill M. Destournelles' sheep."

"Not such a first-rate one, then, for the gray wolf ate up your bait, and then bolted."

"You know why he was not caught, General?"

"No, I do not."

"Because it was the black wolf that belonged to old Thibault, the sabot maker."

"It could not have been Thibault's black wolf, for you said yourself just this moment that the wolf that used to come and kill M. Destournelles' sheep was a gray one."

"He is gray now, General; but thirty years ago, when Thibault the sabot maker was alive, he was black; and, to assure you of the truth of this, look at my hair, which was black as a raven's thirty years ago, and now is as gray as the Doctor's."

The Doctor was a cat, an animal of some fame, that you will

find mentioned in my memoirs and known as the Doctor on account of the magnificent fur which nature had given it for a coat.

"Yes," replied my father. "I know your tale about Thibault, the sabot maker; but, if the black wolf is the devil, Mocquet, as you say he is, he would not change color."

"Not at all, General; only it takes him a hundred years to become quite white, and the last midnight of every hundred years, he turns black as a coal again."

"I give up the case, then, Mocquet; all I ask is that you will not tell my son this fine tale of yours, until he is fifteen at least."

"And why, General?"

"Because it is no use stuffing his mind with nonsense of that kind, until he is old enough to laugh at wolves, whether they are white, gray, or black."

"It shall be as you say, General; he shall hear nothing of this matter."

"Go on, then."

"Where had we got to, General?"

"We had got to your trarp, which you had put on your stomach, and you were saying that it was a first-rate trarp."

"By my faith, General, that was a first-rate trarp! It weighed a good ten pounds. What am I saying! Fifteen pounds at least with its chain! I put the chain over my wrist."

"And what happened that night?"

"That night? Why, it was worse than ever! Generally, it was in her leather overshoes she came and kneaded my chest, but that night she came in her wooden sabots."

"And she comes like this …?"

"Every blessed one of God's nights, and it is making me quite thin; you can see for yourself, General, I am growing as thin as a lath. However, this morning I made up my mind."

"And what did you decide upon, Mocquet?"

"Well, then, I made up my mind I would let fly at her with my gun."

"That was a wise decision to come to. And when do you think of carrying it out?"

"This evening, or tomorrow at latest, General."

"Confound it! And just as I was wanting to send you over to Villers-Hellon."

"That won't matter, General. Was it something that you wanted done at once?"

"Yes, at once."

"Very well, then, I can go over to Villers-Hellon. It's not above a few miles, if I go through the wood—and get back here this evening; the journey both ways is only twenty-four miles, and we have covered a few more than that before now out shooting, General."

"That's settled, then; I will write a letter for you to give to M. Collard, and then you can start."

"I will start, General, without a moment's delay."

My father rose, and wrote to M. Collard; the letter was as follows:

My Dear Collard,

    I am sending you that idiot of a
keeper of mine, whom you know; he has
taken into his head that an old woman
nightmares him every night, and, to rid
himself of this vampire, he intends nothing
more nor less than to kill her.
Justice, however, might not look
favorably on this method of his for curing
himself of indigestion, and so I am going
to start him off to you on a pretext of
some kind or other. Will you, also, on
some pretext or other, send him on, as
soon as he gets to you, to Danré, at
Vouty, who will send him on to Dulauloy,
who, with or without pretext, may then,

as far as I care, send him on to the devil?
In short, he must be kept going for a
fortnight at least. By that time we shall
have moved out of here and shall be at
Antilly, and as he will then no longer be
in the district of Haramont, and as his
nightmare will probably have left him on
the way, Mother Durand will be able to
sleep in peace, which I should certainly
not advise her to do if Mocquet were
remaining anywhere in her neighborhood.
He is bringing you six brace of snipe
and a hare, which we shot while out
yesterday on the marshes of Vallue.
A thousand-and-one of my tenderest
remembrances to the fair Herminie, and
as many kisses to the dear little Caroline.
Your friend,
Alex. Dumas.

An hour later Mocquet was on his way, and, at the end of three weeks, he rejoined us at Antilly.

"Well," asked my father, seeing him reappear in robust health, "well, and how about Mother Durand?"

"Well, General," replied Mocquet cheerfully. "I've got rid of the old mole; it seems she has no power except in her own district."

VII

Twelve years had passed since Mocquet's nightmare, and I was now over fifteen years of age. It was the winter of 1817 to 1818; ten years before that date I had lost my father.

We no longer had a Pierre for gardener, a Hippolyte for valet, or a Mocquet for keeper; we no longer lived at the Château of

Les Fossés or in the villa at Antilly, but in the marketplace of Villers-Cotterets, in a little house opposite the fountain, where my mother kept a bureau de tabac, selling powder and shot as well over the same counter.

As you have already read in my memoirs, although still young, I was an enthusiastic sportsman. As far as sport went, however, that is according to the usual acceptation of the word, I had none, except when my cousin, M. Deviolaine, the ranger of the forest at Villers-Cotterets, was kind enough to ask leave of my mother to take me with him. I filled up the remainder of my time with poaching.

For this double function of sportsman and poacher I was well provided with a delightful single-barreled gun, on which was engraved the monogram of the Princess Borghese, to whom it had originally belonged.

My father had given it me when I was a child, and when, after his death, everything had to be sold, I implored so urgently to be allowed to keep my gun, that it was not sold with the other weapons and the horses and carriages.

The most enjoyable time for me was the winter; then the snow lay on the ground, and the birds, in their search for food, were ready to come wherever grain was sprinkled for them. Some of my father's old friends had fine gardens, and I was at liberty to go and shoot the birds there as I liked. So I used to sweep the snow away, spread some grain, and, hiding myself within easy gunshot, fire at the birds, sometimes killing six, eight, or even ten at a time.

Then, if the snow lasted, there was another thing to look forward to—the chance of tracing a wolf to its lair, and a wolf so traced was everybody's property. The wolf, being a public enemy, a murderer beyond the pale of the law, might be shot at by all or anyone, and so, in spite of my mother's cries, who dreaded the double danger for me, you need not ask if I seized my gun, and was first on the spot ready for sport.

The winter of 1817 to 1818 had been long and severe; the

snow was lying a foot deep on the ground, and so hard frozen that it had held for a fortnight past, and still there were no tidings of anything.

Towards four o'clock one afternoon Mocquet called upon us; he had come to lay in his stock of powder. While so doing, he looked at me and winked with one eye. When he went out, I followed.

"What is it, Mocquet?" I asked. "Tell me."

"Can't you guess, Monsieur Alexandre?"

"No, Mocquet."

"You don't guess, then, that if I come and buy powder here from Madame, your mother, instead of going to Haramont for it —in short, if I walk three miles instead of only a quarter that distance, that I might possibly have a bit of a shoot to propose to you?"

"Oh, you good Mocquet! And what and where?"

"There's a wolf, Monsieur Alexandre."

"Not really?"

"He carried off one of M. Destournelles' sheep last night, I have traced him to the Tillet woods."

"And what then?"

"Why then, I am certain to see him again tonight, and shall find out where his lair is, and tomorrow morning we'll finish his business for him."

"Oh, this is luck!"

"Only, we must first ask leave."

"Of whom, Mocquet?"

"Leave of Madame."

"All right, come in, then, we will ask her at once."

My mother had been watching us through the window; she suspected that some plot was hatching between us.

"I have no patience with you, Mocquet," she said, as we went in. "You have no sense or discretion."

"In what way, Madame?" asked Mocquet.

"To go exciting him in the way you do; he thinks too much of sport as it is."

"Nay, Madame, it is with him, as with dogs of breed; his father was a sportsman, he is a sportsman, and his son will be a sportsman after him; you must make up your mind to that."

"And supposing some harm should come to him?"

"Harm come to him with me? With Mocquet? No, indeed! I will answer for it with my own life, that he shall be safe. Harm happen to him, to him, the General's son? Never, never, never!"

But my poor mother shook her head. I went to her and flung my arms round her neck.

"Mother, dearest," I cried, "please let me go."

"You will load his gun for him, then, Mocquet?"

"Have no fear, sixty grains of powder, not a grain more or less, and a twenty to the pound bullet."

"And you will not leave him?"

"I will stay by him like his shadow."

"You will keep him near you?"

"Between my legs."

"I give him into your sole charge, Mocquet."

"And he shall be given back to you safe and sound. Now, Monsieur Alexandre, gather up your traps, and let us be off; your mother has given her permission."

"You are not taking him away this evening, Mocquet."

"I must, Madame, tomorrow morning will be too late to fetch him; we must hunt the wolf at dawn."

"The wolf! It is for a wolf hunt that you are asking for him to go with you?"

"Are you afraid that the wolf will eat him?"

"Mocquet! Mocquet!"

"But when I tell you that I will be answerable for everything!"

"And where will the poor child sleep?"

"With father Mocquet, of course, he will have a good mattress laid on the floor, and sheets white as those which God has spread over the fields, and two good warm coverlids; I promise you that he shall not catch cold."

"I shall be all right, Mother, you may be sure! Now then, Mocquet, I am ready."

"And you don't even give me a kiss, you poor boy, you!"

"Indeed, yes, dear Mother, and a good many more than one!" And I threw myself on my mother's neck, stifling her with my caresses as I clasped her in my arms.

"And when shall I see you again?"

"Oh, do not be uneasy if he does not return before tomorrow evening."

"How, tomorrow evening! And you spoke of starting at dawn!"

"At dawn for the wolf; but if we miss him, the lad must have a shot or two at the wild ducks on the marshes of Vallue."

"I see! You are going to drown him for me!"

"By the name of all that's good, Madame, if I was not speaking to the General's widow, I should say."

"What Mocquet? What would you say?"

"That you will make nothing but a wretched milksop of your boy ... If the General's mother had been always behind him, pulling at his coattails, as you are behind this child, he would never even have had the courage to cross the sea to France."

"You are right, Mocquet! Take him away! I am a poor fool."

And my mother turned aside to wipe away a tear.

A mother's tear, that heart's diamond, more precious than all the pearls of Ophir! I saw it running down her cheek. I ran to the poor woman, and whispered to her, "Mother, if you like, I will stay at home."

"No, no, go, my child," she said. "Mocquet is right; you must, sooner or later, learn to be a man."

I gave her another last kiss; then I ran after Mocquet, who had already started.

After I had gone a few paces, I looked round; my mother

had run into the middle of the road, that she might keep me in sight as long as possible; it was my turn now to wipe away a tear.

"How now?" said Mocquet. "You crying too, Monsieur Alexandre!"

"Nonsense, Mocquet! It's only the cold makes my eyes run."

But Thou, O God, who gavest me that tear, Thou knowest that it was not because of the cold that I was crying.

VIII

It was pitch dark when we reached Mocquet's house. We had a savory omelet and stewed rabbit for supper, and then Mocquet made my bed ready for me. He kept his word to my mother, for I had a good mattress, two white sheets, and two good warm coverlids.

"Now," said Mocquet, "tuck yourself in there, and go to sleep; we may probably have to be off at four o'clock tomorrow morning."

"At any hour you like, Mocquet."

"Yes, I know, you are a capital riser overnight, and tomorrow morning I shall have to throw a jug of cold water over you to make you get up."

"You are welcome to do that, Mocquet, if you have to call me twice."

"Well, we'll see about that."

"Are you in a hurry to go to sleep, Mocquet?"

"Why, whatever do you want me to do at this hour of the night?"

"I thought, perhaps, Mocquet, you would tell me one of those stories that I used to find so amusing when I was a child."

"And who is going to get up for me at two o'clock tomorrow, if I sit telling you tales till midnight? Our good priest, perhaps?"

"You are right, Mocquet."

"It's fortunate you think so!"

So I undressed and went to bed. Five minutes later Mocquet was snoring like a bass viol.

I turned and twisted for a good two hours before I could get to sleep. How many sleepless nights have I not passed on the eve of the first shoot of the season! At last, towards midnight fatigue gained the mastery over me. A sudden sensation of cold awoke me with a start at four o'clock in the morning; I opened my eyes. Mocquet had thrown my bedclothes off over the foot of the bed, and was standing beside me, leaning both hands on his gun, his face beaming out upon me, as, at every fresh puff of his short pipe, the light from it illuminated his features.

"Well, how have you got on, Mocquet?"

"He has been tracked to his lair."

"The wolf? And who tracked him?"

"This foolish old Mocquet."

"Bravo!"

"But guess where he has chosen to take covert, this most accommodating of good wolves!"

"Where was it then, Mocquet?"

"If I gave you a hundred chances you wouldn't guess! In the Three Oaks Covert."

"We've got him, then?"

"I should rather think so."

The Three Oaks Covert is a patch of trees and undergrowth, about two acres in extent, situated in the middle of the plain of Largny, about five hundred paces from the forest.

"And the keepers?" I went on.

"All had notice sent them," replied Mocquet; "Moynat, Mildet, Vatrin, Lafeuille, all the best shots in short, are waiting in readiness just outside the forest. You and I, with Monsieur Charpentier, from Vallue, Monsieur Hochedez, from Largny, Monsieur Destournelles, from Les Fossés, are to surround the Covert; the dogs will be slipped, the field keeper will go with them, and we shall have him, that's certain."

"You'll put me in a good place, Mocquet?"

"Haven't I said that you will be near me; but you must get up first."

"That's true—Brrou!"

"And I am going to have pity on your youth and put a bundle of wood in the fireplace."

"I didn't dare ask for it; but, on my word of honor, it will be kind of you if you will."

Mocquet went out and brought in an armful of wood from the timber yard, and threw it on to the hearth, poking it down with his foot; then he threw a lighted match among the twigs, and in another moment the clear bright flames were dancing and crackling up the chimney. I went and sat on the stool by the fireside, and there dressed myself; you may be sure that I was not long over my grooming; even Mocquet was astonished at my celerity.

"Now, then," he said, "a drop of this, and then off!" And saying this, he filled two small glasses with a yellowish colored liquor, which did not require any tasting on my part to recognize.

"You know I never drink brandy, Mocquet."

"Ah, you are your father's son, all over! What will you have, then?"

"Nothing, Mocquet, nothing."

"You know the proverb: 'Leave the house empty; the devil will be there.' Believe me, you had better put something into your stomach, while I load your gun, for I must keep my promise to that poor mother of yours."

"Well, then, I will have a crust of bread and a glass of pignolet."

Pignolet is a light wine made in non-winegrowing districts, generally said to require three men to drink it, one to drink, and two to hold him; I was, however, pretty well accustomed to pignolet, and could drink it up without help. So I swallowed my glass of wine while Mocquet loaded my gun.

"What are you doing, Mocquet?" I asked him.

"Making a cross on your bullet," he replied. "As you will be near me, we shall probably let fly together, and, although I know you would give me up your share, still, for the glory of it, it will be as well to know which of us killed him, if the wolf falls. So, mind you aim straight."

"I'll do my best, Mocquet."

"Here's your gun, then, loaded for bird shooting; and now, gun over your shoulder, and off we start."

IX

The meeting place was on the road leading to Chavigny. Here we found the keepers and some of the huntsmen, and within another ten minutes those who were missing had also joined us. Before five o'clock struck, our number was complete, and then we held a council of war to decide our further proceedings. It was finally arranged that we should first take up our position round the Three Oaks Covert at some considerable distance from it, and then gradually advance so as to form a cordon round it. Everything was to be done with the utmost silence, it being well known that wolves decamp on hearing the slightest noise. Each of us was ordered to look carefully along the path he followed, to make quite sure that the wolf had not left the covert. Meanwhile the field keeper was holding Mocquet's hounds in leash.

One by one we took our stand facing the covert, on the spot to which our particular path had conducted us. As it happened, Mocquet and I found ourselves on the north side of the warren, which was parallel with the forest.

Mocquet had rightly said that we should be in the best place, for the wolf would in all probability try and make for the forest, and so would break covert on our side of it.

We took our stand, each in front of an oak tree, fifty paces apart from one another, and then we waited, without moving, and hardly daring to breathe. The dogs on the farther side of the warren were now uncoupled; they gave two short barks, and were then silent. The keeper followed them into the covert, calling halloo as he beat the trees with his stick. But the dogs, their eyes starting out of their heads, their lips drawn back, and their coats bristling, remained as if nailed to the ground. Nothing would induce them to move a step further.

"Halloa, Mocquet!" cried the keeper. "This wolf of yours must be an extra plucky one, Rocador and Tombelle refuse to tackle him."

But Mocquet was too wise to make any answer, for the sound of his voice would have warned the wolf that there were enemies in that direction.

The keeper went forward, still beating the trees, the two dogs after him cautiously advancing step by step, without a bark, only now and then giving a low growl.

All of a sudden there was a loud exclamation from the keeper, who called out, "I nearly trod on his tail! The wolf! The wolf! Look out, Mocquet, look out!"

And at that moment something came rushing towards us, and the animal leapt out of the covert, passing between us like a flash of lightning.

It was an enormous wolf, nearly white with age. Mocquet turned and sent two bullets after him; I saw them bound and rebound along the snow.

"Shoot, shoot!" he called out to me.

Only then did I bring my gun to the shoulder; I took aim, and fired; the wolf made a movement as if he wanted to bite his shoulder.

"We have him! We have him!" cried Mocquet. "The lad has hit his mark! Success to the innocent!"

But the wolf ran on, making straight for Moynat and Mildet, the two best shots in the country round.

Both their first shots were fired at him in the open; the second, after he had entered the forest.

The two first bullets were seen to cross one another, and ran along the ground, sending up spurts of snow; the wolf had escaped them both, but he had no doubt been struck down by the others; that the two keepers who had just fired should miss their aim, was an unheard of thing. I had seen Moynat kill seventeen snipe one after the other; I had seen Mildet cut a squirrel in two as he was jumping from tree to tree.

The keepers went into the forest after the wolf; we looked anxiously towards the spot where they had disappeared. We saw them reappear, dejected, and shaking their heads.

"Well?" cried Mocquet interrogatively.

"Bah!" answered Mildet, with an impatient movement of his arm. "He's at Taille-Fontaine by this time."

"At Taille-Fontaine!" exclaimed Mocquet, completely taken aback. "What! The fools have gone and missed him, then!"

"Well, what of that? You missed him yourself, did you not?"

Mocquet shook his head.

"Well, well, there's some devilry about this," he said. "That I should miss him was surprising, but it was perhaps possible; but that Moynat should have shot twice and missed him is not possible, no, I say, no."

"Nevertheless, so it is, my good Mocquet."

"Besides, you, you hit him," he said to me.

"I! ... are you sure?"

"We others may well be ashamed to say it. But as sure as my name is Mocquet, you hit the wolf."

"Well, it's easy to find out if I did hit him, there would be blood on the snow. Come, Mocquet, let us run and see." And suiting the action to the word, I set off running.

"Stop, stop, do not run, whatever you do," cried Mocquet, clenching his teeth and stamping. "We must go quietly, until we know better what we have to deal with."

"Well, we will go quietly, then; but at any rate, let us go!"

Mocquet then began to follow the wolf's track, step by step.

"There's not much fear of losing it," I said.

"It's plain enough."

"Yes, but that's not what I am looking for."

"What are you looking for, then?"

"You will know in a minute or two."

The other huntsmen had now joined us, and as they came along after us, the keeper related to them what had taken place. Meanwhile, Mocquet and I continued to follow the wolf's footprints, which were deeply indented in the snow. At last we came to the spot where he had received my fire.

"There, Mocquet," I said to him. "You see I did miss him after all!"

"How do you know that you missed him?"

"Because there are no blood marks."

"Look for the mark of your bullet, then, in the snow."

I looked to see which way my bullet would have sped if it had not hit the wolf, and then went in that direction; but I tracked for more than a quarter of a mile to no purpose, so I thought I might as well go back to Mocquet. He beckoned to the keepers to approach, and then turning to me, said: "Well, and the bullet?"

"I cannot find it."

"I have been luckier than you, then, for I have found it."

"What, you found it?"

"Right about and come behind me."

I did as I was told, and the huntsmen having come up, Mocquet pointed out a line to them beyond which they were not to pass. The keepers Mildet and Moynat now joined us. "Well?" said Mocquet to them in their turn.

"Missed," they both answered at once.

"I saw you had missed him in the open, but when he had reached covert ...?"

"Missed him there too."

"Are you sure?"

"Both the bullets have been found, each of them in the trunk of a tree."

"It is almost past belief," said Vatrin.

"Yes," rejoined Mocquet. "It is almost past belief, but I have something to show you which is even more difficult to believe."

"Show it us, then."

"Look there, what do you see on the snow?"

"The track of a wolf; what of that?"

"And close to the mark of the right foot—there—what do you see?"

"A little hole."

"Well, do you understand?"

The keepers looked at each other in astonishment.

"Do you understand now?" repeated Mocquet.

"The thing's impossible!" exclaimed the keepers.

"Nevertheless it is so, and I will prove it to you."

And so saying, Mocquet plunged his hand into the snow, felt about a moment or two, and then, with a cry of triumph, pulled out a flattened bullet.

"Why, that's my bullet," I said.

"You recognize it, then?"

"Of course I do, you marked it for me."

"And what mark did I put on it?"

"A cross."

"You see, sirs," said Mocquet.

"Yes, but explain how this happened."

"This is it; he could turn aside the ordinary bullets, but he had no power over the youngster's, which was marked with a cross; it hit him in the shoulder, I saw him make a movement as if to try and bite himself."

"But," I broke in, astonished at the silence and amazement which had fallen on the keepers, "if my bullet hit him in the shoulder, why did it not kill him?"

"Because it was made neither of gold nor of silver, my dear boy; and because no bullets but those that are made of gold or silver can pierce the skin of the devil, or kill those who have made a compact with him."

"But, Mocquet," said the keepers, shuddering, "do you really think ...?"

"Think? Yes, I do! I could swear that we have had to do this morning with Thibault, the sabot maker's wolf."

The huntsman and keepers looked at one another; two or three of them made the sign of the cross; and they all appeared to share Mocquet's opinion, and to know quite well what he meant by Thibault's wolf.

I, alone, knew nothing about it, and therefore asked impatiently, "What is this wolf, and who is this Thibault, the sabot maker?"

Mocquet hesitated before replying, then, "Ah! To be sure!" he exclaimed. "The General told me that I might let you know about it when you were fifteen. You are that age now, are you not?"

"I am sixteen," I replied with some pride.

"Well, then, my dear Monsieur Alexandre, Thibault, the sabot maker's wolf, is the devil. You were asking me last night for a tale, were you not?"

"Yes."

"Come back home with me this morning, then, and I will tell you a tale, and a fine one too."

The keepers and huntsmen shook hands with one another in silence and separated, each going his own way; I went back with Mocquet, who then told me the tale which you shall now hear.

Perhaps you will ask me why, having heard it so long ago, I have not told it before. I can only answer you by saying it has remained hidden away in a drawer of my memory, which has remained closed ever since, and which I only opened again three days ago. I would tell you what induced me to do this, but you might, I fear, find the recital somewhat tedious, and as it would take time, I prefer starting at once upon my tale.

I say my tale; I ought perhaps to call it Mocquet's tale—but, upon my word! When you have been sitting on an egg for thirty-eight years, you may be excused for coming to believe at last that you've laid it yourself!

THE GRAND MASTER OF HIS HIGHNESS'S WOLF HOUNDS

The Seigneur Jean, Baron of Vez, was a hardy and indefatigable sportsman.

If you follow the beautiful valley which runs between Berval and Longpré, you will see, on your left hand, an old tower, which by reason of its isolated position will appear doubly high and formidable to you.

At the present moment it belongs to an old friend of the writer of this tale, and everyone is now so accustomed to its forbidding aspect, that the peasant passing that way in summer has no more fear of seeking shelter from the heat beneath its walls than the martins with their long black wings and shrill cries, and the swallows with their soft chirrupings, have of building their nests under its eaves.

But at the time we are now speaking of, somewhere about 1780, this lordly dwelling of Vez was looked upon with different eyes, and, it must be confessed, it did not then offer so safe a place of retreat. It was a building of the twelfth or thirteenth century, rugged and gloomy, its terrifying exterior having assumed no kindlier aspect as the years rolled by. True, the sentinel with his measured tread and flashing steel cap no longer paced its ramparts, the archer with his shrill sounding horn no longer kept watch and ward on the battlements; true the postern was no longer guarded by true men at arms, ready at the least signal of danger to lower the portcullis and draw up the bridge; but the solitude alone which surrounded this grim giant of granite was sufficient to inspire the feeling of awe-inspiring majesty awakened by all mute and motionless things.

The lord of this old fortress, however, was by no means so much to be dreaded; those who were more intimately acquainted with him than were the peasants, and could do him more justice, asserted that his bark was worse than his bite, and that he caused more fear than harm—that is, among his fellow Christians. With the animals of the forest it was different, for he was avowedly their mortal and implacable enemy.

He was chief wolf hunter to his Royal Highness Louis Philippe of Orleans, the fourth of that name—a post which allowed him to gratify the inordinate passion he had for the chase. Although it was not easy, it was yet possible to bring the baron to listen to reason in other matters; but as regards the chase, if once he had got a fixed idea in his head, nothing would satisfy him until he had carried it out and had achieved his purpose.

His wife, according to report, was the natural daughter of the prince, which, in conjunction with his title of chief wolf hunter, gave him almost absolute power throughout the domains of his illustrious father-in-law, a power which no one dared to contest with him, especially after the remarriage of his royal highness with Madame de Montesson. This had taken place in 1773, since which date he had almost abandoned his castle at Villers-Cotterets for his delightful residence at Bagnolet, where he entertained all the first wits of the day and amused himself with playacting.

And so, whether the sun was shining to rejoice the earth, or the rain was saddening it, whether the winter fields lay hidden beneath a shroud of snow, or the spring had spread her fresh green carpet over the meadows, it was rare, on any day of the year, not to see the great gates of the castle thrown wide open between eight and nine o'clock in the morning, and first the baron come forth, and immediately after him his chief pricker, Marcotte, followed by the other prickers. Then appeared the dogs, coupled and held in leash by the keepers of the hounds, under the superintendence of Engoulevent, who aspired to become a pricker.

Even as the German executioner walks alone, behind the nobles and in front of the citizens, to show that he is the least of the former and the first of the latter, so he walked immediately after the prickers and ahead of the keepers of the hounds, as being the chief of the whippers-in and least of the prickers.

The whole procession filed out of the castle court in full hunting array, with the English horses and the French hounds; twelve horses, and forty dogs.

Before we go any farther, let me say that with these twelve horses and forty dogs the baron hunted every sort of quarry, but more especially the wolf, in order no doubt to do honor to his title.

No further proof will be needed by the genuine sportsman of the fine faith he had in the general quality of his hounds, and in their keenness of scent, than the fact that next to the wolf he gave preference to the boar, then to the red deer, then to the fallow deer, and lastly to the roebuck; finally, if the keepers of the pack failed to sight the animal they had tracked, he uncoupled at random, and went after the first hare that crossed his path. For, as we have already stated, the worthy baron went out hunting every day, and he would sooner have gone for four-and-twenty hours without food or drink, although he was often thirsty, than have spent that time without seeing his hounds run.

But, as everybody knows, however swift the horses, and however keen the dogs, hunting has its bad times as well as its good.

One day, Marcotte came up to where the baron was awaiting him, with a crestfallen expression of countenance.

"How now, Marcotte," asked the baron frowning. "What is the matter this time? I see by your face we are to expect bad sport today."

Marcotte shook his head.

"Speak up, man," continued the baron with a gesture of impatience.

"The matter is, my lord, that the black wolf is about."

"Ah! ah!" exclaimed the baron, his eyes sparkling; for you must know that this made the fifth or sixth time that the worthy baron had started the animal in question, but never once had he been able to get within gunshot of him or to run him down.

"Yes," Marcotte went on, "but the damned beast has employed himself so well all night crossing his track and doubling, that after having traced him over half the forest, I found myself at the place from which I started."

"You think then, Marcotte, that there is no chance of getting near him."

"I am afraid not."

"By all the devils in hell!" exclaimed the Lord of Vez, who had not had his equal in swearing since the mighty Nimrod, "However, I am not feeling well today, and I must have a burst of some kind to get rid of these bad humors. What do you think we can hunt, Marcotte, in place of this damned black wolf?"

"Well, having been so taken up with the wolf," answered Marcotte, "I have not traced any other animal. Will my lord uncouple at random and hunt the first animal that we come across?"

The baron was about to express his willingness to agree to this proposal when he caught sight of little Engoulevent coming towards them cap in hand.

"Wait a moment," he said. "Here comes Engoulevent, who, I fancy, has some advice to give us."

"I have no advice to give to a noble lord like yourself," replied Engoulevent, assuming an expression of humility on his sly and crafty face. "It is, however, my duty to inform you that there is a splendid buck in the neighborhood."

"Let us see your buck, Engoulevent," replied the chief wolf hunter, "and if you are not mistaken about it, there will be a new crown for you."

"Where is this buck of yours?" asked Marcotte. "But look to your skin, if you make us uncouple to no purpose."

"Let me have Matador and Jupiter, and then we shall see." Matador and Jupiter were the finest among the hounds belonging to the Lord of Vez.

And indeed, Engoulevent had not gone a hundred paces with them through the thicket, before, by the lashing of their tails, and their repeated yelping, he knew that they were on the right scent. In another minute or two a magnificent ten-tined stag came into view. Marcotte cried Tally-ho, sounded his horn, and the hunt began, to the great satisfaction of the Lord of Vez, who, although regretting the black wolf, was willing to make the best of a fine buck in its stead.

The hunt had lasted two hours, and the quarry still held on. It had first led its pursuers from the little wood of Haramont to the Chemin du Pendu, and thence straight to the back of Oigny, and it still showed no sign of fatigue; for it was not one of those poor animals of the flat country who get their tails pulled by every wretched terrier.

As it neared the low grounds of Bourg-Fontaine, however, it evidently decided that it was being run rather hard, for it gave up the bolder measures which had hitherto enabled it to keep ahead, and began to double.

Its first maneuver was to go down to the brook which joins the ponds of Baisemont and Bourg, then to walk against stream with the water up to its haunches, for nearly half a mile; it then sprang on to the right bank, back again into the bed of the stream, made another leap to the left, and with a succession of bounds, as vigorous as its failing strength allowed, continued to outdistance its pursuers. But the dogs of my lord baron were not animals to be put out by such trifles as these. Being both saga-cious and well bred, they, of their own accord, divided the task between themselves, half going up stream, and half down, these hunting on the right those on the left, and so effectually that they long put the animal off its changes, for they soon recovered the scent, rallying at the first cry given by one of the pack, and starting afresh on the chase, as ready and eager as if the deer had been only twenty paces in front of them.

And so with galloping of horses, with cry of hounds and blare of horn, the baron and his huntsmen reached the ponds of Saint Antoine, a hundred paces or so from the Confines of Oigny. Between these and the Osier beds stood the hut of Thibault, the sabot maker.

We must pause to give some description of this Thibault, the shoe maker, the real hero of the tale.

You will ask why I, who have summoned kings to appear upon the stage, who have obliged princes, dukes, and barons to play secondary parts in my romances, should take a simple shoe maker for the hero of this tale.

First, I will reply by saying that, in my dear home country of Villers-Cotterets, there are more sabot makers than barons, dukes and princes, and that, as soon as I decided to make the forest the scene of the events I am about to record, I was obliged to choose one of the actual inhabitants of this forest as hero, unless I had wished to represent such fantastic persons as the Incas of Marmontel or the Abencerrages of M. de Florian.

More than that, it is not the author who decides on the subject, but the subject which takes possession of the author, and, good or bad, this particular subject has taken possession of me. I will therefore endeavor to draw Thibault's portrait for you, plain shoe maker as he was, as exactly as the artist paints the portrait which a prince desires to send to his ladylove.

Thibault was a man between twenty-five and twenty-seven years of age, tall, well made, physically robust, but by nature melancholy and sad of heart. This depression of spirits arose from a little grain of envy, which, in spite of himself, perhaps unconsciously to himself, he harbored towards all such of his neighbors as had been more favored by fortune than himself.

His father had committed a fault, a serious one at all times, but more especially in those days of absolutism, when a man was not able to rise above his station as now-a-days, when with sufficient capacity he may attain to any rank. Thibault had been educated above his position; he had been at school under the Abbé Fortier, at Villers-Cotterets, and had learnt to read, write, and cypher; moreover he knew a little Latin, which made him inordinately proud of himself. Thibault had spent a great part of his time in reading, and his books had been chiefly those which were in vogue at the close of the preceding century. But he had not been a sufficiently clever analyst to know how to separate the good from the bad, or rather he had separated what was bad, and swallowed it in large doses, leaving the good to precipitate itself at the bottom of the glass.

At twenty years of age Thibault had certainly had dreams of being something other than a sabot maker. He had, for instance, for a very little while, cast his eyes towards the army. But his comrades who had worn the double livery of king and country, had left the service as they entered it, mere soldiers of the ranks, having failed during five or six years of slavery to obtain promotion, even to the not very exalted grade of corporal.

Thibault had also thought of becoming a sailor. But a career in the navy was as much forbidden to the plebeian as one in the army. Possibly after enduring danger, and storm and battle for fifteen or twenty years, he might be made a boatswain's mate, that was all, besides, it was by no means Thibault's ambition to wear a short vest and sail-cloth trousers, but the blue uniform of the king with red vest and gold epaulettes. He had moreover known of no single case in which the son of a mere shoe maker had become Master of a Frigate, or even Lieutenant. So he was forced to give up all idea of joining the king's Navy.

Thibault would not have minded being a Notary, and at one

time thought of apprenticing himself to the Royal Scrivener, Maître Niquet, as a steppingstone, and of making his way up on the strength of his own legs and with the help of his pen. But supposing him to have risen to the position of head clerk with a salary of a hundred crowns, where was he to find the thirty thousand francs which would be required for the purchase of the smallest village practice.

There was, therefore, no better chance of his becoming a scrivener than of becoming an officer on sea or land. Meanwhile, Thibault's father died, leaving very little ready money. There was about enough to bury him. So he was buried, and this done, there remained some thirty or forty francs over for Thibault.

Thibault knew his trade well; indeed, he was a first-rate workman; but he had no inclination to handle either auger or parer. It ended, therefore, by his leaving all his father's tools in the care of a friend, a remnant of prudence still remaining to him, and selling every vestige of furniture; having thus realized a sum of five hundred and forty livres, he determined to make what was then called the tour of France.

Thibault spent three years in travelling; he did not make his fortune during that time, but he learnt a great many things in the course of his journey of which he was previously ignorant, and acquired certain accomplishments which he had previously been without.

He learned amongst other things that, although it was as well to keep one's word on matters of business with a man, it was no use whatever keeping love vows made to a woman.

So much for his character and habits of mind. As to his external accomplishments, he could dance a jig beautifully, could hold his own at quarterstaff against four men, and could handle the boar spear as cleverly as the best huntsman going. All these things had not a little served to increase Thibault's natural self esteem, and, seeing himself handsomer, stronger, and cleverer than many of the nobles, he would exclaim against Providence, crying, "Why was I not nobly born? Why was not that nobleman yonder born a peasant?"

But as Providence took care not to make any answer to these apostrophés, and as Thibault found that dancing, playing at quarter staff, and throwing the boar spear only fatigued the body, without procuring him any material advantage, he began to turn his thoughts towards his ancient trade, humble though it was, saying to himself, if it enabled the father to live, it would also enable the son. So Thibault went and fetched away his tools; and then, tools in hand, he went to ask permission of the steward of his Royal Highness Louis Philippe of Orleans, to build a hut in the forest, in which to carry on his trade.

He had no difficulty in obtaining this, for the steward knew by experience that his master was a very kind-hearted man, expending as much as two hundred and forty thousand francs a year on the poor; he felt sure, therefore, that one who gave away a sum like this, would be willing to let an honest workman who wished to ply his trade, have thirty or forty feet of ground.

As he had leave to establish himself in whatever part of the forest he liked best, Thibault chose the spot near the osier beds, where the roads crossed, one of the most beautiful parts of the woods, less than a mile from Oigny and about three times that distance from Villers-Cotterets.

The shoemaker put up his workshop, built partly of old planks given him by M. Panisis, who had been having a sale in the neighborhood, and partly of the branches which the steward gave him leave to cut in the forest.

When the building of the hut, which consisted of a bedroom, cozily shut in, where he could work during the winter, and of a lean-to, open to the air, where he could work in the summer, was completed, Thibault began to think of making himself a bed. At first, a layer of fern had to serve for this purpose; but after he had made a hundred pairs of wooden shoes and had sold these to Bedeau, who kept a general shop at Villers-Cotterets, he was able to pay a sufficient deposit to get a mattress, to be paid for in full by the end of three months. The framework of the bed was not difficult to make; Thibault was not the shoe maker he was without being a bit of a carpenter into the bargain, and when this was finished he plaited osiers to take the place of sacking, laid the mattress upon them, and found himself at last with a bed to lie upon.

Little by little came the sheets, and then in their turn the coverlids; the next purchase was a chafing dish, and earthenware pots to cook in, and finally some plates and dishes. Before the year was out Thibault had also made additions to his furniture of a fine oak chest and a fine walnut cupboard, both, like the bed, his own handiwork. All the while he was driving a brisk trade, for none could beat Thibault in turning a block of beech into a pair of shoes, and in converting the odd chips into spoons, salt cellars, and natty little bowls.

He had now been settled in his workshop for three years, that is, ever since his return after the completion of his tour round France, and there was nothing for which anyone could have reproached him during this interval except the failing we have already mentioned—that he was rather more envious of the good fortune of his neighbor than was altogether conducive to the welfare of his soul. But this feeling was as yet so inoffensive, that his confessor had no need to do more than awaken in him a sense of shame for harboring thoughts which had, so far, not resulted in any active crime.

THE SEIGNEUR JEAN AND THE SABOT MAKER

A s already said, the buck began to dodge and double on reaching Oigny, turning and twisting round Thibault's hut, and the weather being fine although the autumn was well advanced, the shoe maker was sitting at his work in his open lean-to. Looking up, he suddenly espied the trembling animal, quivering in every limb, standing a few paces in front of him, gazing at him with intelligent and terrified eyes.

Thibault had been for a long time aware that the hunt was circling around Oigny, at one time drawing near to the village, and then receding, only to draw near again.

There was nothing therefore very surprising to him in the sight of the buck, yet he stayed his hand, although he was busy at work, and contemplated the animal.

"Saint Sabot!" he exclaimed—I should explain, that the festival of Saint Sabot is the wooden-shoe fête—"Saint Sabot! But that is a dainty morsel and would taste as fine, I warrant, as the chamois I ate at Vienne once at the grand banquet of the Jolly Shoe makers of Dauphiné. Lucky folk who can dine on the like every day. I tasted such once, it is now nearly four years ago, and my mouth waters now when I think of it.

"Oh! These lords! These lords! With their fresh meats and their old wines at every meal, while I have to be satisfied with potatoes to eat and water to drink from one week's end to the other; and it is a chance if even on Sunday, I can feast myself with a lump of rusty bacon and an old cabbage, and a glass of pignolet fit to make my old goat stand on her head."

It need scarcely be said, that as soon as Thibault began this monologue, the buck had turned and disappeared. Thibault had finished rounding his periods, and had just declaimed his peroration, when he heard himself roughly accosted in forcible terms:

"Ho, there, you scoundrel! Answer me."

It was the baron, who seeing his dogs wavering, was anxious to make sure that they were not on the wrong scent.

"Ho, there, you scoundrel!" repeated the wolf hunter. "Have you seen the beast?"

There was evidently something in the manner of the baron's questioning which did not please our philosophical shoe maker, for although he was perfectly aware what was the matter, he answered: "What beast?"

"Curse you! Why, the buck we are hunting! He must have passed close by here, and standing gaping as you do, you must have seen him. It was a fine stag of ten, was it not? Which way did he go? Speak up, you blackguard, or you shall have a taste of my stirrup leather!"

"The black plague take him, cub of a wolf!" muttered the shoe maker to himself.

Then, aloud, with a fine air of pretended simplicity, "Ah, yes!" he said. "I did see him."

"A buck, was it not? A ten-tiner, eh? With great horns."

"Ah, yes to be sure, a buck, with great horns,—or great corns, was it? Yes, I saw him as plain as I see you, my lord. But there, I can't say if he had any corns, for I did not look at his feet, anyhow," he added, with the air of a perfect simpleton, "if he had corns, they did not prevent him running."

At any other time the baron would have laughed at what he might have taken for genuine stupidity; but the doublings of the animal were beginning to put him into a regular huntsman's fever.

"Now, then, you scoundrel, a truce to this jesting! If you are in a humor for jokes, it is more than I am!"

"I will be in whatever humor it may please your lordship I should be."

"Well, then, answer me."

"Your lordship has asked me nothing as yet."

"Did the deer seem tired?"

"Not very."

"Which way did he come?"

"He did not come. He was standing still."

"Well, but he must have come from one side or the other."

"Ah! Very likely, but I did not see him come."

"Which way did he go?"

"I would tell you directly; only I did not see him go."

The Lord of Vez cast an angry look at Thibault.

"Is it some while ago the buck passed this way, Master Simpleton?"

"Not so very long, my lord."

"About how long ago?"

Thibault made as if trying to remember; at last he replied:

"It was, I think, the day before yesterday," but in saying this, the shoe maker, unfortunately, could not suppress a grin. This grin did not escape the baron, who, spurring his horse, rode down on Thibault with lifted whip.

Thibault was agile, and with a single bound he reached the shelter of his lean-to, whither the wolf hunter could not follow, as long as he remained mounted; Thibault was therefore in momentary safety.

"You are only bantering and lying!" cried the huntsman. "For there is Marcassino, my best hound, giving cry not twenty yards off, and if the deer passed by where Marcassino is, he must have come over the hedge, and it is impossible, therefore, that you did not see him."

"Pardon, my lord, but according to our good priest, no one but the pope is infallible, and Monsieur Marcassino may be mistaken."

"Marcassino is never mistaken, do you hear, you rascal! And in proof of it I can see from here the marks where the animal scratched up the ground."

"Nevertheless, my lord, I assure you, I swear," said Thibault, who saw the baron's eyebrows contracting in a way that made him feel uneasy.

"Silence, and come here, blackguard!" cried my lord.

Thibault hesitated a moment, but the black look on the sportsman's face became more and more threatening, and fearing to increase his exasperation by disobeying his command, he thought he had better go forward, hoping that the baron merely wished to ask a service of him.

But it was an unlucky move on his part, for scarcely had he emerged from the protection of the shed, before the horse of the Lord of Vez, urged by bit and spur, gave a leap, which brought his rider swooping down upon Thibault, while at the same moment a furious blow from the butt end of the baron's whip fell upon his head.

The shoe maker, stunned by the blow, tottered a moment, lost his balance and was about to fall face downwards, when the baron, drawing his foot out of the stirrup, with a violent kick in the chest, not only straightened him again, but sent the poor wretch flying in an opposite direction, where he fell with his back against the door of his hut.

"Take that!" said the baron, as he first felled Thibault with his whip, and then kicked him. "Take that for your lie, and that for your banter!"

And then, without troubling himself any further about the man, whom he left lying on his back, the Lord of Vez, seeing that the hounds had rallied on hearing Marcassino's cry, gave them a cheery note on his horn, and cantered away.

Thibault lifted himself up, feeling bruised all over, and began feeling himself from head to foot to make sure that no bones were broken.

Having carefully passed his hand over each limb in succession, "That's all right," he said. "There is nothing broken either above or below, I am glad to find. So, my lord baron, that is how you treat people, because you happen to have married a prince's bastard daughter! But let me tell you, my fine fellow, it is not you who will eat the buck you are hunting today; it will be this blackguard, this scoundrel, this simpleton of a Thibault who will eat it. Yes, it shall be I who eat it, that I vow!" cried Thibault, confirming himself more and more in his bold resolution, and it is no use being a man if having once made a vow, one fails to keep it.

So without further delay, Thibault thrust his bill hook into his belt, seized his boar spear, and after listening for a moment to the cry of the hounds to ascertain in which direction the hunt had gone, he ran off with all the speed of which a man's legs are capable to get the start of them, guessing by the curve which the stag and its pursuers were following what would be the straight line to take so as to intercept them.

There were two ways of doing his deed open to Thibault: either to hide himself beside the path which the buck must take and kill him with his boar spear, or else to surprise the animal just as he was being hunted down by the dogs, and collar him there and then.

And as he ran, the desire to revenge himself on the baron for the latter's brutality, was not so uppermost in Thibault's mind as the thoughts of the sumptuous manner in which he would fare for the next month, on the shoulders, the back, and the haunches of the deer, either salted to a turn, roasted on the spit, or cut in slices and done in the pan. And these two ideas, moreover, of vengeance and gluttony, were so jumbled up in his brain, that while still running at the top of his speed he laughed in his sleeve, as he pictured the dejected mien of the baron and his men returning to the castle after their fruitless day's hunt, and at the same time saw himself seated at table, the door securely fastened, and a pint of wine beside him, tête-à-tête with a haunch of the deer, the rich and delicious gravy escaping as the knife returned for a third or fourth cut.

The deer, as far as Thibault could calculate, was making for the bridge which crosses the Ourcq, between Noroy and Troesne. At the time of which we are now speaking there was a bridge spanning the river, formed of two joists and a few planks. As the river was very high and very rapid, Thibault decided that the deer would not attempt to ford it; so he hid himself behind a rock, within reach of the bridge, and waited.

It was not long before he saw the graceful head of the deer appear above the rock at some ten paces' distance; the animal was bending its ears to the wind, in the endeavor to catch the sound of the enemy's approach as it was borne along the breeze. Thibault, excited by this sudden appearance, rose from behind the rock, poised his boar spear and sent it flying towards the animal.

The buck, with a single bound, reached the middle of the bridge, a second carried him on to the opposite bank, and a third bore him out of sight.

The boar spear had passed within a foot of the animal, and had buried itself in the grass fifteen paces from where Thibault was standing.

Never before had he been known to make such an unskillful throw; he, Thibault, of all the company who made the tour of France, the one known to be surest of his aim! Enraged with himself, therefore, he picked up his weapon, and bounded across the bridge with an agility equal to that of the deer.

Thibault knew the country quite as well as the animal he was pursuing, and so got ahead of the deer and once more concealed himself, this time behind a beech tree, halfway up, and not too far from a little footpath.

The deer now passed so close to him, that Thibault hesitated as to whether it would not be better to knock the animal down with his boar spear than to throw the weapon at it; but his hesitation did not last longer than a flash of lightning, for no lightning could be quicker than the animal itself, which was already twenty paces off when Thibault threw his boar spear, but without better luck than the time before.

And now the baying of the hounds was drawing nearer and nearer; another few minutes, and it would, he felt, be impossible for him to carry out his design. But in honor to his spirit of persistence, be it said, that in proportion as the difficulty increased, the greater became Thibault's desire to get possession of the deer.

"I must have it, come what will," he cried. "I must! And if there is a God who cares for the poor, I shall have satisfaction of this confounded baron, who beat me as if I were a dog, but I am a man notwithstanding, and I am quite ready to prove the same to him." And Thibault picked up his boar spear and once more set off running. But it would appear that the good God whom he had just invoked, either had not heard him, or wished to drive him to extremities, for his third attempt had no greater success than the previous ones.

"By Heaven!" exclaimed Thibault. "God Almighty is assuredly deaf, it seems. Let the devil then open his ears and hear me! In the name of God or of the devil, I want you and I will have you, cursed animal!"

Thibault had hardly finished this double blasphemy when the buck, doubling back, passed close to him for the fourth time, and disappeared among the bushes, but so quickly and unexpectedly, that Thibault had not even time to lift his boar spear.

At that moment he heard the dogs so near him, that he

deemed it would be imprudent to continue his pursuit. He looked round him, saw a thickly-leaved oak tree, threw his boar spear into a bush, swarmed up the trunk, and hid himself among the foliage. He imagined, and with good reason, that since the deer had gone ahead again, the hunt would only pass by following on its track. The dogs had not lost the scent, in spite of the quarry's doublings, and they were not likely to lose it now.

Thibault had not been seated among the branches for above five minutes, when first the hounds came into sight, then the baron, who in spite of his fifty-five years, headed the chase as if he had been a man of twenty. It must be added that the Lord of Vez was in a state of rage that we will not even endeavor to describe.

To lose four hours over a wretched deer and still to be running behind it! Such a thing had never happened to him before.

He stormed at his men, he whipped his dogs, and had so ploughed his horse's sides with his spurs, that the thick coating of mud which covered his gaiters was reddened with blood.

On reaching the bridge over the Ourcq, however, there had been an interval of alleviation for the baron, for the hounds had so unanimously taken up the scent, that the cloak which the wolf hunter carried behind him would have sufficed to cover the whole pack as they crossed the bridge.

Indeed the baron was so pleased, that he was not satisfied with humming a tirra-la, but, unslinging his hunting horn he sounded it with his full lung power, a thing which he only did on great occasions.

But, unfortunately, the joy of my Lord of Vez was destined to be short lived.

All of a sudden, just as the hounds, that were crying in concert in a way which more and more delighted the baron's ears, were passing under the tree where Thibault was perched, the whole pack came to a standstill, and every tongue was silenced as by enchantment. Marcotte, at his master's command, dismounted to see if he could find any traces of the deer, the whippers-in ran up, and they and Marcotte looked about, but they could find nothing.

Then Engoulevent, who had set his heart on a view-halloo being sounded for the animal he had tracked down, joined the others, and he too began to search. Everyone was searching, calling out and trying to rouse the dogs, when above all the other voices, was heard, like the blast of a tempest, the voice of the baron.

"Ten thousand devils!" he thundered.

"Have the dogs fallen into a pit hole, Marcotte?"

"No, my lord, they are here, but they are come to a check."

"How! Come to a standstill!" exclaimed the baron.

"What is to be done, my lord? I cannot understand what has happened, but such is the fact."

"Come to a check!" again exclaimed the baron. "Come to a standstill, here, in the middle of the forest. Here where there is no stream where the animal could have doubled, or rock for it to climb. You must be out of your mind, Marcotte!"

"I, out of my mind, my lord?"

"Yes, you, you fool, as truly as your dogs are all worthless trash!"

As a rule, Marcotte bore with admirable patience the insults which the baron was in the habit of lavishing upon everybody about him at critical moments of the chase, but this word trash, applied to his dogs, was more than his habitual long suffering could bear, and drawing himself up to his full height, he answered vehemently, "Trash, my lord? My dogs worthless trash! Dogs that have brought down an old wolf after such a furious run that the best horse in your stable was foundered! My dogs trash!"

"Yes, trash, worthless trash, I say it again, Marcotte. Only trash would stop at a check like that, after hunting one wretched buck so many hours on end."

"My lord," answered Marcotte, in a tone of mingled dignity

and sorrow. "My lord, say that it is my fault, call me a fool, a blockhead, a scoundrel, a blackguard, an idiot; insult me in my own person, or in that of my wife, of my children, and it is nothing to me; but for the sake of all my past services to you, do not attack me in my office of chief pricker, do not insult your dogs."

"How do you account for their silence, then? Tell me that! How do you account for it? I am quite willing to hear what you have to say, and I am listening."

"I cannot explain it any more than you can, my lord; the damned animal must have flown into the clouds or disappeared in the bowels of the earth."

"What nonsense are you talking!" exclaimed the baron. "Do you want to make out that the deer has burrowed like a rabbit, or risen from the ground like a grouse?"

"My lord, I meant it only as a manner of speech. What is a truth, what is the fact, is that there is some witchcraft behind all this. As sure as it is now daylight, my dogs, every one of them, lay down at the same moment, suddenly, without an instant hesitation. Ask anybody who was near them at the time. And now they are not even trying to recover the scent, but there they lie flat on the ground like so many stags in their lair. I ask you, is it natural?"

"Thrash them, man! Thrash them, then," cried the baron. "Flay the skin off their backs; there is nothing like it for driving out the evil spirit."

And the baron was going forward to emphasize with a few blows from his own whip the exorcisms which Marcotte, according to his orders, was distributing among the poor beasts, when Engoulevent, hat in hand, drew near to the baron and timidly laid his hand on the horse's bridle.

"My lord," said the keeper of the kennel, "I think I have just discovered a cuckoo in that tree who may perhaps be able to give us some explanation of what has happened."

"What the devil are you talking about, with your cuckoo, you ape?" said the baron. "If you wait a moment, you scamp, I will teach you how to come chaffing your master like that!"

And the baron lifted his whip. But with all the heroism of a Spartan, Engoulevent lifted his arm above his head as a shield and continued:

"Strike, if you will, my lord, but after that look up into this tree, and when your lordship has seen the bird that is perched among the branches, I think you will be more ready to give me a crown than a blow."

And the good man pointed to the oak tree in which Thibault had taken refuge on hearing the huntsmen approach. He had climbed up from branch to branch and had finally hoisted himself on to the topmost one.

The baron shaded his eyes with his hand, and, looking up, caught sight of Thibault.

"Well, here's something mighty queer!" he cried. "It seems that in the forest of Villers-Cotterets the deer burrow like foxes, and men perch on trees like crows. However," continued the worthy baron, "we will see what sort of creature we have to deal with." And putting his hand to his mouth, he halloed: "Ho, there, my friend! Would it be particularly disagreeable for you to give me ten minutes' conversation?"

But Thibault maintained the most profound silence.

"My lord" said Engoulevent "if you like." and he made a sign to show that he was ready to climb the tree.

"No, no," said the baron, at the same time putting out his hand to hold him back. "Ho, there, my friend!" repeated the baron still without recognizing Thibault. "Will it please you to answer me, yes or no."

He paused a second.

"I see, it is evidently, no; you pretend to be deaf, my friend; wait a moment, and I will get my speaking trumpet," and he held out his hand to Marcotte, who, guessing his intention, handed him his gun.

Thibault, who wished to put the huntsmen on the wrong

scent, was meanwhile pretending to cut away the dead branches, and he put so much energy into this feigned occupation that he did not perceive the movement on the part of the baron, or, if he saw, only took it as a menace, without attaching the importance to it which it merited.

The wolf hunter waited for a little while to see if the answer would come, but as it did not, he pulled the trigger; the gun went off, and a branch was heard to crack.

The branch which cracked was the one on which Thibault was poised; the baron was a fine shot and had broken it just between the trunk and the shoe maker's foot.

Deprived of his support, Thibault fell, rolling from branch to branch. Fortunately the tree was thick, and the branches strong, so that his fall was broken and less rapid than it might have been, and he finally reached the ground, after many rebounds, without further ill consequences than a feeling of great fear and a few slight bruises on that part of his body which had first come in contact with the earth.

"By Beelzebub's horns!" exclaimed the baron, delighted with his own skill. "If it is not my joker of the morning! Ah! So, you scamp! Did the discourse you had with my whip seem too short to you, that you are so anxious to take it up again where we left off?"

"Oh, as to that, I assure you it is not so, my lord," answered Thibault in a tone of the most perfect sincerity.

"So much the better for your skin, my good fellow. Well, and now tell me what you were doing up there, perched on the top of that oak tree?"

"My lord can see himself," answered Thibault, pointing to a few dry twigs lying here and there on the ground. "I was cutting a little dry wood for fuel."

"Ah! I see. Now then, my good fellow, you will please tell us, without any beating about the bush, what has become of our deer."

"By the devil, he ought to know, seeing that he has been perched up there so as not to lose any of its movements," put in Marcotte.

"But I swear, my lord," said Thibault, "that I don't know what it is you mean about this wretched buck."

"Ah, I thought so," cried Marcotte, delighted to divert his master's ill-humour from himself. "He has not seen it, he has not seen the animal at all, he does not know what we mean by this wretched buck! But look. here, my lord, see, the marks on these leaves where the animal has bitten; it was just here that the dogs came to a full stop, and now, although the ground is good to show every mark, we can find no trace of the animal, for ten, twenty, or a hundred paces even?"

"You hear?" said the baron, joining his words on to those of the pricker. "You were up there, and the deer here at your feet. It did not go by like a mouse without making any sound, and you did not see or hear. You must needs have seen or heard it!"

"He has killed the deer," said Marcotte "and hidden it away in a bush. That's as clear as the day."

"Oh, my lord," cried Thibault, who knew better than anybody else how mistaken the pricker was in making this accusation. "My lord, by all the saints in paradise, I swear to you that I have not killed your deer; I swear it to you on the salvation of my soul, and, may I perish on the spot if I have given him even the slightest scratch. And besides, I could not have killed him without wounding him, and if I had wounded him, blood would have flowed; look, I pray you, sir," continued Thibault turning to the pricker "and God be thanked, you will find no trace of blood. I, kill a poor beast! And, my God, with what? Where is my weapon? God knows I have no other weapon than this billhook. Look yourself, my lord."

But unfortunately for Thibault, he had hardly uttered these words, before Maître Engoulevent, who had been prowling about for some minutes past, reappeared, carrying the boar spear which Thibault had thrown into one of the bushes before climbing up the tree.

He handed the weapon to the baron.

There was no doubt about it—Engoulevent was Thibault's evil genius.

❧ 3 ❧

AGNELETTE

The baron took the weapon which Engoulevent handed him, and carefully and deliberately examined the boar spear from point to handle, without saying a word. On the handle had been carved a little wooden shoe, which had served as Thibault's device while making the tour of France, as thereby he was able to recognize his own weapon. The baron now pointed to this, saying to Thibault as he did so:

"Ah, ah, Master Simpleton! There is something which witnesses terribly against you! I must confess this boar spear smells to me uncommonly of venison, by the devil it does! However, all I have now to say to you is this: You have been poaching, which is a serious crime; you have perjured yourself, which is a great sin; I am going to enforce expiation from you for the one and for the other, to help towards the salvation of that soul by which you have sworn."

Whereupon turning to the pricker, he continued: "Marcotte, strip off that rascal's vest and shirt, and tie him up to a tree with a couple of the dog leashes—and then give him thirty-six strokes across the back with your shoulder belt, a dozen for his perjury, and two dozen for his poaching; no, I make a mistake, a dozen for poaching and two dozen for perjuring himself, God's portion must be the largest."

This order caused great rejoicing among the menials, who thought it good luck to have a culprit on whom they could avenge themselves for the mishaps of the day.

In spite of Thibault's protestations, who swore by all the saints in the calendar, that he had killed neither buck, nor doe, neither goat nor kidling, he was divested of his garments and firmly strapped to the trunk of a tree; then the execution commenced.

The pricker's strokes were so heavy that Thibault, who had sworn not to utter a sound, and bit his lips to enable himself to keep his resolution, was forced at the third blow to open his mouth and cry out.

The baron, as we have already seen, was about the roughest man of his class for a good thirty miles round, but he was not hard-hearted, and it was a distress to him to listen to the cries of the culprit as they became more and more frequent. As, however, the poachers on His Highness's estate had of late grown bolder and more troublesome, he decided that he had better let the sentence be carried out to the full, but he turned his horse with the intention of riding away, determined no longer to remain as a spectator.

As he was on the point of doing this, a young girl suddenly emerged from the underwood, threw herself on her knees beside the horse, and lifting her large, beautiful eyes, all wet with tears, to the baron, cried:

"In the name of the God of mercy, my lord, have pity on that man!"

The Lord of Vez looked down at the young girl. She was indeed a lovely child; hardly sixteen years of age, of a slender and exquisite figure, with a pink and white complexion, large blue eyes, soft and tender in expression, and a crown of fair hair, which fell in luxuriant waves over neck and shoulders, escaping from underneath the shabby little gray linen cap, which endeavored in vain to imprison them.

All this the baron took in with a glance, in spite of the humble clothing of the beautiful suppliant, and as he had no dislike to a pretty face, he smiled down on the charming young peasant girl, in response to the pleading of her eloquent eyes.

But, as he looked without speaking, and all the while the blows were still falling, she cried again, with a voice and gesture of even more earnest supplication.

"Have pity, in the name of Heaven, my lord! Tell your servants to let the poor man go, his cries pierce my heart."

"Ten thousand fiends!" cried the Grand Master; "You take a great interest in that rascal over there, my pretty child. Is he your brother?"

"No, my lord."

"Your cousin?"

"No, my lord."

"Your lover?"

"My lover! My lord is laughing at me."

"Why not? If it were so, my sweet girl, I must confess I should envy him his lot."

The girl lowered her eyes.

"I do not know him, my lord, and have never seen him before today."

"Without counting that now she only sees him wrong side before," Engoulevent ventured to put in, thinking that it was a suitable moment for a little pleasantry.

"Silence, sirrah!" said the baron sternly. Then, once more turning to the girl with a smile.

"Really!" he said. "Well, if he is neither a relation nor a lover, I should like to see how far your love for your neighbor will let you go. Come, a bargain, pretty girl!"

"How, my lord?"

"Grace for that scoundrel in return for a kiss."

"Oh! With all my heart!" cried the young girl. "Save the life of a man with a kiss! I am sure that our good Curé himself would say there was no sin in that."

And without waiting for the baron to stoop and take himself what he had asked for, she threw off her wooden shoe, placed her dainty little foot on the tip of the wolf hunter's boot, and taking hold of the horse's mane, lifted herself up with a spring to the level of the face of the hardy huntsman, and there of her own accord offered him her round cheek, fresh, and velvety as the down of an August peach.

The Lord of Vez had bargained for one kiss, but he took two; then, true to his sworn word, he made a sign to Marcotte to stay the execution.

Marcotte was religiously counting his strokes; the twelfth was about to descend when he received the order to stop, and he did not think it expedient to stay it from falling. It is possible that he also thought it would be as well to give it the weight of two ordinary blows, so as to make up good measure and give a thirteenth in; however that may be, it is certain that it furrowed Thibault's shoulders more cruelly than those that went before. It must be added, however, that he was unbound immediately after.

Meanwhile the baron was conversing with the young girl. "What is your name, my pretty one?"

"Georgine Agnelette, my lord, my mother's name! But the country people are content to call me simply Agnelette."

"Ah, that's an unlucky name, my child," said the baron.

"In what way my lord?" asked the girl.

"Because it makes you a prey for the wolf, my beauty. And from what part of the country do you come, Agnelette?"

"From Préciamont, my lord."

"And you come alone like this into the forest, my child? That's brave for a lambkin."

"I am obliged to do it, my lord, for my mother and I have three goats to feed."

"So you come here to get grass for them?"

"Yes, my lord."

"And you are not afraid, young and pretty as you are?"

"Sometimes, my lord, I cannot help trembling."

"And why do you tremble?"

"Well, my lord, I hear so many tales, during the winter evenings, about werewolves, that when I find myself all alone among the trees, and can hear no sound but the west wind, and the branches creaking as it blows through them, I feel a kind of shiver run through me, and my hair seems to stand on end; but when I hear your hunting horn and the dogs crying, then I feel at once quite safe again."

The baron was pleased beyond measure with this reply of the girl's, and stroking his beard complaisantly, he said:

"Well, we give master wolf a pretty rough time of it; but, there is a way, my pretty one, whereby you may spare yourself all these fears and tremblings."

"And how, my lord?"

"Come in future to the castle of Vez; no werewolf, or any other kind of wolf, has ever crossed the moat there, except when slung by a cord onto a hazel-pole."

Agnelette shook her head.

"You would not like to come? And why not?"

"Because I should find something worse there than the wolf."

On hearing this, the baron broke into a hearty fit of laughter, and, seeing their Master laugh, all the huntsmen followed suit and joined in the chorus. The fact was, that the sight of Agnelette had entirely restored the good humor of the Lord of Vez, and he would, no doubt, have continued for some time laughing and talking with Agnelette, if Marcotte, who had been recalling the dogs, and coupling them, had not respectfully reminded my lord that they had some distance to go on their way back to the castle. The baron made a playful gesture of menace with his finger to the girl, and rode off followed by his train.

Agnelette was left alone with Thibault. We have related what

Agnelette had done for Thibault's sake, and also said that she was pretty.

Nevertheless, for all that, Thibault's first thoughts on finding himself alone with the girl, were not for the one who had saved his life, but were given up to hatred and the contemplation of vengeance.

Thibault, as you see, had, since the morning, been making rapid strides along the path of evil.

"Ah! If the devil will but hear my prayer this time," he cried, as he shook his fist, cursing the while, after the retiring hunts-men, who were just out of view. "If the devil will but hear me, you shall be paid back with usury for all you have made me suffer this day, that I swear."

"Oh, how wicked it is of you to behave like that!" said Agnelette, going up to him. "The baron is a kind lord, very good to the poor, and always gently behaved with women."

"Quite so, and you shall see with what gratitude I will repay him for the blows he has given me."

"Come now, frankly, friend, confess that you deserved those blows," said the girl, laughing.

"So, so!" answered Thibault. "The baron's kiss has turned your head, has it, my pretty Agnelette?"

"You, I should have thought, would have been the last person to reproach me with that kiss, Monsieur Thibault. But what I have said, I say again; my lord baron was within his rights."

"What, in belaboring me with blows!"

"Well, why do you go hunting on the estates of these great lords?"

"Does not the game belong to everybody, to the peasant just as much as to the great lords?"

"No, certainly not; the game is in their woods, it is fed on their grass, and you have no right to throw your boar spear at a buck which belongs to my lord the Duke of Orleans."

"And who told you that I threw a boar spear at his buck?"

replied Thibault, advancing towards Agnelette in an almost threatening manner.

"Who told me? Why, my own eyes, which, let me tell you, do not lie. Yes, I saw you throw your boar spear, when you were hidden there, behind the beech tree."

Thibault's anger subsided at once before the straightforward attitude of the girl, whose truthfulness was in such contrast to his falsehood.

"Well, after all," he said, "supposing a poor devil does once in a way help himself to a good dinner from the super abundance of some great lord! Are you of the same mind, Mademoiselle Agnelette, as the judges who say that a man ought to be hanged just for a wretched rabbit? Come now, do you think God created that buck for the baron more than for me?"

"God, Monsieur Thibault, has told us not to covet other men's goods; obey the law of God, and you will not find yourself any the worse off for it!"

"Ah, I see, my pretty Agnelette, you know me then, since you call me so glibly by my name?"

"Certainly I do; I remember seeing you at Boursonnes, on the day of the fête; they called you the beautiful dancer, and stood round in a circle to watch you."

Thibault, pleased with this compliment, was now quite disarmed.

"Yes, yes, of course," he answered. "I remember now having seen you; and I think we danced together, did we not? But you were not so tall then as you are now, that's why I did not recognize you at first, but I recall you distinctly now. And I remember too that you wore a pink frock, with a pretty little white bodice, and that we danced in the dairy. I wanted to kiss you, but you would not let me, for you said that it was only proper to kiss one's vis-á-vis, and not one's partner."

"You have a good memory, Monsieur Thibault!"

"And do you know, Agnelette, that during these last twelve months, for it is a year since that dance, you have not only grown taller, but grown prettier too; I see you are one of those people who understand how to do two things at once."

The girl blushed and lowered her eyes, and the blush and the shy embarrassment only made her look more charming still.

Thibault's eyes were now turned towards her with more marked attention than before, and, in a voice, not wholly free from a slight agitation, he asked:

"Have you a lover, Agnelette?"

"No, Monsieur Thibault," she answered, "I have never had one, and do not wish to have one."

"And why is that? Is Cupid such a bad lad that you are afraid of him?"

"No, not that, but a lover is not at all what I want."

"And what do you want?"

"A husband."

Thibault made a movement, which Agnelette either did not, or pretended not to see.

"Yes," she repeated, "a husband. Grandmother is old and infirm, and a lover would distract my attention too much from the care which I now give her; whereas, a husband, if I found a nice fellow who would like to marry me, a husband would help me to look after her in her old age, and would share with me the task which God has laid upon me, of making her happy and comfortable in her last years."

"But do you think your husband," said Thibault, "would be willing that you should love your grandmother more than you loved him? And do you not think he might be jealous at seeing you lavish so much tenderness upon her?"

"Oh," replied Agnelette, with an adorable smile, "there is no fear of that, for I will manage so as to let him have such a large share of my love and attention that he will have no cause to complain; the kinder and the more patient he is for the dear old thing, the more I shall devote myself to him, the harder shall I work that there may be nothing wanting to our little household. You see me looking small and delicate, and you doubt that I should have strength for this; but I have plenty of spirit and energy for work, and then, when the heart gives consent, one can work day and night without fatigue. Oh! How I should love the man who loved my grandmother! I promise you, that she, and my husband, and I, we should be three happy folks together."

"You mean that you would be three very poor folks together, Agnelette!"

"And do you think the loves and friendships of the rich are worth a farthing more than those of the poor? At times, when I have been loving and caressing my grandmother, Monsieur Thibault, and she takes me on her lap and clasps me in her poor weak trembling arms, and puts her dear old wrinkled face against mine, and I feel my cheek wet with the loving tears she sheds, I begin to cry myself, and, I tell you, Monsieur Thibault, so soft and sweet are my tears, that there is no woman or girl, be she queen or princess, who has ever, I am sure, even in her happiest days, known such a real joy as mine. And, yet, there is no one in all the country round who is so destitute as we two are."

Thibault listened to what Agnelette was saying without answering; his mind was occupied with many thoughts, such thoughts as are indulged in by the ambitious; but his dreams of ambition were disturbed at moments by a passing sensation of depression and disillusionment.

He, the man who had spent hours at a time watching the beautiful and aristocratic dames belonging to the Court of the Duke of Orleans, as they swept up and down the wide entrance stairs; who had often passed whole nights gazing at the arched windows of the Keep at Vez, when the whole place was lit up for some festivity, he, that same man, now asked himself, if what he had so ambitiously desired to have, a lady of rank and a rich dwelling, would, after all, be so much worth possessing as a thatched roof and this sweet and gentle girl called Agnelette. And it was certain that if this dear and charming little woman were to become his, that he would be envied in turn by all the earls and barons in the countryside.

"Well, Agnelette," said Thibault "and suppose a man like myself were to offer himself as your husband, would you accept him?"

It has been already stated that Thibault was a handsome young fellow, with fine eyes and black hair, and that his travels had left him something better than a mere workman. And it must further be borne in mind that we readily become attached to those on whom we have conferred a benefit, and Agnelette had, in all probability, saved Thibault's life; for, under such strokes as Marcotte's, the victim would certainly have been dead before the thirty-sixth had been given.

"Yes," she said. "If it would be a good thing for my grandmother?"

Thibault took hold of her hand.

"Well then, Agnelette," he said, "we will speak again about this, dear child, and that as soon as may be."

"Whenever you like, Monsieur Thibault."

"And you will promise faithfully to love me if I marry you, Agnelette?"

"Do you think I should love any man besides my husband?"

"Never mind, I want you just to take a little oath, something of this kind, for instance; Monsieur Thibault, I swear that I will never love anyone but you."

"What need is there to swear? The promise of an honest girl should be sufficient for an honest man."

"And when shall we have the wedding, Agnelette?" and in saying this, Thibault tried to put his arm round her waist.

But Agnelette gently disengaged herself.

"Come and see my grandmother," she said. "It is for her to decide about it; you must content yourself this evening with helping me up with my load of heath, for it is getting late, and it is nearly three miles from here to Préciamont."

So Thibault helped her as desired, and then accompanied her

on her way home as far as the forest fence of Billemont, that is until they came in sight of the village steeple. Before parting, he so begged of pretty Agnelette to give him one kiss as an earnest of his future happiness, that at last she consented, and then, far more agitated by this one kiss than she had been by the baron's double embrace, Agnelette hastened on her way, in spite of the load which she was carrying on her head, and which seemed far too heavy for so slender and delicate a creature.

Thibault stood for some time looking after her as she walked away across the moor. All the flexibility and grace of her youthful figure were brought into relief as the girl lifted her pretty rounded arms to support the burden upon her head, and thus silhouetted against the dark blue of the sky she made a delightful picture. At last, having reached the outskirts of the village, the land dipping at that point, she suddenly disappeared, passing out of sight of Thibault's admiring eyes.

He gave a sigh, and stood still, plunged in thought; but it was not the satisfaction of thinking that this sweet and good young creature might one day be his that had caused his sigh. Quite the contrary; he had wished for Agnelette, because Agnelette was young and pretty, and because it was part of his unfortunate disposition to long for everything that belonged or might belong to another. His desire to possess Agnelette had been quickened by the innocent frankness with which she had talked to him; but it had been a matter of fancy rather than of any deeper feeling, of the mind, and not of the heart. For Thibault was incapable of loving as a man ought to love, who, being poor himself, loves a poor girl; in such a case there should be no thought, no ambition on his part beyond the wish that his love may be returned.

But it was not so with Thibault; on the contrary, I repeat, the farther he walked away from Agnelette, leaving it would seem his good genius farther behind him with every step, the more urgently did his envious longings begin again as usual to torment his soul. It was dark when he reached home.

✂ 4 ✂

THE BLACK WOLF

T hibault's first thought was to get himself some supper, for he was terribly tired. The past day had been an eventful one for him, and certain things which had happened to him had evidently been calculated to produce a craving for food. The supper, it must be said, was not quite such a savory one as he had promised himself, when starting to kill the buck; but the animal, as we know, had not been killed by Thibault, and the ferocious hunger which now consumed him made his black bread taste almost as delicious as venison.

He had hardly, however, begun his frugal repast, when he became conscious that his goat—of which I think we have already spoken—was uttering the most plaintive bleatings. Thinking that she, too, was in want of her supper, he went into the lean-to for some fresh grass, which he then carried to her, but as he opened the little door of the shed, out she rushed with such precipitancy that she nearly knocked Thibault over, and without stopping to take the provender he had brought her, ran towards the house.

Thibault threw down the bundle of grass and went after her, with the intention of reinstalling her in her proper place; but he found that this was more than he was able to do. He had to use all his force to get her along, for the goat, with all the strength of which a beast of her kind is capable, resisted all his efforts to drag her back by the horns, arching her back, and stubbornly refusing to move. At last, however, being vanquished in the struggle, it ended by the goat being once more shut up in her shed, but, in spite of the plentiful supper which Thibault left her with, she continued to utter the most lamentable cries. Perplexed, and cross at the same time, the shoe maker again rose from his supper and went to the shed, this time opening the door so cautiously that the goat could not escape.

Once inside he began feeling about with his hands in all the nooks and corners to try and discover the cause of her alarm. Suddenly his fingers came in contact with the warm, thick coat of some other animal. Thibault was not a coward, far from it, none the less, he drew back hastily. He returned to the house and got a light, but it almost fell from his hand, when, on reentering the shed, he recognized in the animal that had so frightened the goat, the buck of the Lord of Vez; the same buck that he had followed, had failed to kill, that he had prayed for in the devil's name, if he could not have it in God's; the same that had thrown the hounds out; the very same in short which had cost him such hard blows.

Thibault, after assuring himself that the door was fastened, went gently up to the animal; the poor thing was either so tired, or so tame, that it did not make the slightest attempt to move, but merely gazed out at Thibault with its large dark velvety eyes, rendered more appealing than ever by the fear which agitated it.

"I must have left the door open," muttered the shoe maker to himself. "And the creature, not knowing where to hide itself, must have taken refuge here." But on thinking further over the matter, it came back to him that when he had gone to open the door, only ten minutes before, for the first time, he had found the wooden bolt pushed so firmly into the staple that he had had to get a stone to hammer it back; and then, besides, the goat, which, as we have seen, did not at all relish the society of the newcomer, would certainly have run out of the shed before, if the door had been open. What was, however, still more surprising was that Thibault, looking more closely at the buck, saw that it had been fastened up to the rack by a cord.

Thibault, as we have said, was no coward, but now a cold sweat began to break out in large drops on his brow, a curious kind of a shiver ran through his body, and his teeth chattered violently. He went out of the shed, shutting the door after him, and began looking for his goat, which had taken advantage of the moment when the shoe maker had gone to fetch a light, and ran again into the house, where she was now lying beside the hearth, having evidently quite made up her mind this time not to forsake a resting place, which, for that night at least, she found preferable to her usual abode.

Thibault had a perfect remembrance of the unholy invocation he had addressed to Satan, and although his prayer had been miraculously answered, he still could not bring himself to believe that there was any diabolic intervention in the matter.

As the idea, however, of being under the protection of the spirit of darkness filled him with an instinctive fear, he tried to pray; but when he wished to raise his hand to make the sign of the cross on his forehead, his arm refused to bend, and although up to that time he had never missed a day saying his Ave Maria, he could not remember a single word of it.

These fruitless efforts were accompanied by a terrible turmoil in poor Thibault's brain; evil thoughts came rushing in upon him, and he seemed to hear them whispering all around him, as one hears the murmur of the rising tide, or the laughing of the winter wind through the leafless branches of the trees.

"After all," he muttered to himself, as he sat pale, and staring before him, "the buck is a fine windfall, whether it comes from God or the devil, and I should be a fool not to profit by it. If I am afraid of it as being food sent from the nether regions, I am in no way forced to eat it, and what is more, I could not eat it alone, and if I asked anyone to partake of it with me, I should be betrayed; the best thing I can do is to take the live beast over to the Nunnery of Saint-Rémy, where it will serve as a pet for the Nuns and where the Abbess will give me a good round sum for it. The atmosphere of that holy place will drive the evil out of it, and I shall run no risk to my soul in taking a handful of consecrated crown pieces.

"What days of sweating over my work, and turning my auger, it would take, to earn even the quarter of what I shall get by just leading the beast to its new fold! The devil who helps one is certainly better worth than the angel who forsakes one. If my lord Satan wants to go too far with me, it will then be time enough to free myself from his claws: bless me! I am not a child, nor a young lamb like Georgine, and I am able to walk straight in front of me and go where I like." He had forgotten, unhappy man, as he boasted of being able to go where and how he liked, that only five minutes before he had tried in vain to lift his hand to his head.

Thibault had such convincing and excellent reasons ready to hand, that he quite made up his mind to keep the buck, come whence it might, and even went so far as to decide that the money he received for it should be devoted to buying a wedding dress for his betrothed. For, strange to say, by some freak of memory, his thoughts would keep returning towards Agnelette; and he seemed to see her clad in a long white dress with a crown of white lilies on her head and a long veil. If, he said to himself, he could have such a charming guardian angel in his house, no devil, however strong and cunning he might be, would ever dare to cross the threshold. "So," he went on, "there is always that remedy at hand, and if my lord Satan begins to be too trouble-some, I shall be off to the grandmother to ask for Agnelette; I shall marry her, and if I cannot remember my prayers or am unable to make the sign of the cross, there will be a dear pretty little woman, who has had no traffic with Satan, who will do all that sort of thing for me."

Having more or less reassured himself with the idea of this compromise, Thibault, in order that the buck should not run down in value, and might be as fine an animal as possible to offer to the holy ladies, to whom he calculated to sell it, went and filled the rack with fodder and looked to see that the litter was soft and thick enough for the buck to rest fully at its ease. The remainder of the night passed without further incident, and without even a bad dream.

The next morning, my lord baron again went hunting, but this time it was not a timid deer that headed the hounds, but the wolf which Marcotte had tracked the day before and had again that morning traced to his lair.

And this wolf was a genuine wolf, and no mistake; it must have seen many and many a year, although those who had that morning caught sight of it while on its track, had noted with astonishment that it was black all over. Black or gray, however, it was a bold and enterprising beast, and promised some rough work to the baron and his huntsmen. First started near Verte-feuille, in the Dargent covert, it had made over the plain of Meutard, leaving Fleury and Dampleux to the left, crossed the road to Ferté-Milou, and finally begun to run cunning in the Ivors coppices. Then, instead of continuing in the same direction, it doubled, returning along the same track it had come, and so exactly retracing its own steps, that the baron, as he galloped along, could actually distinguish the prints left by his horse's hoofs that same morning.

Back again in the district of Bourg-Fontaine, he ranged the country, leading the hunt right to the very spot where the misadventures of the previous day had had their start, the vicinity of the shoe maker's hut.

Thibault, we know, had made up his mind what to do in regard to certain matters, and as he intended going over to see Agnelette in the evening, he had started work early.

You will naturally ask why, instead of sitting down to a work which brought in so little, as he himself acknowledged, Thibault did not start off at once to take his buck to the ladies of Saint-Rémy. Thibault took very good care to do nothing of the sort; the day was not the time to be leading a buck through the forest of Villers-Cotterets; the first keeper he met would have stopped him, and what explanation could he have given?

No, Thibault had arranged in his own mind to leave home one evening about dusk to follow the road to the right, then go down the sandpit lane which led into the Chemin du Pendu, and he would then be on the common of Saint-Rémy, only a hundred paces or so from the convent.

Thibault no sooner caught the first sound of the horn and the dogs, than he immediately gathered together a huge bundle of dried heather, which he hastily piled up in front of the shed, where his prisoner was confined, so as to hide the door, in case the huntsmen and their master should halt in front of his hut, as they had the day before. He then sat down again to his work, applying to it an energy unknown even to himself before, bending over the shoe he was making with an intentness which prevented him from even lifting his eyes.

All at once he thought he detected a sound like something scratching at the door; he was just going through from his lean-to to open it when the door fell back, and to Thibault's great astonishment an immense black wolf entered the room, walking on its hind legs. On reaching the middle of the floor, it sat down after the fashion of wolves, and looked hard and fixedly at the sabot maker.

Thibault seized a hatchet which was within reach, and in order to give a fit reception to his strange visitor, and to terrify him, he flourished the weapon above his head.

A curious mocking expression passed over the face of the wolf, and then it began to laugh.

It was the first time that Thibault had ever heard a wolf laugh. He had often heard tell that wolves barked like dogs, but never that they laughed like human beings. And what a laugh it was! If a man had laughed such a laugh, Thibault would verily and indeed have been scared out of his wits.

He brought his lifted arm down again.

"By my lord of the cloven foot," said the wolf, in a full and sonorous voice, "you are a fine fellow! At your request, I send you the finest buck from his royal highness's forests, and in return, you want to split my head open with your hatchet; human gratitude is worthy to rank with that of wolves." On hearing a voice exactly like his own coming forth from a beast's mouth, Thibault's knees began to shake under him, and the hatchet fell out of his hand.

"Now then," continued the wolf, "let us be sensible and talk together like two good friends. Yesterday you wanted the baron's buck, and I led it myself into your shed, and for fear it should escape, I tied it up myself to the rack. And for all this you take your hatchet to me!"

"How should I know who you were?" asked Thibault.

"I see, you did not recognize me! A nice sort of excuse to give."

"Well, I ask you, was it likely I should take you for a friend under that ugly coat?"

"Ugly coat, indeed!" said the wolf, licking his fur with a long tongue as red as blood. "Confound you! You are hard to please. However, it's not a matter of my coat; what I want to know is, are you willing to make me some return for the service I have done you?"

"Certainly," said the shoemaker, feeling rather uncomfortable, "but I ought to know what your demands are. What is it? What do you want? Speak!"

"First of all, and above all things, I should like a glass of water, for those confounded dogs have run me until I am out of breath."

"You shall have it in a moment, my lord wolf."

And Thibault ran and fetched a bowl of fresh, clear water

from a brook which ran some ten paces from the hut. The eager readiness with which he complied with the wolf's request betrayed his feeling of relief at getting out of the bargain so cheaply.

As he placed the bowl in front of the wolf, he made the animal a low bow. The wolf lapped up the contents with evident delight, and then stretched himself on the floor with his paws straight out in front of him, looking like a sphinx.

"Now," he said, "listen to me."

"There is something else you wish me to do?" asked Thibault, inwardly quaking.

"Yes, a very urgent something," replied the wolf. "Do you hear the baying of the dogs?"

"Indeed I do, they are coming nearer and nearer, and in five minutes they will be here."

"And what I want you to do is to get me out of their way."

"Get you out of their way! And how?" cried Thibault, who but too well remembered what it had cost him to meddle with the baron's hunting the day before.

"Look about you. Think. Invent some way of delivering me!"

"The baron's dogs are rough customers to deal with, and you are asking neither more nor less than that I should save your life; for I warn you, if they once get hold of you, and they will probably scent you out, they will make short work of pulling you to pieces. And now supposing I spare you this disagreeable business," continued Thibault, who imagined that he had now got the upper hand, "what will you do for me in return?"

"Do for you in return?" said the wolf. "And how about the buck?"

"And how about the bowl of water?" said Thibault.

"We are quits there, my good sir. Let us start a fresh business altogether; if you are agreeable to it, I am quite willing."

"Let it be so then; tell me quickly what you want of me."

"There are folks," proceeded Thibault, "who might take advantage of the position you are now in, and ask for all kinds of extravagant things, riches, power, titles, and what not, but I am not going to do anything of the kind; yesterday I wanted the buck, and you gave it me, it is true; tomorrow, I shall want something else. For some time past I have been possessed by a kind of mania, and I do nothing but wish first for one thing and then for another, and you will not always be able to spare time to listen to my demands. So what I ask for is, that, as you are the devil in person or someone very like it, you will grant me the fulfilment of every wish I may have from this day forth."

The wolf put on a mocking expression of countenance. "Is that all?" he said. "Your peroration does not accord very well with your exordium."

"Oh!" continued Thibault. "My wishes are honest and moderate ones, and such as become a poor peasant like myself. I want just a little corner of ground, and a few timbers, and planks; that's all that a man of my sort can possibly desire."

"I should have the greatest pleasure in doing what you ask," said the wolf, "but it is simply impossible, you know."

"Then I am afraid you must make up your mind to put up with what the dogs may do to you."

"You think so, and you suppose I have need of your help, and so you can ask what you please?"

"I do not suppose it, I am sure of it."

"Indeed! Well then, look."

"Look where?" asked Thibault.

"Look at the spot where I was," said the wolf. Thibault drew back in horror. The place where the wolf had been lying was empty; the wolf had disappeared, where or how it was impossible to say. The room was intact, there was not a hole in the roof large enough to let a needle through, nor a crack in the floor through which a drop of water could have filtered.

"Well, do you still think that I require your assistance to get out of trouble," said the wolf.

"Where the devil are you?"

"If you put a question to me in my real name," said the wolf with a sneer in his voice, "I shall be obliged to answer you. I am still in the same place."

"But I can no longer see you!"

"Simply because I am invisible."

"But the dogs, the huntsmen, the baron, will come in here after you?"

"No doubt they will, but they will not find me."

"But if they do not find you, they will set upon me."

"As they did yesterday; only yesterday you were sentenced to thirty-six strokes of the strap for having carried off the buck; today, you will be sentenced to seventy-two, for having hidden the wolf, and Agnelette will not be on the spot to buy you off with a kiss."

"Phew! What am I to do?"

"Let the buck loose; the dogs will mistake the scent, and they will get the blows instead of you."

"But is it likely such trained hounds will follow the scent of a deer in mistake for that of a wolf?"

"You can leave that to me," replied the voice. "Only do not lose any time, or the dogs will be here before you have reached the shed, and that would make matters unpleasant, not for me, whom they would not find, but for you, whom they would."

Thibault did not wait to be warned a second time, but was off like a shot to the shed. He unfastened the buck, which, as if propelled by some hidden force, leapt from the house, ran round it, crossing the track of the wolf, and plunged into the Baisemont coppice. The dogs were within a hundred paces of the hut; Thibault heard them with trepidation; the whole pack came full force against the door, one hound after the other.

Then, all at once, two or three gave cry and went off in the direction of Baisemont, the rest of the hounds after them.

The dogs were on the wrong scent; they were on the scent of the buck, and had abandoned that of the wolf.

Thibault gave a deep sigh of relief; he watched the hunt gradually disappearing in the distance, and went back to his room to the full and joyous notes of the baron's horn.

He found the wolf lying composedly on the same spot as before, but how it had found its way in again was quite as impossible to discover as how it had found its way out.

5

THE PACT WITH SATAN

Thibault stopped short on the threshold, overcome with astonishment at this re-apparition.

"I was saying," began the wolf, as if nothing had happened to interrupt the conversation, "that it is out of my power to grant you the accomplishment of all the wishes you may have in future for your own comfort and advancement."

"Then I am to expect nothing from you?"

"Not so, for the ill you wish your neighbor can be carried out with my help."

"And, pray, what good would that do me personally?"

"You fool! Has not a moralist said, 'There is always something sweet to us in the misfortune of our friends—even the dearest.'"

"Was it a wolf said that? I did not know wolves could boast of moralists among their number."

"No, it was not a wolf, it was a man."

"And was the man hanged?"

"On the contrary, he was made Governor of part of Poitou; there are, to be sure, a good many wolves in that province—well then, if there is something pleasant in the misfortune of our best friend, cannot you understand what a subject of rejoicing the misfortune of our worst enemy must be!"

"There is some truth in that, certainly," said Thibault. "Without taking into consideration that there is always an opportunity of profiting by our neighbor's calamity, whether he be friend or foe." Thibault paused for a minute or two to consider before he answered, "By my faith, you are right there, friend wolf, and suppose, then, you do me this service, what shall you expect in exchange? I suppose it will have to be a case of give and take, eh?"

"Certainly. Every time that you express a wish that is not to your own immediate advantage, you will have to repay me with a small portion of your person."

Thibault drew back with an exclamation of fear.

"Oh! Do not be alarmed! I shall not demand a pound of flesh, as a certain Jew of my acquaintance did from his debtor."

"What is it then you ask of me?"

"For the fulfilment of your first wish, one of your hairs; two hairs for the second wish, four for the third, and so on, doubling the number each time."

Thibault broke into a laugh. "If that is all you require, master wolf, I accept on the spot; and I shall try to start with such a comprehensive wish, that I shall never need to wear a wig. So let it be agreed between us!" and Thibault held out his hand.

The black wolf lifted his paw, but he kept it raised.

"Well?" said Thibault.

"I was only thinking," replied the wolf, "that I have rather sharp claws, and, without wishing to do so, I might hurt you badly; but I see a way whereby to clinch the bargain without any damage done to you. You have a silver ring, I have a gold one; let us exchange; the barter will be to your advantage, as you see." And the wolf held out its paw.

Thibault saw a ring of the purest gold shining under the fur of what corresponded to the ring finger, and accepted the bargain without hesitation; the respective rings then changed ownership.

"Good!" said the wolf. "Now we two are married."

"You mean betrothed, master wolf," put in Thibault. "Plague upon you! You go too fast."

"We shall see about that, Master Thibault. And now you go back to your work, and I'll go back to mine."

"Good-bye, my lord wolf."

"Till we meet again, Master Thibault."

The wolf had hardly uttered these last words, on which it had laid an unmistakable emphasis, ere it disappeared like a pinch of lighted gunpowder, and like the gunpowder, left behind a strong smell of sulfur.

Thibault again stood for a moment dumbfounded. He had not yet grown accustomed to this manner of making one's exit, to use a theatrical expression; he looked round him on every side, but the wolf was not there.

At first he thought the whole thing must have been a dream, but, looking down, he saw the devil's ring on the third finger of his right hand; he drew it off and examined it. He saw a monogram engraved on the inner side, and looking more closely, perceived that it was formed of two letters, T. and S.

"Ah!" he exclaimed, in a cold sweat. "Thibault and Satan, the family names of the two contracting parties. So much the worse for me! But when one gives oneself to the devil, one has to do it without reserve."

And Thibault began humming a song, trying to drown his thoughts, but his voice filled him with fear, for there was a new and curious sound in it, even to his own ears. So he fell silent, and went back to his work as a distraction.

He had only just begun, however, to shape his wooden shoe, when, some distance off, from the direction of Baisemont, he again heard the baying of the hounds, and the notes of the baron's horn. Thibault left off working to listen to these various sounds.

"Ah, my fine lord, you may chase your wolf as long as you like; but I can tell you, you won't get this one's paw to nail up over the door of your castle. What a lucky beggar I am! Here am I, almost as good as a magician, and while you ride on, suspecting nothing, my brave dispenser of blows, I have but to say the word, and a spell will be cast over you whereby I shall be amply avenged." And in thinking thus, Thibault suddenly paused.

"And, after all," he went on, "why shouldn't I revenge myself on this damned baron and Master Marcotte? Pshaw! With only a hair at stake I may well gratify myself on this score." And so saying Thibault passed his hand through the thick, silky hair which covered his head like a lion's mane.

"I shall have plenty of hairs left to lose," he continued. "Why bother about one! And, besides, it will be an opportunity for seeing whether my friend the devil has been playing false with me or not. Very well then, I wish a serious accident to befall the baron, and as for that good-for-nothing of a Marcotte, who laid on to me so roughly yesterday, it is only fair that something as bad again should happen to him."

While expressing this double wish, Thibault felt anxious and agitated to the last degree; for in spite of what he had already seen of the wolf's power, he still feared the devil might only have been playing on his credulity. After uttering his wish, he tried in vain to return to his work, he took hold of his parer, wrong side up, and took the skin off his fingers, and still going on with his paring he spoilt a pair of shoes worth a good twelve sous.

As he was lamenting over this misfortune, and wiping the blood off his hand, he heard a great commotion in the direction of the valley; he ran into the Chrétiennelle road and saw a number of men walking slowly two and two in his direction. These men were the prickers and kennelmen of the Lord of Vez. The road they were traversing was about two miles long, so that it was some time before Thibault could distinguish what the men were doing, who were walking as slowly and solemnly as if forming part of a funeral procession. When, however, they got to within five hundred paces of him, he saw that they were carrying two rough litters, on which were stretched two lifeless bodies, those of the baron and of Marcotte. A cold sweat broke out over Thibault's forehead. "Ah!" he exclaimed. "What do I see here?"

What had happened was this:

Thibault's expedient for putting the dogs on the wrong scent had succeeded, and all had gone well as long as the buck remained in covert; but it doubled, when near Marolle, and while crossing the heath passed within ten paces of the baron. The latter thought at first that the animal had been startled by hearing the hounds, and was trying to hide itself.

But at that moment, not more than a hundred paces behind him, the whole pack of hounds appeared, forty dogs, running, yelping, yelling, crying, some in a deep bass like great cathedral bells, others with the full sound of a gong, and again others in a falsetto key, like clarinets out of tune, all giving cry at the top of their voices, as eagerly and merrily as if they had never followed the scent of any other beast.

Then the baron gave way to one of his wild fits of rage, fits only worthy of Polichinello tearing a passion to tatters in a puppet show. He did not shout, he yelled; he did not swear, he cursed. Not satisfied with lashing his dogs, he rode them down, trampling them beneath his horse's hoofs, flinging himself about in his saddle like a devil in a stoup of holy water.

All his maledictions were hurled at his chief pricker, whom he held responsible for the stupid blunder that had occurred. This time Marcotte had not a word to say either in explanation or excuse, and the poor man was terribly ashamed of the mistake his hounds had made, and mighty uneasy at the towering passion into which it had thrown my lord. He made up his mind therefore to do everything in the power of man, if possible more, to repair the one and calm the other, and so started off at full gallop, dashing among the trees and over the brushwood, crying out at the top of his voice, while he slashed right and left with such vigor, that every stroke of his whip cut into the flesh of the poor animals.

"Back, dogs! Back!"

But in vain he rode, and whipped, and called aloud, the dogs only seemed to become more wildly anxious to follow up the new found scent, as if they recognized the buck of the day before, and were determined that their wounded self-esteem should have its revenge. Then Marcotte grew desperate, and determined on the only course that seemed left. The river Ourcq was close by, the dogs were already on the point of crossing the water, and the one chance of breaking up the pack was to get across himself and whip back the dogs as they began to climb the opposite bank. He spurred his horse in the direction of the river, and leaped with it into the very middle of the stream, both horse and rider arriving safely in the water; but, unfortunately, as we have already mentioned, the river just at this time was terribly swollen with the rains, the horse was unable to stand against the violence of the current, and after being swept round two or three times finally disappeared. Seeing that it was useless trying to save his horse, Marcotte endeavored to disengage himself, but his feet were so firmly fixed in the stirrups that he could not draw them out, and three seconds after his horse had disappeared, Marcotte himself was no longer to be seen.

Meanwhile, the baron, with the remainder of the huntsmen, had ridden up to the water's edge, and his anger was in an instant converted into grief and alarm as soon as he became aware of the perilous situation of his pricker; for the Lord of Vez had a sincere love towards those who ministered to his pleasure, whether man or beast. In a loud voice he shouted to his followers: "By all the powers of hell! Save Marcotte! Five and twenty louis, fifty louis, a hundred louis, to anyone who will save him!"

And men and horses, like so many startled frogs, leaped into the water, vying with each other who should be first. The baron was for riding into the river himself, but his henchmen held him back, and so anxious were they to prevent the worthy baron from carrying out his heroic intention, that their affection for their master was fatal to the poor pricker. For one moment he was forgotten, but that last moment meant his death. He appeared once more above the surface, just where the river makes a bend; he was seen to battle against the water, and his face for an instant rose into view, as with one last cry he called to his hounds, "Back! Dogs, back!" But the water again closed over him, stifling the last syllable of the last word, and it was not till a quarter of an hour later that his body was found lying on a little beach of sand on to which the current had washed him. Marcotte was dead; there was no doubt about it!

This accident was disastrous in its effect on the Lord of Vez. Being the noble lord he was, he had somewhat of a liking for good wine; and this predisposed him ever so little to apoplexy, and now, as he came face to face with the corpse of his good servitor, the emotion was so great, that the blood rushed to his head and brought on a fit.

Thibault felt appalled as he realized with what scrupulous exactness the black wolf had fulfilled his part of the contract, and not without a shudder did he think of the right Master Isengrin now had to claim an equal punctuality of payment in return. He began to wonder uneasily whether the wolf, after all, was the kind of being that would continue to be satisfied with a few hairs —and this the more that both at the moment of his wish and during the succeeding minutes during which it was being accomplished, he had not been conscious of the slightest sensation anywhere about the roots of his hair, not even of the least little tickling. He was far from being pleasantly affected by the sight of poor Marcotte's corpse; he had not loved him, it was true, and he had felt that he had good reason for not doing so; but his dislike to the defunct had never gone so far as to make him wish for his death, and the wolf had certainly gone far beyond his desires. At the same time, Thibault had never precisely said what he did wish, and had left the wolf a wide margin for the exercise of his malice; evidently he would have to be more careful in future in stating exactly what he wanted, and above all, more circumspect as regards any wish he might formulate.

As to the baron, although still alive, he was almost as good as dead. From the moment when, as the result of Thibault's wish, he had been struck down as it were by lightning, he had remained unconscious. His men had laid him on the heap of heather which the shoe maker had piled up to hide the door of the shed, and troubled and frightened, were ransacking the place to try and find some restorative which might bring their master back to life. One asked for vinegar to put on his temples, another for a key to put down his back, this one for a bit of board to slap his hands with, that for some sulfur to burn under his nose.

In the midst of all this confusion was heard the voice of little Engoulevent, calling out, "In the name of all that's good, we don't want all this truck, we want a goat. Ah! If only we had a goat!"

"A goat?" cried Thibault, who would have rejoiced to see the baron recover, for it would lift at least part of the burden now weighing on his conscience, and would also rid his dwelling of these marauders. "A goat? I have a goat!"

"Really! You have a goat?" cried Engoulevent. "Oh! My friends! Now our dear master is saved!"

And so overcome with joy was he, that he flung his arms round Thibault's neck, saying, "Bring out your goat, my friend! Bring out your goat!"

Thibault went to the shed and led out the goat, which ran after him bleating.

"Hold it firmly by the horns," said the huntsman, "and lift up one of its front feet." And as he gave the word, the second huntsman drew from its sheath a little knife which he carried in his belt, and began carefully sharpening it on the grindstone which Thibault used for his tools.

"What are you going to do?" asked the shoe maker, feeling somewhat uneasy about these preparations.

"What! Don't you know," said Engoulevent, "that there is a little bone in the shape of a cross inside a goat's heart, which, if crushed into powder, is a sovereign remedy for apoplexy?"

"You intend to kill my goat?" exclaimed Thibault, at the same time leaving hold of the goat's horns, and dropping its foot. "But I will not have it killed."

"Fie, fie!" said Engoulevent. "That is not at all a becoming speech, Monsieur Thibault, would you value the life of our good master as of no more worth than that of your wretched goat? I am truly ashamed for you."

"It's easy for you to talk. This goat is all I have to depend upon, the only thing I possess. She gives me milk, and I am fond of her."

"Ah! Monsieur Thibault, you cannot be thinking of what you are saying—it is fortunate that the baron does not hear you—for he would be broken-hearted to know that his precious life was being bargained for in that miserly way."

"And besides," said one of the prickers with a sneering laugh, "if Master Thibault values his goat at a price which he thinks only my lord can pay, there is nothing to prevent him coming to the castle of Vez to claim this payment. The account can be settled with what was left over as due to him yesterday."

Thibault knew that he could not get the better of these men, unless he again called the devil to his aid; but he had just received such a lesson from Satan, that there was no fear of his exposing himself, at all events for a second time the same day, to similar good offices. His one desire for the time being was not to wish any sort of ill to anyone of those present.

One man dead, another nearly so—Thibault found this lesson enough. Consequently, he kept his eyes turned away from the menacing and jeering countenances around him, for fear of being aggravated beyond control. While his back was turned, the poor goat's throat was cut, her piteous cry alone informing him of the fact; and it was no sooner killed than its heart, which had hardly ceased throbbing, was opened in search of the little bone of which Engoulevent had spoken. This found, it was ground into powder, mixed with vinegar diluted with thirteen drops of gall from the bladder containing it, the whole stirred together in a glass with the cross of a rosary, and then poured gently down the baron's throat, after his teeth had been forced apart with the blade of a dagger.

The effect of the draught was immediate and truly miraculous. The Lord of Vez sneezed, sat up, and said in a voice, intelligible though still a little husky: "Give me something to drink."

Engoulevent handed him some water in a wooden drinking cup, a family possession, of which Thibault was very proud. But the baron had no sooner put his lips to it and become aware of what the vile, abominable liquid was, which they had had the impudence to offer him, than, with an exclamation of disgust, he flung the vessel and its contents violently against the wall, and the cup fell, smashed into a thousand pieces. Then in a loud and sonorous voice, which left no doubt of his perfect recovery, he called out: "Bring me some wine." One of the prickers mounted and rode at full speed to the castle of Oigny, and there requested the lord of the place to give him a flask or two of sound old Burgundy; ten minutes after he was back again. Two bottles were uncorked, and there being no glasses at hand, the baron put them in turn to his mouth, draining each at a single draught.

Then he turned himself round with his face to the wall, and murmuring—Mâcon, 1743—fell into a profound slumber.

6

THE BEDEVILLED HAIR

The huntsmen, being reassured with regard to their master's health, now went in search of the dogs, which had been left to carry on the chase alone. They were found lying asleep, the ground around them stained with blood. It was evident that they had run down the buck and eaten it; if any doubt on the matter remained, it was done away with by the sight of the antlers, and a portion of the jaw bone, the only parts of the animal which they could not crunch up, and which had therefore not disappeared. In short, they were the only ones who had cause to be satisfied with the day's work. The huntsmen, after shutting up the hounds in Thibault's shed, seeing that their master was still sleeping, began to turn their thoughts to getting some supper. They laid hands on everything they could find in the poor wretch's cupboard, and roasted the goat, politely inviting Thibault to take a share in the meal towards the cost of which he had not a little contributed. He refused, giving as a plausible excuse, the great agitation he still was under, owing to Marcotte's death and the baron's accident.

He gathered up the fragments of his beloved drinking cup, and seeing that it was useless to think of ever being able to put it together again, he began turning over in his mind what it might be possible for him to do, so as to free himself from the miserable existence which the events of the last two days had rendered more insupportable than ever.

The first image that appeared to him, was that of Agnelette. Like the beautiful angels that pass before the eyes of children in their dreams, he saw her figure, dressed all in white, with large white wings, floating across a blue sky. She seemed happy and beckoned to him to follow, saying the while "Those who come with me will be very happy."

But the only answer which Thibault vouchsafed to this charming vision was a movement of the head and shoulders, which interpreted, meant, "Yes, yes, Agnelette, I see you, and recognize you; yesterday, it would have been all very well to follow you; but today I am, like a king, the arbiter of life and death, and I am not the man to make foolish concessions to a love only born a day ago, and which has hardly learnt to stammer out its first words. To marry you, my poor child, far from lessening the bitter hardships of our lives, would only double or treble the burden under which we are both borne down. No, Agnelette, no! You would make a charming mistress; but, a wife—she must be in a position to bring money to support the household, equal in proportion to the power which I should contribute."

His conscience told him plainly that he was engaged to marry Agnelette; but he quieted it with the assurance that if he broke the engagement, it would be for the good of that gentle creature.

"I am an upright man," he murmured to himself. "And it is my duty to sacrifice my personal pleasure to the welfare of the dear child. And more than that, she is sufficiently young and pretty and good, to find a better fate than what would await her as the wife of a plain sabot maker." And the end of all these fine reflections was, that Thibault felt himself bound to allow his foolish promises of the day before to melt away into air, and to forget the betrothal, of which the only witnesses had been the quivering leaves of the birch trees, and the pink blossom of the heather. It should be added that there was another mental vision, not wholly irresponsible for the resolution at which Thibault had arrived—the vision of a certain young widow, owner of the mill at Croyolles, a woman between twenty-six and twenty-eight, fresh and plump, with fine, rolling eyes, not devoid of mischief. Moreover, she was credibly supposed to be the richest match in all the country side, for her mill was never idle, and so, for all reasons, as one can clearly see, it was the very thing for Thibault.

Formerly, it would never have occurred to Thibault to aspire to anyone in the position of the rich and beautiful Madame Polet, for such was the name of the owner of the mill; and this will explain why her name is introduced here for the first time. And, in truth, it was the first time that she had ever occurred as a subject of serious consideration to our hero. He was astonished at himself for not having thought of her before, but then, as he said to himself, he had often thought about her, but without hope, while now, seeing that he was under the protection of the wolf, and that he had been endowed with a supernatural power, which he had already had occasion to exercise, it seemed to him an easy matter to get rid of all his rivals and achieve his purpose. True there were evil tongues that spoke of the owner of the mill as having something of an ill temper and a hard heart; but the shoe maker came to the conclusion that, with the devil up his sleeve, he need not trouble himself about any wicked spirit, any petty little second class demon that might find a corner in Widow Polet's disposition. And so, by the time the day broke, he had decided to go to Croyolles, for all these visions had of course visited him during the night.

The Lord of Vez awoke with the first song of the birds; he had entirely recovered from his indisposition of the day before, and woke up his followers with loud slashings of his whip. Having sent off Marcotte's body to Vez, he decided that he would not return home without having killed something, but that he would hunt the boar, just as if nothing out of the way had taken place on the previous day. At last, about six o'clock in the morning, they all went off, the baron assuring Thibault that he was most grateful to him for the hospitality that he himself and his men and dogs had met with under his poor roof, in consideration of which he was quite willing, he swore, to forget all the grievances which he had against the shoe maker.

It will be easily guessed that Thibault experienced little regret at the departure of lord, dogs, and huntsmen. All these having at last disappeared, he stood a few moments contemplating his ransacked home, his empty cupboard, his broken furniture, his empty shed, the ground scattered with fragments of his belongings. But, as he told himself, all this was the ordinary thing to happen whenever one of the great lords went through a place, and the future, as it appeared to him, was far too brilliant to allow him to dwell long on this spectacle. He dressed himself in his Sunday attire, smartening himself as best he could, ate his last bit of bread with the last morsel left of his goat, went to the spring and drank a large glass of water, and started off for Croyolles.

Thibault was determined to try his fortune with Madame Polet before the day was over, and therefore set out about nine o'clock in the morning.

The shortest way to Croyolles was round by the rear of Oigny and Pisseleu. Now Thibault knew every in and out of the forest of Villers-Cotterets as well as any tailor knows the pockets he has made; why, therefore, did he take the Chrétiennelle track, seeing that it lengthened his journey by a good mile and a half? Reader, it was because this lane would bring him near to the spot where he had first seen Agnelette, for, although practical considerations were carrying him in the direction of Croyolles Mill, his heart was drawing him towards Préciamont. And there, as fate would have it, just after crossing the road that runs to La Ferté-Milou, he came upon Agnelette, cutting grass by the wayside for her goats. He might easily have passed her without being seen, for her back was turned towards him; but the evil spirit prompted him, and he went straight up to her. She was stooping to cut the grass with her sickle, but hearing someone approaching she lifted her head, and blushed as she recognized that it was Thibault. With the blush a happy smile rose to her face, which showed that the rising color was not due to any feeling of hostility towards him.

"Ah! There you are," she said. "I dreamt much of you last night, and prayed many prayers for you also." And as she spoke, the vision of Agnelette passing along the sky, with the dress and wings of an Angel, and her hands joined in supplication, as he had seen her the previous night, returned to him.

"And what made you dream of me and pray for me, my pretty child?" asked Thibault with as unconcerned an air as a young lord at Court. Agnelette looked at him with her large eyes of heavenly blue.

"I dreamed of you, Thibault, because I love you," she said. "And I prayed for you, because I saw the accident that happened to the baron and his huntsmen, and all the trouble that you were put to in consequence. Ah! If I had been able to obey the dictates of my heart, I should have run to you at once to give you help."

"It is a pity you did not come; you would have found a merry company, I can tell you."

"Oh! It was not for that I should have liked to be with you, but to be of use to you in receiving the baron and his train. Oh! What a beautiful ring you have, Monsieur Thibault, where did you get it?"

And the girl pointed to the ring which had been given to Thibault by the wolf.

Thibault felt his blood run cold. "This ring?" he said.

"Yes, that ring," and seeing that Thibault appeared unwilling to answer her, Agnelette turned her head aside, and sighed. "A present from some fine lady, I suppose," she said in a low voice.

"There you are mistaken, Agnelette," replied Thibault with all the assurance of a consummate liar. "It is our betrothal ring,

87

the one I have bought to put on your finger the day we are married."

"Why not tell me the truth, Monsieur Thibault?" said Agnelette, shaking her head sadly.

"I am speaking the truth, Agnelette."

"No," and she shook her head more sadly than before.

"And what makes you think that I am telling a lie?"

"Because the ring is large enough to go over two of my fingers." And Thibault's finger would certainly have made two of Agnelette's.

"If it is too large, Agnelette," he said, "we can have it made smaller."

"Goodbye, Monsieur Thibault."

"What! Goodbye?"

"Yes."

"You are going to leave me?"

"Yes, I am going."

"And why, Agnelette?"

"Because I do not love liars."

Thibault tried to think of some vow he could make to reassure Agnelette, but in vain.

"Listen," said Agnelette, with tears in her eyes, for it was not without a great effort of self-control that she was turning away, "if that ring is really meant for me—"

"Agnelette, I swear to you that it is."

"Well then, give it me to keep till our wedding day, and on that day I will give it back to you, that you may have it blessed."

"I will give it you with all my heart," replied Thibault, "but I want to see it on your pretty hand. You were right in saying that it was too large for you, and I am going into Villers-Cotterets today, we will take the measure of your finger, and I will get Monsieur Dugué, the goldsmith there, to alter it for us."

The smile returned to Agnelette's face and her tears were dried up at once. She put out her little hand; Thibault took it between his own, turned it over and looked at it, first on the back and then on the palm, and stooping, kissed it.

"Oh!" said Agnelette "you should not kiss my hand, Monsieur Thibault, it is not pretty enough."

"Give me something else then to kiss."

And Agnelette lifted her face that he might kiss her on the forehead.

"And now," she said joyously, and with childish eagerness, "let me see the ring."

Thibault drew off the ring, and laughing, tried to put it on Agnelette's thumb; but, to his great astonishment, he could not get it over the joint.

"Well, well," he exclaimed "who would ever have thought such a thing?"

Agnelette began to laugh. "It is funny, isn't it!" she said.

Then Thibault tried to pass it over the first finger, but with the same result as when he put it on the thumb. He next tried the middle finger, but the ring seemed to grow smaller and smaller, as if fearing to sully this virgin hand; then the third finger, the same on which he wore it himself, but it was equally impossible to get it on. And as he made these vain attempts to fit the ring, Thibault felt Agnelette's hand trembling more and more violently within his own, while the sweat fell from his own brow, as if he were engaged in the most arduous work; there was something diabolic at the bottom of it, as he knew quite well. At last he came to the little finger and endeavored to pass the ring over it. This little finger, so small and transparent, that the ring should have hung as loosely upon it as a bracelet on one of Thibault's, this little finger, in spite of all Agnelette's efforts, refused to pass through the ring.

"Ah! My God, Monsieur Thibault," cried the child "what does this mean?"

"Ring of the devil, return to the devil!" cried Thibault, flinging the ring against a rock, in the hope that it would be broken. As it struck the rock, it emitted flame; then it rebounded, and in rebounding, fitted itself on to Thibault's finger. Agnelette who saw this strange evolution of the ring, looked at Thibault in horrified amazement. "Well," he said, trying to brave it out, "what is the matter?"

Agnelette did not answer, but as she continued to look at Thibault, her eye grew more and more wild and frightened. Thibault could not think what she was looking at, but slowly lifting her hand and pointing with her finger at Thibault's head, she said, "Oh! Monsieur Thibault, Monsieur Thibault, what have you got there?"

"Where?" asked Thibault.

"There! There!" cried Agnelette, growing paler and paler.

"Well, but where?" cried the shoe maker, stamping with his foot. "Tell me what you see."

But instead of replying, Agnelette covered her face with her hands, and uttering a cry of terror, turned, and fled with all her might.

Thibault, stunned by what had happened, did not even attempt to follow her; he stood rooted to the spot, unable to move or speak, as if thunderstruck. What had Agnelette seen that had alarmed her so? What was it that she pointed to with her finger? Had God branded him, as He branded the first murderer? And why not? Had not he, like Cain, killed a man? And in the last sermon he had heard at Oigny had not the preacher said that all men were brothers? Thibault felt wild with misgivings; what had so terrified Agnelette? That he must find out without delay. At first he thought he would go into the town of Bourg-Fontaine and look at himself in a glass. But then, supposing the fatal mark was upon him, and others, besides Agnelette, were to see it! No, he must think of some other way of finding out. He could, of course, pull his hat over his brow, and run back to Oigny, where he had a fragment of mirror in which he could see himself; but Oigny was a long way off. Then he remembered that only a few paces from where he stood, there was a spring as transparent as crystal, which fed the pond near

Baisemont, and those at Bourg; he would be able to see himself in that as clearly as in the finest mirror from Saint-Gobain.

So Thibault went to the side of the stream and, kneeling down, looked at himself. He saw the same eyes, the same nose, and the same mouth, and not even the slightest little mark upon the forehead—he drew a breath of relief. But still, there must have been something.

Agnelette had certainly not taken fright as she had, for nothing. Thibault bent over closer to the crystal water; and now he saw there was something bright that shone amid the dark curls on his head and fell over his forehead. He leaned closer still—it was a red hair. A red hair, but of a most peculiar red—not sandy colored or carroty; neither of a light shade nor a dark; but a red of the color of blood, with a brightness of the most vivid flame.

Without stopping to consider how a hair of such a phenomenal color could possibly have grown there, he began trying to pull it out. He drew forward the curl where gleamed the terrible red hair, that it might hang over the water, and then taking hold of it carefully between his finger and thumb gave it a violent pull; but the hair refused to come away. Thinking that he had not got sufficient hold of it, he tried another way, winding the hair round his finger and again giving it a vigorous jerk—the hair cut into his fingers but remained as firmly rooted as ever.

Thibault then turned it round two of his fingers and pulled again; the hair lifted a little bit of his scalp, but as to moving, Thibault might as well have tried to move the oak that threw its shady branches across the stream. Thibault began to think that he would do better to continue his walk to Croyolles; after all, as he remarked to himself, the questionable color of a single hair would not hardly upset his plans of marriage.

Nevertheless, the wretched hair caused him a great deal of worry; he could not get it out of his mind. It seemed to dance before his eyes, dazzling him like flames of running fire, until at last, out of all patience, he stamped his foot, exclaiming, "By all the devils in hell! I am not far from home yet, and I'll get the better of this confounded hair somehow." Whereupon he set off running back towards his hut, went in and found his fragment of mirror, got hold of his hair again, seized a carpenter's chisel, placed it so as to cut off the hair as close to the head as possible, and keeping hair and tool in this position, leant over his bench, and dug the chisel down with as much force as possible.

The tool cut deeply into the wood of the bench, but the hair remained intact. He tried the same plan again, only this time he armed himself with a mallet, which he swung over his head and brought down with redoubled blows on the handle of the chisel —but he was as far as ever from carrying out his purpose.

He noticed, however, that there was a little notch in the sharp edge of the chisel, just the width of a hair.

Thibault sighed; he understood now that this hair, the price he had paid in return for his wish, belonged to the black wolf, and he gave up all further attempts to get rid of it.

❦ 7 ❧

THE BOY AT THE MILL

F inding it impossible either to cut off or pull out the accursed hair, the only thing left for Thibault to do was to hide it as well as he could, by bringing the other hair over it; everybody would not, he hoped, have such eyes as Agnelette.

As we have already said, Thibault had a fine head of black hair, and by parting it down the side, and giving a certain turn to the front lock, he trusted that the one hair would pass unobserved.

He recalled with envy the young lords whom he had seen at the court of Madame de Maintenon, for, with their powdered wigs to cover it, the color of their hair, whatever it might be, was of no moment. He, unfortunately, could not make use of powder to hide his, being prohibited from doing so by the sumptuary laws of the period.

However, having successfully managed, by an adroit turn of the comb, to hide his one red hair artistically under the others, Thibault decided to start again on his premeditated visit to the fair owner of the mill. He was careful this time, instead of inclining to the left, to verge towards the right, fearing to meet

93

Agnelette if he followed the same path as he had taken that morning.

Emerging, therefore, on to the road leading to La Ferté-Milou, he then took the footpath which runs direct to Pisseleu across the fields.

Arriving at Pisseleu, he continued along the valley in the direction of Croyolles, but had scarcely pursued this lower road for more than a few minutes, when, walking just ahead of him, he saw two donkeys being driven by a tall youth, whom he recognized as a cousin of his, named Landry. Cousin Landry was head boy at the mill, in the service of the owner whom Thibault was on his way to visit, and as the latter had but an indirect acquaintance with the widow Polet, he had counted on Landry to introduce him. It was a lucky chance therefore to come across his cousin like this, and Thibault hastened to overtake him.

Hearing footsteps behind him echoing his own, Landry turned and recognized Thibault. Thibault had always found Landry a pleasant and cheerful companion, and he was therefore very much astonished to see him looking sad and troubled. Landry waited for Thibault to come up to him, letting his donkeys go on alone. Thibault was the first to speak:

"Why, Cousin Landry," he asked, "what's the meaning of this? Here am I, putting myself out and leaving my work to come and shake hands with a friend and relation that I have not seen for more than six weeks, and you greet me with a face like that!"

"Ah, my dear Thibault," replied Landry, "what would you have of me! I may greet you with a gloomy face, but, believe me or not as you will, I am truly delighted to see you."

"That may be as you say, but you do not appear so."

"What do you mean?"

"You tell me you are delighted to see me in a tone of voice fit to bring on the blue devils. Why, my dear Landry, you are generally as bright and lively as the click-clack of your mill, and singing songs to accompany it, and today you are as melancholy as the crosses in the cemetery. How now then! Has the mill stopped for want of water?"

"Oh! Not that! There is no want of water; on the contrary, there is more than usual, and the sluice is kept constantly at work. But, you see, instead of corn, it is my heart that is in the mill, and the mill works so well and so incessantly, and my heart is so ground between the stones that there is nothing left of it but a little powder."

"Indeed! Are you so miserable then at the mill?"

"Ah! Would to God I had been dragged under the wheel the first day I put my foot inside it!"

"But what is it? You frighten me, Landry! ... Tell me all your troubles, my dear lad."

Landry gave a deep sigh.

"We are cousins," continued Thibault, "and if I am too poor to give you a few crowns to help you out of any money trouble you are in, well, I can at least give you some words of good advice if it is a matter of the heart that is causing you grief."

"Thank you, Thibault; but neither money nor advice can do me any good."

"Well, anyhow, tell me what is the matter; it eases trouble to speak of it."

"No, no; it would be useless; I will say nothing."

Thibault began to laugh.

"You laugh?" said Landry, both angry and astonished. "My trouble makes you laugh?"

"I am not laughing at your trouble, Landry, but at your thinking that you can hide the cause of it from me, when it is as easy as anything to guess what it is."

"Guess then."

"Why, you are in love; nothing more difficult than that to guess, I can swear."

"I, in love!" exclaimed Landry; "Why who has been telling you lies like that?"

"It is not a lie, it is the truth."

Landry again drew a deep sigh, more laden with despair even than his former one.

"Well, yes!" he said. "It is so, I am in love!"

"Ah! That's right! You have spoken out at last!" said Thibault, not without a certain quickening of the pulse, for he foresaw a rival in his cousin. "And with whom are you in love?"

"With whom?"

"Yes, I ask you with whom?"

"As to that, Cousin Thibault, you will have to drag the heart out of my breast before I tell you."

"You have told me already."

"What? I have told you who it is?" cried Landry, staring at Thibault with astonished eyes.

"Certainly you have."

"Surely you cannot mean it!"

"Did you not say that it would have been better for you to have been dragged under by the mill wheel the first day you entered into the service of Madame Polet, than to have been taken on by her as chief hand? You are unhappy at the mill, and you are in love; therefore, you are in love with the mistress of the mill, and it is this love which is causing your unhappiness."

"Ah, Thibault, pray hush! What if she were to overhear us!"

"How is it possible that she can overhear us; where do you imagine her to be, unless she is able to make herself invisible, or to change herself into a butterfly or a flower?"

"Never mind, Thibault, you keep quiet."

"Your mistress of the mill is hard-hearted then, is she? And takes no pity on your despair, poor fellow?" was Thibault's rejoinder; but his words, though seemingly expressive of great commiseration, had a shade of satisfaction and amusement in them.

"Hard-hearted! I should think so indeed!" said Landry. "In the beginning, I was foolish enough to fancy that she did not repulse my love ... All day long I was devouring her with my eyes, and now and then, she too would fix her eyes on me, and after looking at me a while, would smile ... Alas! My dear Thibault, what happiness those looks and smiles were to me! ... Ah! Why did I not content myself with them?"

"Well, there it is," said Thibault philosophically. "Man is so insatiable."

"Alas! Yes; I forgot that I had to do with someone above me in position, and I spoke. Then Madame Polet flew into a great rage; called me an insolent beggar, and threatened to turn me out of doors the very next week."

"Phew!" said Thibault. "And how long ago is that?"

"Nearly three weeks."

"And the following week is still to come?" The shoe maker as he put the question began to feel a revival of the uneasiness which had been momentarily allayed, for he understood women better than his cousin Landry. After a minute's silence, he continued: "Well, well, you are not so unhappy after all as I thought you."

"Not so unhappy as you thought me?"

"No."

"Ah! If you only knew the life I lead! Never a look, or a smile! When she meets me she turns away, when I speak to her on matters concerning the mill, she listens with such a disdainful air, that instead of talking of bran and wheat and rye, of barley and oats, of first and second crops, I begin to cry, and then she says to me, 'Take care!' in such a menacing tone, that I run away and hide myself behind the bolters."

"Well, but why do you pay your addresses to this mistress of yours? There are plenty of girls in the country round who would be glad to have you for their wooer."

"Because I love her in spite of myself, I cannot help it, so there!"

"Take up with someone else; I'd think no more about her."

"I could not do it."

"At any rate, you might try. It's just possible that if she saw you transferring your affections to another, the mistress of the

Mill might grow jealous, and might then run after you, as you are now running after her. Women are such curious creatures."

"Oh, if I was sure of that, I would begin to try at once ... although now." and Landry shook his head.

"Well, what about ... now?"

"Although now, after all that has happened, it would be of no use."

"What has happened then?" asked Thibault, who was anxious to ascertain all particulars.

"Oh! As to that, nothing," replied Landry, "and I do not even dare speak of it."

"Why?"

"Because, as they say with us, 'Best let sleeping dogs lie.'"

Thibault would have continued to urge Landry to tell him what the trouble was to which he referred, but they were now near the Mill, and their explanation would have to remain unfinished, even if once begun.

What was more, Thibault thought that he already knew enough; Landry was in love with the fair owner of the Mill, but the fair owner of the Mill was not in love with Landry. And, in truth, he feared no danger from a rival such as this. It was with a certain pride and self-complacency that he compared the timid, boyish looks of his cousin, a mere lad of eighteen, with his own five feet six and well set figure, and he was naturally led into thinking, that, however little of a woman of taste Madame Polet might be, Landry's failure was a good reason for believing that his own success was assured. The Mill at Croyolles is charmingly situated at the bottom of a cool green valley; the stream that works it forms a little pond, which is shaded by pollard willows, and slender poplars; and between these dwarfed and giant trees stand magnificent alders, and immense walnut trees with their fragrant foliage. After turning the wheel of the mill, the foaming water runs off in a little rivulet, which never ceases its hymn of joy as it goes leaping over the pebbles of its bed, starring the flowers that lean coquettishly over to look at themselves in its clear shallows with the liquid diamonds that are scattered by its tiny waterfalls.

The Mill itself lies so hidden in a bower of shrubs, behind the sycamores and weeping willows, that until one is within a short distance of it, nothing is to be seen but the chimney from which the smoke rises against the background of trees like a column of blue tinted alabaster.

Although Thibault was familiar with the spot, the sight of it filled him, as he now looked upon it, with a feeling of delight which he had not hitherto experienced; but then he had never before gazed on it under the conditions in which he now found himself, for he was already conscious of that sense of personal satisfaction which the proprietor feels on visiting an estate which has been obtained for him by proxy. On entering the farmyard, where the scene was more animated, he was moved to even greater ecstasy of enjoyment.

The blue and purple-throated pigeons were cooing on the roofs, the ducks quacking, and going through sundry evolutions in the stream, the hens were clucking on the dung heap, and the turkey cocks bridling and strutting as they courted the turkey hens, while the brown and white cows came slowly in from the fields, their udders full of milk. Here, on one side, a cart was being unloaded, there, as they were being unharnessed, two splendid horses neighed and stretched their necks, now freed from the collar, towards their mangers; a boy was carrying a sack up into the granary, and a girl was bringing another sack filled with crusts and the refuse water to an enormous pig, that lay basking in the sun waiting to be transformed into salt-pork, sausages, and black puddings; all the animals of the ark were there, from the braying donkey to the crowing cock, mingling their discordant voices in this rural concert, while the mill with its regular click-clack, seemed to be beating time.

Thibault felt quite dazzled; he saw himself the owner of all that he now looked upon, and he rubbed his hands together with such evident pleasure, that Landry, if he had not been so absorbed in his own trouble, which grew ever greater as they drew nearer to the house, would certainly have noticed this apparently causeless emotion of joy on his cousin's part. As they entered the farmyard, the widow, who was in the dining room, became aware of their presence, and seemed very inquisitive to know who the stranger was who had returned with her head boy.

Thibault, with an easy and confident sort of manner, went up to the dwelling house, gave his name, and explained to her, that, having a great wish to see his cousin Landry, he had decided to come over and introduce himself to her.

The mistress of the Mill was extremely gracious, and invited the new comer to spend the day at the Mill, accompanying her invitation with a smile that Thibault took as a most favorable augury.

Thibault had not come unprovided with a present. He had unhooked some thrushes which he had found caught in a snare set with rowan-berries, as he came through the forest; and the widow sent them at once to be plucked, saying as she did so, that she hoped Thibault would stay to eat his share of them. But he could not help noticing that all the while she was speaking to him, she kept on looking over his shoulder at something which seemed to attract her attention, and turning quickly, he saw that the preoccupation of the fair owner of the Mill had evidently been caused by watching Landry, who was unloading his asses.

Becoming conscious that Thibault had noticed the wandering of her looks and attention, Madame Polet turned as red as a cherry, but, immediately recovering herself she said to her new acquaintance:

"Monsieur Thibault, it would be kind of you, who appear so robust, to go and help your cousin; you can see that the job is too heavy a one for him alone," and so saying, she went back into the house.

"Now, the devil!" muttered Thibault, as he looked first after Madame Polet and then at Landry. "Is the fellow after all more fortunate than he suspects himself, and shall I be forced to call the black wolf to my assistance to get rid of him?"

However, he went as the owner of the mill had asked him, and gave the required assistance. Feeling quite sure that the pretty widow was looking at him through some chink or other of the curtain, he put forth all his strength, and displayed to the full his athletic grace, in the accomplishment of the task in which he was sharing. The unloading finished, they all assembled in the dining room where a waiting-maid was busy setting the table. As soon as dinner was served, Madame Polet took her place at the head of the table, with Thibault to her right. She was all attention and politeness to the latter, so much so indeed that Thibault, who had been temporarily crestfallen, took heart again, filled with hope. In order to do honor to Thibault's present, she had herself dressed the birds with juniper berries, and so prepared, no more delicate or appetizing dish could well have been provided. While laughing at Thibault's sallies, however, she cast stealthy glances now and again at Landry, who she saw had not touched what she herself had placed on the poor boy's plate, and also that great tears were rolling down his cheeks, and falling into the untasted juniper sauce.

This mute sorrow touched her heart; a look almost of tenderness came into her face, as she made a sign to him with her head, which seemed to say, so expressive was it, "Eat, Landry, I beg of you."

There was a whole world of loving promises in this little pantomime. Landry understood the gesture, for he nearly choked himself trying to swallow the bird at one mouthful, so eager was he to obey the orders of his fair mistress.

Nothing of all this escaped Thibault's eye.

He swore to himself, using an oath that he had heard in the mouth of the Seigneur Jean, and which, now that he was the friend of the devil, he fancied he might use like any other great lord: "Can it be possible," he thought, "that she is really in love with this slip of a youth? Well, if so, it does not say much for her taste, and more than that, it does not suit my plans at all. No, no, my fair mistress, what you need is a man who will know how to look well after the affairs of the mill, and that man will be myself or the black wolf will find himself in the wrong box."

Noticing a minute later that Madame Polet had finally gone back to the earlier stage of sidelong glances and smiles which Landry had described to him, he continued, "I see I shall have to resort to stronger measures, for lose her I will not; there is not another match in all the countryside that would suit me equally well. But then, what am I to do with Cousin Landry? His love, it is true, upsets my arrangements; but I really cannot for so small a thing send him to join the wretched Marcotte in the other world. But what a fool I am to bother my brains about finding a way to help myself! It's the wolf's business, not mine."

Then in a low voice: "Black Wolf," he said, "arrange matters in such a way, that without any accident or harm happening to my Cousin Landry, I may get rid of him." The prayer was scarcely uttered, when he caught sight of a small body of four or five men in military uniform, walking down the hillside and coming towards the mill. Landry also saw them; for he uttered a loud cry, got up as if to run away, and then fell back in his chair, as if all power of movement had forsaken him.

❧ 8 ❧

THIBAULT'S WHISHES

The widow, on perceiving the effect which the sight of the soldiers advancing towards the mill had upon Landry, was almost as frightened as the lad himself.

"Ah! Dear God!" she cried. "What is the matter, my poor Landry?"

"Say, what is the matter?" asked Thibault in his turn.

"Alas I," replied Landry, "last Thursday, in a moment of despair, meeting the recruiting sergeant at the Dauphin Inn, I enlisted."

"In a moment of despair?" exclaimed the mistress of the mill. "And why were you in despair?"

"I was in despair," said Landry, with a mighty effort, "I was in despair because I love you."

"And it is because you loved me, unhappy boy! That you enlisted?"

"Did you not say that you would turn me away from the mill?"

"And have I turned you away?" asked Madame Polet, with an expression which it was impossible to misinterpret.

"Ah! God! Then you would not really have sent me away?" asked Landry.

"Poor boy!" said the mistress of the mill, with a smile and a pitying movement of the shoulders, which, at any other time, would have made Landry almost die of joy, but, as it was, only doubled his distress.

"Perhaps even now I might have time to hide," he said.

"Hide!" said Thibault. "That will be of no use, I can tell you."

"And why not?" said Madame Polet. "I am going to try, anyhow. Come, dear Landry."

And she led the young man away, with every mark of the most loving sympathy.

Thibault followed them with his eyes: "It's going badly for you, Thibault, my friend," he said; "fortunately, let her hide him as cleverly as she may, they have a good scent, and will find him out."

In saying this, Thibault was unconscious that he was giving utterance to a fresh wish.

The widow had evidently not hidden Landry very far away, for she returned after a few seconds of absence; the hiding place was probably all the safer for being near. She had scarcely had time to take breath when the recruiting sergeant and his companions appeared at the door.

Two remained outside, no doubt to catch Landry if he should attempt to escape, the sergeant and the other soldier walked in with the confidence of men who are conscious of acting under authority. The sergeant cast a searching glance round the room, brought back his right foot into the third position and lifted his hand to the peak of his cap. The mistress of the Mill did not wait for the sergeant to address her, but with one of her most fascinating smiles, asked him if he would like some refreshment, an offer which no recruiting sergeant is ever known to refuse. Then, thinking it a favorable moment to put the question, she asked them while they were drinking their wine, what had brought them to Croyolles Mill. The sergeant replied that he had come in search of a lad, belonging to the Mill, who, after drinking with him to his Majesty's health and signed his engagement, had not reappeared. The lad in question, interrogated as to his name and dwelling place, had declared himself to be one Landry, living with Madame Polet, a widow, owner of the Mill at Croyolles. On the strength of this declaration, he had now come to Madame Polet, widow, of Croyolles Mill, to reclaim the defaulter.

The widow, quite convinced that it was permissible to lie for a good cause, assured the sergeant that she knew nothing of Landry, nor had any one of that name ever been at the Mill.

The sergeant in reply said that Madame had the finest eyes and the most charming mouth in the world, but that was no reason why he should implicitly believe the glances of the one or the words of the other. He was bound, therefore, he continued, "To ask the fair widow to allow him to search the Mill."

The search was begun, in about five minutes the sergeant came back into the room and asked Madam Polet for the key of her room. The widow appeared very much surprised and shocked at such a request, but the sergeant was so persistent and determined that at last she was forced to give up the key. A minute or two later, and the sergeant walked in again, dragging Landry in after him by the collar of his coat. When the widow saw them both enter, she turned deadly pale. As for Thibault, his heart beat so violently, that he thought it would burst, for without the black wolf's assistance, he was sure the sergeant would never have gone to look for Landry where he had found him.

"Ah! Ah! My good fellow!" cried the sergeant in a mocking voice. "So we prefer the service of beauty to the king's service? That is easy to understand; but when one has the good fortune to be born in his Majesty's domains and to have drunk his health, one has to give him a share of service, when his turn comes. So you must come along with us, my fine fellow, and after a few years in the king's uniform, you can come back and serve under your old flag. So, now then, march!"

"But," cried the widow, "Landry is not yet twenty, and you have not the right to take him under twenty."

"She is right," added Landry. "I am not twenty yet."

"And when will you be twenty?"

"Not until tomorrow."

"Good," said the sergeant. "We will put you tonight on a bed of straw, like a medlar, and by tomorrow, at daybreak, when we wake you up, you will be ripe."

Landry wept. The widow prayed, pleaded, implored, allowed herself to be kissed by the soldiers, patiently endured the coarse pleasantry excited by her sorrow, and at last offered a hundred crowns to buy him off. But all was of no avail. Landry's wrists were bound, and then one of the soldiers taking hold of the end of the cord, the party started off, but not before the lad of the mill had found time to assure his dear mistress, that far or near, he would always love her, and that, if he died, her name would be the last upon his lips. The beautiful widow, on her side, had lost all thought of the world's opinion in face of this great catastrophe, and before he was led away, she clasped Landry to her heart in a tender embrace.

When the little party had disappeared behind the willows, and she lost sight of them, the widow's distress became so over-powering that she became insensible, and had to be carried and laid on her bed. Thibault lavished upon her the most devoted attention. He was somewhat taken aback at the strong feeling of affection which the widow evinced for his cousin; however, as this only made him applaud himself the more for having cut at the root of the evil, he still cherished the most sanguine hopes.

On coming to herself, the first name the widow uttered was that of Landry, to which Thibault replied with a hypocritical gesture of commiseration. Then the mistress of the mill began to sob.

"Poor lad!" she cried, while the hot tears flowed down her cheeks. "What will become of him, so weak and delicate as he is? The mere weight of his gun and knapsack will kill him!"

Then turning to her guest, she continued:

"Ah! Monsieur Thibault, this is a terrible trouble to me, for you no doubt have perceived that I love him? He was gentle, he was kind, he had no faults; he was not a gambler, nor a drinker; he would never have opposed my wishes, would never have tyrannized over his wife, and that would have seemed very sweet to me after the two cruel years that I lived with the late M. Polet. Ah! Monsieur Thibault, Monsieur Thibault! It is a sad grief indeed for a poor miserable woman to see all her anticipations of future happiness and peace thus suddenly swallowed up!"

Thibault thought this would be a good moment to declare himself; whenever he saw a woman crying, he immediately thought, most erroneously, that she only cried because she wished to be consoled.

He decided, however, that he would not be able to attain his object without a certain circumlocution.

"Indeed," he answered. "I quite understand your sorrow, nay, more than that, I share it with you, for you cannot doubt the affection I bear my cousin. But we must resign ourselves, and without wishing to deny Landry's good qualities, I would still ask you, Madame, to find someone else who is his equal."

"His equal!" exclaimed the widow. "There is no such person. Where shall I find so nice and so good a youth? It was a pleasure to me to look at his smooth young face, and with it all, he was so self-composed, so steady in his habits! He was working night and day, and yet I could with a glance make him shrink away and hide. No, no, Monsieur Thibault, I tell you frankly, the remembrance of him will prevent me ever wishing to look at another man, and I know that I must resign myself to remaining a widow for the rest of my life."

"Phew!" said Thibault; "but Landry was very young!"

"There is no disadvantage in that," replied the widow.

"But who knows if he would always have retained his good qualities. Take my advice, Madame, do not grieve any more, but, as I say, look out for someone who will make you forget him. What you really need is not a babyface like that, but a grown man, possessing all the qualities that you admire and regret in

Landry, but, at the same time sufficiently mature to prevent the chance of finding one fine day that all your illusions are dispersed, and that you are left face to face with a libertine and a bully."

The mistress of the Mill shook her head; but Thibault went on:

"In short, what you need, is a man who while earning your respect, will, at the same time make the Mill work profitably. You have but to say the word, and you would not have to wait long before you found yourself well provided for, my fair Madame, a good bit better than you were just now."

"And where am I to find this miracle of a man?" asked the widow, as she rose to her feet, looking defiantly at the shoe maker, as if throwing down a challenge. The latter, mistaking the tone in which these last words were said, thought it an excellent occasion to make known his own proposals, and accordingly hastened to profit by it.

"Well, I confess," he answered, "that when I said that a handsome widow like you would not have to go far before finding the man who would be just the very husband for her, I was thinking of myself, for I should reckon myself fortunate, and should feel proud, to call myself your husband. Ah! I assure you," he went on, while the mistress of the Mill stood looking at him with ever increasing displeasure in her eyes, "I assure you that with me you would have no occasion to fear any opposition to your wishes: I am a perfect lamb in the way of gentleness, and I should have but one law and one desire, my law would be to obey you, my desire to please you! And as to your fortune, I have means of adding to it which I will make known to you later on."

But the end of Thibault's sentence remained unspoken.

"What!" cried the widow, whose fury was the greater for having been kept in check until then. "What! You, whom I thought my friend, you dare to speak of replacing him in my heart! You try to dissuade me from keeping my faith to your cousin. Get out of the place, you worthless scoundrel! Out of the place, I say! Or I will not answer for the consequences; I have a good mind to get four of my men to collar you and throw you under the mill wheel."

Thibault was anxious to make some sort of response, but, although ready with an answer on ordinary occasions, he could not for the moment think of a single word whereby to justify himself. True, Madame Polet, gave him no time to think, but seizing hold of a beautiful new jug that stood near her, she flung it at Thibault's head. Luckily for him, Thibault dodged to the left and escaped the missile, which flew past him, crashing to pieces against the chimneypiece. Then the mistress of the house took up a stool, and aimed it at him with equal violence; this time Thibault dodged to the right, and the stool went against the window, smashing two or three panes of glass. At the sound of the falling glass, all the youths and maids of the Mill came running up.

They found their mistress flinging bottles, water jugs, salt cellars, plates, everything in short that came to hand, with all her might at Thibault's head. Fortunately for him widow Polet was too much incensed to be able to speak; if she had been able to do so, she would have called out; "Kill him! Strangle him! Kill the rascal! The scoundrel! The villain!"

On seeing the reinforcements arriving to help the widow, Thibault endeavored to escape by the door that had been left open by the recruiting party, but just as he was running out, the good pig, that we saw taking its siesta in the sun, being roused out of its first sleep by all this hullabaloo, and thinking the farm people were after it, made a dash for its sty, and in so doing charged right against Thibault's legs. The latter lost his balance, and went rolling over and over for a good ten paces in the dirt and slush. "Devil take you, you beast!" cried the shoe maker, bruised by his fall, but even more furious at seeing his new clothes covered with mud. The wish was hardly out of his mouth, when the pig was suddenly taken with a fit of frenzy, and began rushing about the farmyard like a mad animal, breaking, shattering, and turning over everything that came in its way. The farm hands, who had run to their mistress on hearing her cries, thought the pig's behavior was the cause of them—and started off in pursuit of the animal. But it eluded all their attempts to seize hold of it, knocking over boys and girls, as it had knocked Thibault over, until, at last, coming to where the mill was separated from the sluice by a wooden partition, it crashed through the latter as easily as if it were made of paper, threw itself under the mill wheel ... and disappeared as if sucked down by a whirlpool.

The mistress of the mill had by this time recovered her speech. "Lay hold of Thibault!" she cried, for she had heard Thibault's curse, and had been amazed and horrified at the instantaneous way in which it had worked. "Lay hold of him! Knock him down! He is a wizard, a sorcerer! A werewolf!"—applying to Thibault with this last word, one of the most terrible epithets that can be given to a man in our forest lands.

Thibault, who scarcely knew where he was, seeing the momentary stupefaction which took possession of the farm people on hearing their mistress's final invective, made use of the opportunity to dash past them, and while one went to get a pitchfork and another a spade, he darted through the farmyard gate, and began running up an almost perpendicular hill-side at full speed, with an ease which only confirmed Madame Polet's suspicions, for the hill had always hitherto been looked upon as absolutely inaccessible, at any rate by the way Thibault had chosen to climb it.

"What?" she cried. "You give in like that! You should make after him, and seize hold of him, and knock him down!" But the farm servants shook their heads.

"Ah! Madame!" they said. "What is the use, what can we do against a werewolf?"

❧ 9 ❧

THE WOLF LEADER

Thibault, fleeing from before Madame Polet's threats and her farm servants' weapons, turned instinctively towards the forest, thinking to take shelter within it, should he chance to come across one of the enemy, for he knew that no one would venture to follow him there, for fear of any lurking dangers. Not that Thibault had much to fear, whatever kind of enemy he met, now that he was armed with the diabolical power which he had received from the wolf. He had only to send them where he had sent the widow's pig, and he was sure of being rid of them. Nevertheless, conscious of a certain tightening of the heart when from time to time the thought of Marcotte came back to him, he acknowledged to himself that, however anxious to be rid of them, one could not send men to the devil quite as readily as one sent pigs.

While thus reflecting on the terrible power he possessed, and looking back at intervals to see if there were any immediate need to put it into use, Thibault, by the time night fell, had reached the rear of Pisseleu.

It was an autumn night, dark and stormy, with a wind that tore the yellowing leaves from the trees, and wandered through the forest ways with melancholy sighs and moanings. These funereal voices of the wind were interrupted from time to time by the hooting of the owls, which sounded like the cries of lost travelers, hailing one another. But all these sounds were familiar to Thibault and made very little impression upon him. Moreover he had taken the precaution, on first entering the forest, of cutting a stick, four feet long, from a chestnut tree, and adept as he was with the quarterstaff, he was ready, armed thus, to withstand the attack of any four men. So he entered the forest with all boldness of heart, at the spot which is known to this day as the wolf's Heath.

He had been walking for some minutes along a dark and narrow glade, cursing as he went the foolish whims of women, who, for no reason whatever, preferred a weak and timid child to a brave, strong, full grown man, when all of a sudden, at some few paces behind him, he heard a crackling among the leaves. He turned and the first thing he could distinguish in the darkness was the glowing light in a pair of eyes which shone like live coals. Then, looking more closely, and forcing his eyes, so to speak, to penetrate the gloom, he saw that a great wolf was following him, step by step. But it was not the wolf that he had entertained in his hut; that was black, while this was a reddish-brown.

There was no mistaking one for the other, either as to color or size. As Thibault had no reason to suppose that all the wolves he came across would be animated with such benevolent feelings towards him as the first with which he had had dealings, he grasped his quarterstaff in both hands, and began twirling it about to make sure he had not forgotten the knack of using it. But to his great surprise the wolf went on trotting quietly behind him, without evincing any hostile intention, pausing when he paused, and going on again when he did, only now and then giving a howl as if to summon reinforcements. Thibault was not altogether without uneasiness as regards these occasional howls, and presently he became aware of two other bright spots of light in front of him, shining at intervals through the darkness which was growing thicker and thicker.

Holding his stick up in readiness to hit, he went forward towards these two lights, which remained stationary, and as he did so, his foot seemed to stumble against something lying across the path ... it was another wolf. Not pausing to reflect whether it might not be unwise now to attack the first wolf, Thibault brought down his staff, giving the fellow a violent blow on the head.

The animal uttered a howl of pain, then shaking his ears like a dog that has been beaten by its master, began walking on in front of the shoe maker. Thibault then turned to see what had become of the first wolf: it was still following him, still keeping step with him. Bringing his eyes back again to the front, he now perceived that a third wolf was walking alongside to the right, and turning instinctively to the left, saw a fourth flanking him on that side too. Before he had gone a mile, a dozen of the animals had formed a circle round him. The situation was critical, and Thibault was fully conscious of its gravity. At first he tried to sing, hoping that the sound of the human voice might frighten away the animals; but the expedient was vain. Not a single animal swerved from its place in the circle, which was as exactly formed as if drawn with compasses. Then he thought he would climb up into the first thick-leaved tree he came to, and there wait for daylight; but on further deliberation, he decided that the wisest course was to try to get home, as the wolves, in spite of their number, still appeared as well intentioned as when there was only one. It would be time enough to climb up into a tree when they began to show signs of any change of behavior towards him.

At the same time we are bound to add that Thibault was so disquieted in mind and that he had reached his own door before he knew where he was, he did not at first recognize his own house. But a still greater surprise awaited him, for the wolves who were in front now respectfully drew back into two lines, sitting up on their hind legs and making a lane for him to pass along. Thibault did not waste time in stopping to thank them for this act of courtesy, but dashed into the house, banging the door to after him. Having firmly shut and bolted the door, he pushed the great chest against it, that it might be better able to resist any assault that might be made upon it. Then he flung himself into a chair, and began at length to find himself able to breathe more freely.

As soon as he was somewhat recovered, he went and peeped through the little window that looked out on the forest. A row of gleaming eyes assured him that far from having retired, the wolves had arranged themselves symmetrically in file in front of his dwelling.

To anyone else the mere proximity of the animals would have been most alarming, but, Thibault who shortly before, had been obliged to walk escorted by this terrible troop, found comfort in the thought that a wall, however thin, now separated him from his formidable companions.

Thibault lit his little iron lamp and put it on the table; drew the scattered ashes of his hearth together and threw on them a bundle of chips, and then made a good fire, hoping that the reflection of the blaze would frighten away the wolves. But Thibault's wolves were evidently wolves of a special sort, accustomed to fire, for they did not budge an inch from the post they had taken up. The state of uneasiness he was in prevented Thibault from sleeping, and directly dawn broke, he was able to look out and count them. They seemed, just as on the night before, to be waiting, some seated, some lying down, others sleeping or walking up and down like sentinels. But at length, as the last star melted away, drowned in the waves of purple light ebbing up from the east, all the wolves with one accord rose, and uttering the mournful howl with which animals of darkness are wont to salute the day, they dispersed in various directions and disappeared. Thibault was now able to sit down and think over the misadventure of the previous

day, and he began by asking himself how it was that the
mistress of the Mill had not preferred him to his cousin Landry.
Was he no longer the handsome Thibault, or had some disad-
vantageous change come over his personal appearance? There
was only one way of ascertaining whether this was so or not,
namely, by consulting his mirror. So he took down the fragment
of looking glass hanging over the chimneypiece, and carried it
towards the light, smiling to himself the while like a vain
woman. But he had hardly given the first glance at himself in
the mirror, before he uttered a cry, half of astonishment, half of
horror. True, he was still the handsome Thibault, but the one
red hair, thanks to the hasty wishes which had so imprudently
escaped him, had now grown to a regular lock of hair, of a
color and brilliancy that vied with the brightest flames upon his
hearth.

His forehead grew cold with sweat. Knowing, however, that
all attempts to pluck it out or cut it off would be futile, he made
up his mind to make the best of the matter as it stood, and in
future to forbear as far as possible from framing any wishes. The
best thing was to put out of his mind all the ambitious desires
that had worked so fatally for him, and go back to his humble
trade. So Thibault sat down and tried to work, but he had no
heart for the job. In vain he tried to remember the carols he had
been in the habit of singing in the happier days when the beech
and the birch shaped themselves so quickly beneath his fingers;
his tools lay untouched for hours together. He pondered over
matters, asking himself whether it was not a miserable thing to
be sweating one's heart out merely for the privilege of leading a
painful and wretched existence, when, by judiciously directing
one's wishes one might so easily attain to happiness. Formerly,
even the preparation of his frugal meal had been an agreeable
distraction, but it was so no longer; when hunger seized him and
he was forced to eat his piece of black bread, he did it with a
feeling of repugnance, and the envy, which had hitherto been
nothing more than a vague aspiration after ease and comfort,

was now developed into a blind and violent hatred towards his fellow creatures.

Still the day, long as it seemed to Thibault, passed away like all its fellows. When twilight fell, he went outside and sat down on the bench which he had made himself and placed in front of the door, and there he remained, lost in gloomy reflections. Scarcely had the shadows begun to darken, before a wolf emerged from the underwood, and, as on the previous evening, went and lay down at a short distance from the house. As on the evening before, this wolf was followed by a second, by a third, in short by the whole pack, and once more they all took up their respective posts preparatory to the night's watch. As soon as Thibault saw the third wolf appear, he went indoors and barricaded himself in as carefully as the evening before; but this evening he was even more unhappy and low spirited, and felt that he had not the strength to keep awake all night. So he lighted his fire, and piled it up in such a way that it would last till the morning, and throwing himself on his bed, fell fast asleep. When he awoke, it was broad daylight, the sun having risen some hours before. Its rays fell in many colors on the quivering autumn leaves, dyeing them with a thousand shades of gold and purple.

Thibault ran to the window, the wolves had disappeared, leaving behind only the mark of where their bodies had lain on the dew-covered grass.

Next evening they again congregated before his dwelling; but he was now growing gradually accustomed to their presence, and had come to the conclusion that his relations with the large black wolf had somehow awakened sympathetic feelings towards him in all other individuals of the same species, and he determined to find out, once for all, what their designs towards him really were. Accordingly, thrusting a freshly sharpened billhook into his belt, and taking his boar spear in his hand, the shoe maker opened his door and walked resolutely out to face them. Having half expected that they would spring upon him, he was greatly surprised to see them begin to wag their tails like so many dogs on seeing their master approach. Their greetings were so expressive of friendliness, that Thibault even ventured to stroke one or two of them on the back, which they not only allowed him to do, but actually gave signs of the greatest pleasure at being thus noticed.

"Oh! Ho!" muttered Thibault, whose wandering imagination always went ahead at a gallop. "If these queer friends of mine are as obedient as they are gentle, why, here I am, the owner of a pack unequalled by any my lord baron has ever possessed, and I shall have no difficulty whatever now in dining on venison whenever the fancy so takes me."

He had hardly said the words, when four of the strongest and most alert of the four-footed beasts separated themselves from the others and galloped off into the forest. A few minutes later a howl was heard, sounding from the depths of the underwood, and half an hour afterwards one of the wolves reappeared dragging with it a fine kid which left behind it a long trail of blood on the grass. The wolf laid the animal at Thibault's feet, who delighted beyond measure at seeing his wishes, not only accomplished, but forestalled, broke up the kid, giving each of the wolves an equal share, and keeping the back and haunches for himself. Then with the gesture of an emperor, which showed that he now at last understood the position he held, he ordered the wolves away until the morrow.

Early next morning, before the day broke, he went off to Villers-Cotterets, and at the price of a couple of crowns, the innkeeper of the Boule-d'Or, took the two haunches off his hands.

The following day, it was half of a boar that Thibault conveyed to the innkeeper, and it was not long before he became the latter's chief purveyor.

Thibault, taking a taste for this sort of business, now passed his whole day hanging about the taverns, and gave no more thought to the making of shoes. One or two of his acquaintances began to make fun of his red lock, for however assiduously he covered it with the rest of his hair, it always found a way of getting through the curls that hid it, and making itself visible. But Thibault soon gave it plainly to be understood that he would take no joking about the unfortunate disfigurement.

Meanwhile, as ill luck would have it, the Duke of Orleans and Madame de Montesson came to spend a few days at Villers-Cotterets. This was a fresh incentive to Thibault's madly ambitious spirit. All the fine and beautiful ladies and all the gay young lords from the neighboring estates, the Montbretons, the Montesquious, the Courvals, hastened to Villers-Cotterets. The ladies brought their richest attire, the young lords their most elegant costumes. The baron's hunting horn resounded through the forest louder and gayer than ever. Graceful amazons and dashing cavaliers, in red coats laced with gold, passed like radiant visions, as they were borne along on their magnificent English horses, illuminating the somber depths of the wood like brilliant flashes of light.

In the evening it was different; then all this aristocratic company assembled for feasting and dancing, or at other times drove out in beautiful gilt carriages bedizened with coats of arms of every color.

Thibault always took his stand in the front rank of the onlookers, gazing with avidity on these clouds of satin and lace, which lifted now and then to disclose the delicate ankles encased in their fine silk stockings, and the little shoes with their red heels. Thus the whole cavalcade swept past in front of the astonished peasantry, leaving a faint exhalation of scent and powder and delicate perfumes. And then Thibault would ask himself why he was not one of those young lords in their embroidered coats; why he had not one of these beautiful women in their rustling satins for his mistress. Then his thoughts would turn to Agnelette and Madame Polet, and he saw them just as they were, the one a poor little peasant girl, the other nothing more than the owner of a rustic mill.

But it was when he was walking home at night through the forest, accompanied by his pack of wolves, which, from the moment the night fell and he set foot inside the forest, no more thought of leaving him than the king's bodyguard would dream of leaving their royal master, that his broodings took their most disastrous turn. Surrounded by the temptations which now assailed him, it was only what was to be expected that Thibault who had already gone so far in the direction of evil, should break away from what little good was still left in him, losing even the very remembrance of having once led an honest life. What were the few paltry crowns that the landlord of the Boule-d'Or gave him in payment for the game which his good friends the wolves procured for him? Saved up for months, even for years, they would still be insufficient to satisfy a single one of the humblest of the desires which kept tormenting his brain. It would be scarcely safe to say that Thibault, who had first wished for a haunch of the baron's buck, then for Agnelette's heart, and then for the widow Polet's mill, would now be satisfied even with the castle at Oigny or Longpont, to such extravagant issues had his ambition been excited by those dainty feet, those trim ankles, those exquisite scents exhaled from all those velvet and satin gowns.

At last one day he said to himself definitely that it would be the veriest folly to go on living his poor life when a power so tremendous as he now possessed, was at his disposal. From that moment he made up his mind that, no matter if his hair should grow as red as the crown of fire which is seen at night hanging over the great chimney at the glass works of Saint Gobain, he would exercise this power of his to the accomplishing of the most high flown of his ambitions.

10

MAÎTRE MAGLOIRE

I n this reckless state of mind Thibault, who had not as yet decided on any special course of action, spent the last days of the old year and the first of the new. Still, remembering the heavy expenses entailed on each and all by New Year's Day, he had exacted double rations from his usual purveyor's, as the trying time drew nearer and nearer, simultaneously, drawing double profits from the landlord of the Boule-d'Or.

Thus it came about that, apart from the disquieting fact that his mesh of red hair was getting larger and larger almost every day, Thibault entered upon the New Year in a better condition as to material matters than he had ever known before. Observe, I say, as to material matters, and material matters only; for albeit the body might seem in good plight, the soul was already alarmingly compromised. The body, at any rate was well clothed, and ten crowns or more made a merry jingling in his waistcoat pocket; and so dressed, and so accompanied by this silvery music, Thibault no longer appeared like a wooden shoe maker's apprentice, but like some well-to-do farmer, or even a comfortable citizen, carrying on a trade maybe, but simply for his own pleasure. Looking such as he now did, Thibault went to one of those village functions, which are fête-days for the whole province. The magnificent ponds of Berval and Poudron were to be drawn. Now the drawing of a pond is a grand affair for the owner, or for the one who farms it, not to mention the great pleasure it affords to the spectators. Such an event therefore is advertised a month in advance, and people come from thirty miles round to enjoy this fine entertainment. And to those of my readers who are not accustomed to the manners and customs of the provinces, let me explain that the fishing which takes place is not a fishing with the line, baited with worms, or scented wheat, or with the cast net, or the sweep net, nothing of the kind; this fishing consists in emptying a pond, sometimes nearly a mile, or even three miles long, of every fish from the largest pike to the smallest minnow. This is how the thing is managed. In all probability, not a single one of my readers has ever seen the kind of pond to which I refer. I will describe it; to begin with, it always has two issues, that by which the water flows in, that by which the water flows out; that by which the water enters has no particular name, that by which it is let out is called the sluice. The water as it leaves the sluice falls into a large reservoir whence it escapes through the meshes of a strong net; the water flows away, but the fish remain. Everyone knows that it takes several days to empty a pond, therefore those who wish to take a share in the fishing, and the onlookers, are not summoned to attend before the second, third, or fourth day, according to the volume of water which the pond has to disgorge before it is ready for the final act, and this takes place as soon as the fish appear at the sluice.

At the hour announced for the fishing, a crowd assembles, varying in number according to the size and the celebrity of the pond, but comparatively as large and as fashionable as that to be seen at the Champ de Mars or Chantilly on race days when favorite horses are to run and favorite jockeys to ride. Only here the spectators do not look on from grand stands and carriages; on the contrary, they come as they can, or as they like, in gigs, pleasure vans, phaëtons, carts, on horseback, on donkeyback, but once on the spot everyone rushes to find a place, stationing him or herself either in order of arrival, or according to the amount of elbowing and pushing of which each is capable, always, however, with that due respect for authority which is observed even in the least civilized districts. A sort of stout trelliswork, however, firmly sunk into the ground, prevents the onlookers from falling into the reservoir.

The color and the smell of the water betoken the arrival of the fish. Every kind of show has its drawbacks: the larger and grander the audience at the opera house, the more carbon dioxide is there to draw into the lungs; at the drawing of a pond, the nearer the supreme moment approaches, the more marsh gas is there to inhale.

When the sluice is first opened, the water that pours through is beautifully clear, and slightly green in color, like the water of a brook; this is the upper layer, which, carried along by its weight, is the first to appear. By degrees the water becomes less transparent, and takes on a grayish hue; this is the second layer, emptying itself in turn, and every now and then, more frequently as the water becomes muddier, a ray of silver is seen to dart through it; it is some fish, too small and weak to resist the current, which flashes past as if acting as scout for its stronger brethren. Nobody troubles to pick it up; it is allowed to lie gasping, and trying to find some little stagnant puddle of water at the bottom of the pond, flapping, floundering and capering like an acrobat going through his antics.

Then the black water comes pouring through; this is the last act, the final catastrophe.

Each fish, according to its power of resistance, struggles against the current which is bearing it along in this unusual manner. Instinctively they feel there is danger, and each strives its hardest to swim in an opposite direction; the pike struggles beside the carp which it was yesterday pursuing so hard; the perch is reconciled to the tench, and as they swim side by side, does not so much as think of taking a bite out of the flesh he finds so palatable at other times. So the Arabs at times find huddled together in the pits they dig to catch game, gazelles and jackals, antelopes and hyenas, the jackals and hyenas having grown as gentle and as timid as the gazelles and antelopes.

But the strength of the struggling and dying fish begins at last to fail. The scouts that we noticed a few minutes ago become more numerous; the size of the fish becomes more respectable, which is proved to them by the attention they receive from the pickers-up. These pickers-up are men, clad in plain linen trousers and cotton shirts; the trousers are rolled up to above the knee, and the shirt sleeves turned up to the shoulders. The fish are gathered up in baskets; those destined to be sold alive, or kept for restocking the pond, are poured off into tanks; those condemned to death are simply spread out on the grass, and will be sold before the day is out. As the fish grow more and more abundant the cries of delight from the spectators become louder and more frequent; for these onlookers are not like the audiences in our theatres; they have no idea of stifling their feelings, or showing good taste by appearing indifferent. No, they come to amuse themselves, and every fine tench, or fine carp, or fine pike, calls forth loud, undisguised and delighted applause. As in a well-ordered review, the troops file past in order, according to their weight, if we may use the expression, first the fight sharp-shooters, then the somewhat heavier dragoons, and finally the ponderous cuirassiers and heavy artillery to bring up the rear, so the fish sweep by according to their several species; the smallest, that is the weakest, first, the heaviest, that is the strongest, last.

At last the moment comes when the water ceases to flow; the passage is literally obstructed by the remainder of the fish, the bigwigs of the pond, and the pickers-up have veritable monsters to fight with. This is the supreme moment. Now comes the climax of applause, the last vociferous bravos. Then, the play being over, everyone goes to examine the actors; the latter are mostly lying gasping to death on the grass of the field, while a certain number are recovering themselves in the water. You look about for the eels; where are the eels you ask? Then three or four eels, about as big round as your thumb and half the length of your arm, are pointed out to you; for the eels, thanks to their peculiar organization, have momentarily at least, escaped the general carnage. The eels have taken a header into the mud and disappeared; and this is the reason why you may see men with guns walking up and down at the edge of the pond, and hear a report from time to time. If you ask the reason for this shooting, you will be told that it is to bring the eels out of their hiding places. But why do eels come out of the mud when they hear the report of a gun? Why do they make for the water which still runs in little rivulets at the bottom of the pond? Why, in short, being safe at the bottom of the mud, like other good friends of our acquaintance who have the good sense to remain there, do the eels not stay there, instead of wriggling back into a stream of water, which carries them along with it, and finally lands them in the reservoir, that is in the common grave? The Collège de France would find nothing easier than to answer this question, under existing circumstances; so I put this question to its learned members: Is not the idea of the gun a pure superstition, and is not the following solution the right and simple one? The mud in which the eel takes refuge is at first liquid, but gradually becomes drier and drier, like a sponge when squeezed, and so becomes more and more uninhabitable for it, and so, in the long run, it is obliged to get back to its natural element—the water. The water once reached, the eel is lost; but it is not till the fifth or sixth day after the emptying of the pond, that the eels are caught.

It was to a fête of this kind that everyone at Villers-Cotterets, at Crespy, at Mont-Gobert, and in the surrounding villages had been invited. Thibault went like everybody else; he had now no need to work, finding it simpler to allow the wolves to work for him. From a workman he had risen to be a man at ease, it now only remained to make himself a gentleman, and Thibault counted upon being able to do this. He was not a man to allow himself to remain in the rear, and he therefore made good use of his arms and legs so as to secure a place in the front row. In the course of this maneuver he happened to rumple the dress of a tall, fine woman, next to whom he was trying to install himself. The lady was fond of her clothes, and no doubt, also, she was in the habit of commanding, which naturally produces an attitude of disdain, for, turning to see who had brushed past her, she let fall the uncompromising word, "lout!" Notwithstanding the rudeness of the remark, the mouth that uttered the words was so beautiful, the lady so pretty, and her momentary anger in such ugly contrast to the charming expression of her face, that Thibault, instead of retorting in similar, or even more objectionable style, only drew back, stammering some sort of excuse.

There is no need to remind the reader that of all aristocracies, beauty is still the chief. If the woman had been old and ugly, she might have been a Marquise, but Thibault would certainly have called her by some opprobrious title. It is possible also that Thibault's ideas were somewhat distracted by the strange appearance of the man who served as knight to this lady, He was a stout man of about sixty years of age, dressed entirely in black, and of a perfectly dazzling exactness of toilet; but therewith, so extremely short, that his head scarcely reached the lady's elbow, and as she would have been unable to take his arm, without positive torture to herself, she was content to lean majestically upon his shoulder. Seeing them thus together, one might have taken her for an ancient Cybele leaning on one of those grotesque little modern figures of Chinese idols. And what a fascinating idol it was with those short legs, that bulgy stomach, those little fat podgy arms, those white hands under the lace ruffles, that plump, rubicund head and face, that well-combed, well-powdered, well-curled head of hair, and that tiny pigtail, which with every movement of its wearer's, went bobbing up and down with its neat bow of ribbon against the coat collar. It reminded one of those black beetles of which the legs seem so little in harmony with the body, that the insects seem rather to roll than to walk. And with it all, the face was so jovial, the little eyes level with the forehead, were so full of kindness, that one felt involuntarily drawn towards him; one could be sure that the pleasant little man was too intent on giving himself a good time, by every means in his power, to think of quarrelling with that vague and indefinite person known as one's neighbor. Wherefore, on hearing his companion speak so cavalierly to Thibault, the good fat little man appeared to be in despair.

"Gently, Madame Magloire! Gently, madame bailiff!" he said, contriving in these few words to let his neighbors know what and who he was; "Gently! Those were ugly words to use to the poor fellow, who is more sorry than you are for the accident."

"And may I ask, Monsieur Magloire," replied the lady, "if I am not at liberty to thank him for so nicely crumpling my beautiful blue damask dress, which is now entirely spoilt, not taking into consideration that he also trod on my little toe?"

"I beg you, Madame, to pardon my clumsiness," replied Thibault; "when you turned your face towards me, its wonderful beauty dazzled me like a ray of May sunshine, so that I could not see where I was treading."

It was not a badly turned compliment for a man who for three months past had been in the daily society of a pack of wolves; nevertheless it did not produce any great effect upon the lady, who only responded with a haughty little pouting of the mouth. The truth was, that in spite of Thibault being so decently dressed, she had, with the curious insight which women of all ranks possess in these matters, detected at once to what class he belonged.

Her stout little companion however, was more indulgent, for he clapped loudly with his podgy hands, which the pose adopted by his wife left him free to use as he liked.

"Ah! bravo, bravo!" he said. "You have hit the mark, Monsieur; you are a clever young fellow, and seem to have studied the style to address women in. My love, I hope you appreciated the compliment as I did, and to prove to this gentlemen that we are good Christians and bear no ill will towards him, he will, I hope, if he is living in this neighborhood and it would not be too far out of his way, accompany us home, and we will drink a bottle of old wine together, if Perrine will get one out for us from the back of the wood shed."

"Ah! There I know you, Master Népomucène; any excuse serves you to be clinking glasses with somebody, and when no genuine occasion offers, you are very clever at ferreting out one, it does not matter where. But you know, Monsieur Magloire, that the doctor has expressly forbidden you to drink between meals."

"True, madame bailiff, true," replied her husband, "but he did not forbid me to show politeness to an agreeable young fellow such as Monsieur appears to me to be. Be lenient, I pray, Suzanne; give up this surly manner, which suits you so ill. Why, Madame, those who do not know you, would think, to hear you, that we had nearly got to quarrelling over a gown. However, to prove the contrary to Monsieur, I promise that if you can get him to go back with us, I will, the very minute we get home, give you the money to buy that figured silk dress, which you have been wishing for so long."

The effect of this promise was like magic. Madame Magloire was instantly mollified, and as the fishing was now drawing to a close, she accepted with less ungraciousness the arm which Thibault, somewhat awkwardly we must confess, now offered her.

As to Thibault himself, struck with the beauty of the lady, and gathering from words which had fallen from her and her husband, that she was the wife of a magistrate, he parted the crowd before him with an air of command, holding his head high the while, and making his way with as much determination as if he were starting on the conquest of the Golden Fleece.

And in truth, Thibault, the bridegroom elect of Agnelette, the lover who had been so ignominiously expelled her house by the mistress of the mill, was thinking not only of all the pleasure he could enjoy, but of the proud position he would hold as the beloved of a bailiff's wife, and of all the advantages to be drawn from the good fortune which had so unexpectedly befallen him, and which he had so long desired.

As on her side also, Madame Magloire was not only very much preoccupied with her own thoughts, but also paid very little attention to him, looking to right and left, first in front of her and then behind, as if in search of someone, the conversation would have lagged terribly as they walked along if their excellent little companion had not been at the expense of the best part of it, as he jogged along now beside Thibault and now beside Suzanne, waddling like a duck jogging home after a big feed.

And so with Thibault engaged in his calculations, and the bailiff's wife with her dreams, the bailiff trotting beside them talking and wiping his forehead with a fine cambric handkerchief, they arrived at the village of Erneville, which is situated about a mile and a half from the Poudron ponds. It was here, in this charming village, which lies halfway between Haramont and Bonneuil, within a stone's throw or two of the castle of Vez, the dwelling of my lord the baron, that Monsieur Magloire sat as magistrate.

11

DAVID AND GOLIATH

A fter walking the whole length of the village, they stopped before an imposing looking house at the junction of the roads leading to Longpré and Haramont. As they neared the house—the little host, with all the gallantry of a "preux chevalier" went on ahead, mounted the flight of five or six steps with an agility which one could not have expected, and, by dint of standing on tiptoe, managed to reach the bell with the tips of his fingers. It should be added, that having once got hold of it, he gave it a pull which unmistakably announced the return of the master. It was, in short, no ordinary return, but a triumphal one, for the bailiff was bringing home a guest.

A maid, neatly dressed in her best clothes, opened the door. The bailiff gave her an order in a low voice, and Thibault, whose adoration of beautiful women did not prevent him from liking a good dinner, gathered that these few whispered words referred to the menu which Perrine was to prepare. Then turning round, his host addressed Thibault:

"Welcome, my dear guest, to the house of Bailiff Népomucène Magloire."

Thibault politely allowed Madame to pass in before him, and was then introduced into the drawing room.

But the shoe maker now made a slip. Unaccustomed as yet to luxury, the man of the forest was not adroit enough to hide the admiration which he felt on beholding the bailiff's home. For the first time in his life he found himself in the midst of damask curtains and gilt armchairs; he had not imagined that any one save the king, or at least his Highness the Duke of Orleans, had curtains and armchairs of this magnificence. He was unconscious that all the while Madame Magloire was closely watching him, and that his simple astonishment and delight did not escape her detective eye. However, she appeared now, after mature reflexion, to look with greater favor on the guest whom her husband had imposed upon her, and endeavored to soften for him the glances of her dark eyes. But her affability did not go so far as to lead her to comply with the request of Monsieur Magloire, who begged her to add to the flavor and bouquet of the champagne by pouring it out herself for her guest.

Notwithstanding the entreaties of her august husband, the bailiff's wife refused, and under the pretext of fatigue from her walk, she retired to her own room. Before leaving the room, however, she expressed a hope to Thibault, that, as she owed him some expiation, he would not forget the way to Erneville, ending her speech with a smile which displayed a row of charming teeth. Thibault responded with so much lively pleasure in his voice that it rendered any roughness of speech less noticeable, swearing that he would sooner lose the power to eat and drink than the remembrance of a lady who was as courteous as she was beautiful.

Madame Magloire gave him a curtsey which would have made her known as the bailiff's wife a mile off, and left the room.

She had hardly closed the door behind her, when Monsieur Magloire went through a pirouette in her honor, which though less light, was not less significant than the caper a schoolboy executes when once he has got rid of his master.

"Ah! my dear friend," he said. "Now that we are no longer

hampered by a woman's presence, we will have a good go at the wine! Those women, they are delightful at mass or at a ball; but at table, heaven defend me, there is nobody like the men! What do you say, old fellow?"

Perrine now came in to receive her master's orders as to what wine she was to bring up. But the gay little man was far too fastidious a judge of wines to trust a woman with such a commission as this. Indeed, women never show that reverential respect for certain old bottles which is their due, nor that delicacy of touch with which they love to be handled. He drew Perrine down as if to whisper something in her ear; instead of which he gave a good sound kiss to the cheek which was still young and fresh, and which did not blush sufficiently to lead to the belief that the kiss was a novelty to it.

"Well, sir," said the girl laughing. "What is it?"

"This is it, Perrinette, my love," said the bailiff, "that I alone know the good brands, and as they are many in number, you might get lost among them, and so I am going to the cellar myself." And the good man disappeared trundling off on his little legs, cheerful, alert and fantastic as those Nuremberg toys mounted on a stand, which you wind up with a key, and which, once set going, turn round and round, or go first one way and then the other, till the spring has run down; the only difference being, that this dear little man seemed wound up by the hand of God himself, and gave no sign of ever coming to a standstill.

Thibault was left alone. He rubbed his hands together, congratulating himself on having chanced upon such a well-to-do house, with such a beautiful wife, and such an amiable husband for host and hostess. Five minutes later the door again opened, and in came the bailiff, with a bottle in either hand, and one under each arm. The two under his arms were bottles of sparkling Sillery, of the first quality, which, not being injured by shaking, were safe to be carried in a horizontal position. The two which he carried in his hands, and which he held with a respectful care which was a pleasure to behold, were, one a bottle of very old Chambertin, the other a bottle of Hermitage.

The supper hour had now come; for it must be remembered, that at the period of which we are writing, dinner was at midday, and supper at six. Moreover, it had already been dark for some time before six o'clock, in this month of January, and whether it be six, or twelve o'clock at night, if one has to eat one's meal by candle or lamplight, it always seems to one like supper.

The bailiff put the bottles tenderly down on the table and rang the bell. Perrinette came in.

"When will the table be ready for us, my pretty?" asked Magloire.

"Whenever Monsieur pleases," replied Perrine. "I know Monsieur does not like waiting; so I always have everything ready in good time."

"Go and ask Madame, then, if she is not coming; tell her, Perrine, that we do not wish to sit down without her."

Perrine left the room.

"We may as well go into the dining room to wait," said the little host; "you must be hungry, my dear friend, and when I am hungry, I like to feed my eyes before I feed my stomach."

"You seem to me to be a fine gourmand, you," said Thibault.

"Epicure, epicure, not gourmand—you must not confuse the two things. I go first, but only in order to show you the way."

And so saying, Monsieur Magloire led his guest into the dining room. "Ah!" he exclaimed gaily as he went in, patting his corporation. "Tell me now, do you not think this girl of mine is a capital cook, fit to serve a Cardinal? Just look now at this little supper she has spread for us; quite a simple one, and yet it pleases me more, I am sure, than would have Belshazzar's feast."

"On my honor, bailiff," said Thibault, "you are right; it is a sight to rejoice one's heart." And Thibault's eyes began to shine like carbuncles.

And yet it was, as the bailiff described it, quite an unpretentious little supper, but withal so appetizing to look upon, that it was quite surprising. At one end of the table was a fine carp, boiled in vinegar and herbs, with the roe served on either side of it on a layer of parsley, dotted about with cut carrots. The opposite end was occupied by a boar ham, mellow flavored, and deliciously reposing on a dish of spinach, which lay like a green islet surrounded by an ocean of gravy.

A delicate game pie, made of two partridges only, of which the heads appeared above the upper crust, as if ready to attack one another with their beaks, was placed in the middle of the table; while the intervening spaces were covered with side dishes holding slices of Arles sausage, pieces of tunny fish, swimming in beautiful green oil from Provence, anchovies sliced and arranged in all kinds of strange and fantastic patterns on a white and yellow bed of chopped eggs, and pats of butter that could only have been churned that very day. As accessories to these were two or three sorts of cheese, chosen from among those of which the chief quality is to provoke thirst, some Reims biscuits, of delightful crispness, and pears just fit to eat, showing that the master himself had taken the trouble to preserve them, and to turn them about on the store-room shelf.

Thibault was so taken up in the contemplation of this little amateur supper, that he scarcely heard the message which Perrine brought back from her mistress, who sent word that she had a headache, and begged to make her excuses to her guest, with the hope that she might have the pleasure of entertaining him when he next came.

The little man gave visible signs of rejoicing on hearing his wife's answer, breathed loudly, and clapped his hands, exclaiming:

"She has a headache! She has a headache! Come along then, sit down! Sit down!" And thereupon, besides the two bottles of old Mâcon, which had already been respectively placed within reach of the host and guest, as vin ordinaire, between the hors d'oeuvre and the dessert plates, he introduced the four other bottles which he had just brought up from the cellar.

Madame Magloire had, I think, acted not unwisely in refusing to sup with these stalwart champions of the table, for such was their hunger and thirst, that half the carp and the two bottles of wine disappeared without a word passing between them except such exclamations as:

"Good fish! Isn't it?"

"Capital!"

"Fine wine! Isn't it?"

"Excellent!"

The carp and the Mâcon being consumed, they passed on to the game pie and the Chambertin, and now their tongues began to be unloosed, especially the bailiff's.

By the time half the game pie, and the first bottle of Chambertin were finished, Thibault knew the history of Népomucène Magloire; not a very complicated one, it must be confessed.

Monsieur Magloire was son to a church ornament manufacturer who had worked for the chapel belonging to his Highness the Duke of Orleans, the latter, in his religious zeal having a burning desire to obtain pictures by Albano and Titian for the sum of four to five thousand francs.

Chrysostom Magloire had placed his son Népomucène Magloire, as head cook with Louis' son, his Highness the Duke of Orleans.

The young man had, from infancy almost, manifested a decided taste for cooking; he had been especially attached to the castle at Villers-Cotterets, and for thirty years presided over his Highness's dinners, the latter introducing him to his friends as a thorough artist, and from time to time, sending for him to come upstairs to talk over culinary matters with Marshal Richelieu.

When fifty-five years of age, Magloire found himself so rounded in bulk, that it was only with some difficulty he could get through the narrow doors of the passages and offices.

Fearing to be caught some day like the weasel of the fable, he asked permission to resign his post.

The Duke consented, not without regret, but with less regret than he would have felt at any other time, for he had just married Madame de Montesson, and it was only rarely now that he visited his castle at Villers-Cotterets.

His Highness had fine old-fashioned ideas as regards super-annuated retainers. He, therefore, sent for Magloire, and asked him how much he had been able to save while in his service. Magloire replied that he was happily able to retire with a compe-tence; the prince, however, insisted upon knowing the exact amount of his little fortune, and Magloire confessed to an income of nine thousand livres.

"A man who has provided me with such a good table for thirty years," said the prince, "should have enough to live well upon himself for the remainder of his life." And he made up the income to twelve thousand, so that Magloire might have a thou-sand livres a month to spend. Added to this, he allowed him to choose furniture for the whole of his house from his own old lumber room; and thence came the damask curtains and gilt arm chairs, which, although just a little bit faded and worn, had nevertheless preserved that appearance of grandeur which had made such an impression on Thibault.

By the time the whole of the first partridge was finished, and half the second bottle had been drunk, Thibault knew that Madame Magloire was the host's fourth wife, a fact which seemed in his own eyes to add a good foot or two to his height.

He had also ascertained that he had married her not for her fortune, but for her beauty, having always had as great a predilection for pretty faces and beautiful statues, as for good wines and appetizing victuals, and Monsieur Magloire further stated, with no sign of faltering, that, old as he was, if his wife were to die, he should have no fear in entering on a fifth marriage.

As he now passed from the Chambertin to the Hermitage,

which he alternated with the Sillery, Monsieur Magloire began to speak of his wife's qualities. She was not the personification of docility, no, quite the reverse; she was somewhat opposed to her husband's admiration for the various wines of France, and did everything she could, even using physical force, to prevent his too frequent visits to the cellar; while, for one who believed in living without ceremony, she on her part was too fond of dress, too much given to elaborate head gears, English laces, and such like gewgaws, which women make part of their arsenal; she would gladly have turned the twelve hogsheads of wine, which formed the staple of her husband's cellar, into lace for her arms, and ribands for her throat, if Monsieur Magloire had been the man to allow this metamorphosis. But, with this exception, there was not a virtue which Suzanne did not possess, and these virtues of hers, if the bailiff was to be believed, were carried on so perfectly shaped a pair of legs, that, if by any misfortune she were to lose one, it would be quite impossible throughout the district to find another that would match the leg that remained. The good man was like a regular whale, blowing out self-satisfaction from all his airholes, as the former does seawater.

But even before all these hidden perfections of his wife had been revealed to him by the bailiff, like a modern king Candaules ready to confide in a modern Gyges, her beauty had already made such a deep impression on the shoe maker, that, as we have seen, he could do nothing but think of it in silence as he walked beside her, and since he had been at table, he had continued to dream about it, listening to his host,—eating the while of course,—without answering, as Monsieur Magloire, delighted to have such an accommodating audience, poured forth his tales, linked one to another like a necklace of beads.

But the worthy bailiff, having made a second excursion to the cellar, and this second excursion having produced, as the saying is, a little knot at the tip of his tongue, he began to be rather less appreciative of the rare quality which was required in his disciples by Pythagons.

He, therefore, gave Thibault to understand that he had now said all that he wished to tell him concerning himself and his wife, and that it was Thibault's turn to give him some information as regards his own circumstances, the amiable little man adding that wishing often to visit him, he wished to know more about him. Thibault felt that it was very necessary to disguise the truth; and accordingly gave himself out as a man living at ease in the country, on the revenues of two farms and of a hundred acres of land, situated near Vertefeuille.

There was, he continued, a splendid warren on these hundred acres, with a wonderful supply of red and fallow deer, boars, partridges, pheasants and hares, of which the bailiff should have some to taste. The bailiff was astonished and delighted. As we have seen, by the menu for his table, he was fond of venison, and he was carried away with joy at the thought of obtaining his game without having recourse to the poachers, and through the channel of this new friendship.

And now, the last drop of the seventh bottle having been scrupulously divided between the two glasses, they decided that it was time to stop.

The rosy champagne—prime vintage of Aï, and the last bottle emptied—had brought Népomucène Magloire's habitual good nature to the level of tender affection. He was charmed with his new friend, who tossed off his bottle in almost as good style as he did himself; he addressed him as his bosom friend, he embraced him, he made him promise that there should be a morrow to their pleasant entertainment; he stood a second time on tiptoe to give him a parting hug as he accompanied him to the door, which Thibault on his part, bending down, received with the best grace in the world.

The church clock of Erneville was striking midnight as the door closed behind the shoe maker. The fumes of the heady wine he had been drinking had begun to give him a feeling of oppression before leaving the house, but it was worse when he got into the open air. He staggered, overcome with giddiness, and went and leant with his back against a wall. What followed next was as vague and mysterious to him as the phantasmagoria of a dream. Above his head, about six or eight feet from the ground, was a window, which, as he moved to lean against the wall, had appeared to him to be lighted, although the light was shaded by double curtains. He had hardly taken up his position against the wall when he thought he heard it open. It was, he imagined, the worthy bailiff, unwilling to part with him without sending him a last farewell, and he tried to step forward so as to do honor to this gracious intention, but his attempt was unavailing. At first he thought he was stuck to the wall like a branch of ivy, but he was soon disabused of this idea. He felt a heavy weight planted first on the right shoulder and then on the left, which made his knees give way so that he slid down the wall as if to seat himself. This maneuver on Thibault's part appeared to be just what the individual who was making use of him as a ladder wished him to do, for we can no longer hide the fact that the weight so felt was that of a man. As Thibault made his forced genuflection, the man was also lowered;

"That's right, l'Eveillé! That's right!" he said. "So!" And with this last word, he jumped to the ground, while overhead was heard the sound of a window being shut.

Thibault had sense enough to understand two things: first, that he was mistaken for someone called l'Eveillé, who was probably asleep somewhere about the premises; secondly, that his shoulders had just served some lover as a climbing ladder; both of which things caused Thibault an undefined sense of humiliation.

Accordingly, he seized hold mechanically of some floating piece of stuff which he took to be the lover's cloak, and, with the persistency of a drunken man, continued to hang on to it.

"What are you doing that for, you scoundrel?" asked a voice, which did not seem altogether unfamiliar to the shoe maker. "One would think you were afraid of losing me."

"Most certainly I am afraid of losing you," replied Thibault, "because I wish to know who it is has the impertinence to use my shoulders for a ladder."

"Phew!" said the unknown. "It's not you then, l'Eveillé?"

"No, it is not," replied Thibault.

"Well, whether it is you or not you, I thank you."

"How, thank you? Ah! I dare say! Thank you, indeed! You think the matter is going to rest like that, do you?"

"I had counted upon it being so, certainly."

"Then you counted without your host."

"Now, you blackguard, leave go of me! You are drunk!"

"Drunk! What do you mean? We only drank seven bottles between us, and the bailiff had a good four to his share."

"Leave go of me, you drunkard, do you hear!"

"Drunkard! You call me a drunkard, a drunkard for having drunk three bottles of wine!"

"I don't call you a drunkard because you drank three bottles of wine, but because you let yourself get tipsy over those three unfortunate bottles."

And, with a gesture of commiseration, and trying for the third time to release his cloak, the unknown continued:

"Now then, are you going to let go my cloak or not, you idiot?"

Thibault was at all times touchy as to the way people addressed him, but in his present state of mind his susceptibility amounted to extreme irritation.

"By the devil!" he exclaimed. "Let me tell you, my fine sir, that the only idiot here is the man who gives insults in return for the services of which he has made use, and seeing that is so, I do not know what prevents me planting my fist in the middle of your face."

This menace was scarcely out of his mouth, when, as instantly as a cannon goes off once the flame of the match has touched the powder, the blow with which Thibault had threatened his unknown adversary, came full against his own cheek.

"Take that, you beast," said the voice, which brought back to

Thibault certain recollections in connection with the blow he received. "I am a good Jew, you see, and pay you back your money before weighing your coin."

Thibault's answer was a blow in the chest; it was well directed, and Thibault felt inwardly pleased with it himself. But it had no more effect on his antagonist than the fillip from a child's finger would have on an oak tree. It was returned by a second blow of the fist which so far exceeded the former in the force with which it was delivered, that Thibault felt certain if the giant's strength went on increasing in the same ratio, that a third of the kind would level him with the ground.

But the very violence of his blow brought disaster on Thibault's unknown assailant. The latter had fallen on to one knee, and so doing, his hand, touching the ground, came in contact with a stone. Rising in fury to his feet again, with the stone in his hand, he flung it at his enemy's head. The colossal figure uttered a sound like the bellowing of an ox, turned round on himself, and then, like an oak tree cut off by the roots, fell his whole length on the ground, and lay there insensible.

Not knowing whether he had killed, or only wounded his adversary, Thibault took to his heels and fled, not even turning to look behind him.

♒ 12 ♒

WOLVES IN THE SHEEP FOLD

The forest was not far from the bailiff's house, and in two bounds Thibault found himself on the further side of Les Fossés, and in the wooded path leading to the brickyard. He had no sooner entered the forest than his usual escort surrounded him, fawning and blinking with their eyes and wagging their tails to show their pleasure.

Thibault, who had been so alarmed the first time he found himself in company with this strange body guard, took no more notice of them now than if they had been a pack of poodles. He gave them a word or two of caress, softly scratched the head of the one that was nearest him, and continued on his way, thinking over his double triumph.

He had beaten his host at the bottle, he had vanquished his adversary at fisticuffs, and in this joyous frame of mind, he walked along, saying aloud to himself:

"You must acknowledge, friend Thibault, that you are a lucky rascal! Madame Suzanne is in every possible respect just what you want! A bailiff's wife! My word! That's a conquest worth making! And if he dies first, what a wife to get! But in either case, when she is walking beside me, and taking my arm, whether as wife or mistress, the devil take it, if I am mistaken for anything but a gentleman! And to think that unless I am fool enough to play my cards badly, all this will be mine! For she did not deceive me by the way she went off: those who have nothing to fear have no need to take flight. She was afraid to show her feelings too plainly at first meeting; but how kind she was after she got home! Well, well, it is all working itself out, as I can see; I have only got to push matters a bit; and some fine morning she will find herself rid of her fat little old man, and then the thing is done. Not that I do, or can, wish for the death of poor Monsieur Magloire. If I take his place after he is no more, well and good; but to kill a man who has given you such good wine to drink! To kill him with his good wine still hot in your mouth! Why, even my friend the wolf would blush for me if I were guilty of such a deed."

Then with one of his most roguish smiles, he went on:

"And besides, would it not be as well to have already acquired some rights over Madame Suzanne, by the time Monsieur Magloire passes, in the course of nature, into the other world, which, considering the way in which the old scamp eats and drinks, cannot be a matter of long delay?"

And then, no doubt because the good qualities of the bailiff's wife which had been so highly extolled to him came back to his mind:

"No, no," he continued, "no illness, no death! But just those ordinary disagreeables which happen to everybody; only, as it is to be to my advantage, I should like rather more than the usual share to fall to him; one cannot at his age set up for a smart young buck; no, every one according to their dues … and when these things come to pass, I will give you more than a thank you, cousin wolf."

My readers will doubtless not be of the same way of thinking as Thibault, who saw nothing offensive in this pleasantry of his, but on the contrary, rubbed his hands together smiling at his own thoughts, and indeed so pleased with them that he had reached the town, and found himself at the end of the Rue de

Largny before he was aware that he had left the bailiff's house more than a few hundred paces behind him.

He now made a sign to his wolves, for it was not quite prudent to traverse the whole town of Villers-Cotterets with a dozen wolves walking alongside as a guard of honor; not only might they meet dogs by the way, but the dogs might wake up the inhabitants.

Six of his wolves, therefore, went off to the right, and six to the left, and although the paths they took were not exactly of the same length, and although some of them went more quickly than the others, the whole dozen nevertheless managed to meet, without one missing, at the end of the Rue de Lormet. As soon as Thibault had reached the door of his hut, they took leave of him and disappeared; but, before they dispersed, Thibault requested them to be at the same spot on the morrow, as soon as night fell.

Although it was two o'clock before Thibault got home, he was up with the dawn; it is true, however, that the day does not rise very early in the month of January.

He was hatching a plot. He had not forgotten the promise he had made to the bailiff to send him some game from his warren; his warren being, in fact, the whole of the forest land which belonged to his most serene Highness the Duke of Orleans. This was why he had got up in such good time. It had snowed for two hours before daybreak; and he now went and explored the forest in all directions, with the skill and cunning of a bloodhound.

He tracked the deer to its lair, the wild boar to its soil, the hare to its form; and followed their traces to discover where they went at night.

And then, when darkness again fell on the forest, he gave a howl—a regular wolf's howl—in answer to which came crowding to him the wolves that he had invited the night before, followed by old and young recruits, even to the very cubs of a year old.

Thibault then explained that he expected a more than usually fine night's hunting from his friends, and as an encouragement to them, announced his intention of going with them himself and giving his help in the chase.

It was in very truth a hunt beyond the power of words to describe. The whole night through did the somber glades of the forest resound with hideous cries.

Here, a roebuck pursued by a wolf, fell, caught by the throat by another wolf hidden in ambush; there, Thibault, knife in hand like a butcher, was running to the assistance of three or four of his ferocious companions, that had already fastened on a fine young boar of four years old, which he now finished off.

An old she-wolf came along bringing with her half-a-dozen hares which she had surprised in their love frolics, and she had great difficulty in preventing her cubs from swallowing a whole covey of young partridges which the young marauders had come across with their heads under their wings, without first waiting for the wolf master to levy his dues.

Madame Suzanne Magloire little thought what was taking place at this moment in the forest of Villers-Cotterets, and on her account. In a couple of hours' time the wolves had heaped up a perfect cartload of game in front of Thibault's hut.

Thibault selected what he wanted for his own purposes, and left over sufficient to provide them a sumptuous repast. Borrowing a mule from a charcoal burner, on the pretext that he wanted to convey his shoes to town, he loaded it up with the game and started for Villers-Cotterets. There he sold a part of this booty to the gamedealer, reserving the best pieces and those which had been least mutilated by the wolves' claws, to present to Madame Magloire.

His first intention had been to go in person with his gift to the bailiff; but Thibault was beginning to have a smattering of the ways of the world, and thought it would, therefore, be more becoming to allow his offering of game to precede him. To this end he employed a peasant on payment of a few coppers, to carry the game to the Bailiff of Erneville, merely accompanying it with a slip of paper, on which he wrote: "From Monsieur Thibault." He, himself, was to follow closely on the message; and, indeed, so closely did he do so, that he arrived just as Maître Magloire was having the game he had received spread out on a table.

The bailiff, in the warmth of his gratitude, extended his arms towards his friend of the previous night, and tried to embrace him, uttering loud cries of joy. I say tried, for two things prevented him from carrying out his wish; one, the shortness of his arms, the other, the rotundity of his person.

But thinking that where his capacities were insufficient, Madame Magloire might be of assistance, he ran to the door, calling at the top of his voice: "Suzanne, Suzanne!"

There was so unusual a tone in the bailiff's voice that his wife felt sure something extraordinary had happened, but whether for good or ill she was unable to make sure: and downstairs she came, therefore, in great haste, to see for herself what was taking place.

She found her husband, wild with delight, trotting round to look on all sides at the game spread on the table, and it must be confessed, that no sight could have more greatly rejoiced a gourmand's eye. As soon as he caught sight of Suzanne, "Look, look, Madame!" he cried, clapping his hands together. "See what our friend Thibault has brought us, and thank him for it. Praise be to God! There is one person who knows how to keep his promises! He tells us he will send a hamper of game, and he sends us a cartload. Shake hands with him, embrace him at once, and just look here at this."

Madame Magloire graciously followed out her husband's orders; she gave Thibault her hand, allowed him to kiss her, and cast her beautiful eyes over the supply of food which elicited such exclamations of admiration from the bailiff. And as a supply, which was to make such an acceptable addition to the ordinary daily fare, it was certainly worthy of all admiration.

First, as prime pieces, came a boar's head and ham, firm and savory morsels; then a fine three-year-old kid, which should have been as tender as the dew that only the evening before beaded the grass at which it was nibbling; next came hares, fine fleshy hares from the heath of Gondreville, full fed on wild thyme; and then such scented pheasants, and such delicious red-legged partridges, that once on the spit, the magnificence of their plumage was forgotten in the perfume of their flesh. And all these good things the fat little man enjoyed in advance in his imagination; he already saw the boar broiled on the coals, the kid dressed with sauce piquant, the hares made into a pasty, the pheasants stuffed with truffles, the partridges dressed with cabbage, and he put so much fervor and feeling into his orders and directions, that merely to hear him was enough to set a gourmand's mouthwatering.

It was this enthusiasm on the part of the bailiff which no doubt made Madame Suzanne appear somewhat cold and unappreciative in comparison.

Nevertheless she took the initiative, and with much graciousness assured Thibault that she would on no account allow him to return to his farms until all the provisions, with which, thanks to him, the larder would now overflow, had been consumed. You may guess how delighted Thibault was at having his cherished wishes thus met by Madame herself. He promised himself no end of grand things from this stay at Erneville, and his spirits rose to the point of himself proposing to Maître Magloire that they should indulge in a preparatory whack of liquor to prepare their digestions for the savory dishes that Mademoiselle Perrine was preparing for them.

Maître Magloire was quite gratified to see that Thibault had forgotten nothing, not even the cook's name. He sent for some vermouth, a liqueur as yet but little known in France, having been imported from Holland by the Duke of Orleans and of which a present had been made by his Highness's head cook to his predecessor.

Thibault made a face over it; he did not think this foreign

drink was equal to a nice little glass of native Châblis; but when assured by the bailiff that, thanks to the beverage, he would in an hour's time have a ferocious appetite, he made no further remark, and affably assisted his host to finish the bottle. Madame Suzanne, meanwhile, had returned to her own room to smarten herself up a bit, as women say, which generally means an entire change of raiment.

It was not long before the dinner hour sounded, and Madame Suzanne came down stairs again. She was perfectly dazzling in a splendid dress of gray damask trimmed with pearl, and the transports of amorous admiration into which Thibault was thrown by the sight of her prevented the shoe maker from thinking of the awkwardness of the position in which he now unavoidably found himself, dining as he was for the first time with such handsome and distinguished company. To his credit, be it said, he did not make bad use of his opportunities. Not only did he cast frequent and unmistakable sheep's eyes at his fair hostess, but he gradually brought his knee nearer to hers, and finally went so far as to give it a gentle pressure. Suddenly, and while Thibault was engaged in this performance, Madame Suzanne, who was looking sweetly towards him, opened her eyes and stared fixedly a moment. Then she opened her mouth, and went off into such a violent fit of laughter, that she almost choked, and nearly went into hysterics. Maître Magloire, taking no notice of the effect, turned straight to the cause, and he now looked at Thibault, and was much more concerned and alarmed with what he thought to see, than with the nervous state of excitement into which his wife had been thrown by her hilarity.

"Ah! My dear fellow!" he cried, stretching two little agitated arms towards Thibault. "You are in flames, you are in flames!"

Thibault sprang up hastily.

"Where? How?" he asked.

"Your hair is on fire," answered the bailiff, in all sincerity; and so genuine was his terror, that he seized the water bottle that was in front of his wife in order to put out the conflagration blazing among Thibault's locks.

The shoe maker involuntarily put up his hand to his head, but feeling no heat, he at once guessed what was the matter, and fell back into his chair, turning horribly pale. He had been so preoccupied during the last two days, that he had quite forgotten to take the same precaution he had done before visiting the owner of the mill, and had omitted to give his hair that particular twist whereby he was able to hide the hairs of which the black wolf had acquired the proprietorship under his others.

Added to this, he had during this short period given vent to so many little wishes, one here, and one there, all more or less to the detriment of his neighbor, that the flame-colored hairs had multiplied to an alarming extent, and at this moment, any one of them could vie in brilliancy with the light from the two wax candles which lit the room.

"Well, you did give me a dreadful fright, Monsieur Magloire," said Thibault, trying to conceal his agitation.

"But, but," responded the bailiff, still pointing with a certain remains of fear at Thibault's flaming lock of hair.

"That is nothing," continued Thibault. "Do not be uneasy about the unusual color of some of my hair; it came from a fright my mother had with a pan of hot coals, that nearly set her hair on fire before I was born."

"But what is more strange still," said Madame Suzanne, who had swallowed a whole glassful of water in the effort to control her laughter, "that I have remarked this dazzling peculiarity for the first time today."

"Ah! Really!" said Thibault, scarcely knowing what to say in answer.

"The other day," continued Madame Suzanne, "it seemed to me that your hair was as black as my velvet mantle, and yet, believe me, I did not fail to study you most attentively, Monsieur Thibault."

This last sentence, reviving Thibault's hopes, restored him once more to good humor.

"Ah! Madame," he replied, "you know the proverb: 'Red hair, warm heart,' and the other: 'Some folks are like ill-made sabots—smooth outside, but rough to wear?'"

Madame Magloire made a face at this low proverb about wooden shoes, but, as was often the case with the bailiff, he did not agree with his wife on this point.

"My friend Thibault utters words of gold," he said, "and I need not go far to be able to point the truth of his proverbs ... See for example, this soup we have here, which has nothing much in its appearance to commend it, but never have I found onion and bread fried in goose fat more to my taste."

And after this there was no further talk of Thibault's fiery head.

Nevertheless, it seemed as if Madame Suzanne's eyes were irresistibly attracted to this unfortunate lock, and every time that Thibault's eyes met the mocking look in hers, he thought he detected on her face a reminiscence of the laugh which had not long since made him feel so uncomfortable. He was very much annoyed at this, and, in spite of himself, he kept putting up his hand to try and hide the unfortunate lock under the rest of his hair. But the hairs were not only unusual in color, but also of a phenomenal stiffness—it was no longer human hair, but horse-hair. In vain Thibault endeavored to hide the devil's hairs beneath his own, nothing, not even the hairdresser's tongs could have induced them to lie otherwise than in the way which seemed natural to them. But although so occupied with thinking of his hair, Thibault's legs still continued their tender maneuverings; and although Madame Magloire made no response to their solicitations, she apparently had no wish to escape from them, and Thibault was presumptuously led to believe that he had achieved a conquest.

They sat on pretty late into the night, and Madame Suzanne, who appeared to find the evening drag, rose several times from the table and went backwards and forwards to other parts of the house, which afforded the bailiff opportunities of frequent visits to the cellar.

He hid so many bottles in the lining of his waistcoat, and once on the table, he emptied them so rapidly, that little by little his head sank lower and lower on to his chest, and it was evidently high time to put an end to the bout, if he was to be saved from falling under the table.

Thibault decided to profit by this condition of things, and to declare his love to the bailiff's wife without delay, judging it a good opportunity to speak while the husband was heavy with drink; he therefore expressed a wish to retire for the night. Whereupon they rose from table, and Perrine was called and bidden to show the guest to his room. As he followed her along the corridor, he made enquiries of her concerning the different rooms.

Number one was Maître Magloire's, number two that of his wife, and number three was his. The bailiff's room, and his wife's, communicated with one another by an inner door; Thibault's room had access to the corridor only.

He also noticed that Madame Suzanne was in her husband's room; no doubt some pious sense of conjugal duty had taken her there. The good man was in a condition approaching to that of Noah when his sons took occasion to insult him, and Madame Suzanne's assistance would seem to have been needed to get him into his room.

Thibault left his own room on tiptoe, carefully shut his door behind him, listened for a moment at the door of Madame Suzanne's room, heard no sound within, felt for the key, found it in the lock, paused a second, and then turned it.

The door opened; the room was in total darkness. But having for so long consorted with wolves, Thibault had acquired some of their characteristics, and, among others, that of being able to see in the dark.

He cast a rapid glance round the room; to the right was the

fireplace; facing it a couch with a large mirror above it; behind him, on the side of the fireplace, a large bed, hung with figured silk; in front of him, near the couch, a dressing table covered with a profusion of lace, and, last of all, two large draped windows. He hid himself behind the curtains of one of these, instinctively choosing the window that was farthest removed from the husband's room. After waiting a quarter of an hour, during which time Thibault's heart beat so violently that the sound of it—fatal omen—reminded him of the click-clack of the mill wheel at Croyolles, Madame Suzanne entered the room.

Thibault's original plan had been to leave his hiding place as soon as Madame Suzanne came in and the door was safely shut behind her, and there and then to make avowal of his love. But on consideration, fearing that in her surprise, and before she recognized who it was, she might not be able to suppress a cry which would betray them, he decided that it would be better to wait until Monsieur Magloire was asleep beyond all power of being awakened.

Perhaps, also, this procrastination may have been partly due to that feeling which all men have, however resolute of purpose they may be, of wishing to put off the critical moment, when on this moment depend such chances as hung on the one which was to decide for or against the happiness of the shoe maker. For Thibault, by dint of telling himself that he was madly in love with Madame Magloire, had ended by believing that he really was so, and, in spite of being under the protection of the black wolf, he experienced all the timidity of the genuine lover. So he kept himself concealed behind the curtains.

The bailiff's wife, however, had taken up her position before the mirror of her Pompadour table, and was decking herself out as if she were going to a festival or preparing to make one of a procession.

She tried on ten veils before making choice of one.

She arranged the folds of her dress.

She fastened a triple row of pearls round her neck.

Then she loaded her arms with all the bracelets she possessed.

Finally she dressed her hair with the minutest care.

Thibault was lost in conjectures as to the meaning of all this coquetry, when all of a sudden a dry, grating noise, as if some hard body coming in contact with a pane of glass, made him start. Madame Suzanne started too, and immediately put out the lights. The shoe maker then heard her step softly to the window, and cautiously open it; whereupon there followed some whisperings, of which Thibault could not catch the words, but, by drawing the curtain a little aside, he was able to distinguish in the darkness the figure of a man of gigantic stature, who appeared to be climbing through the window.

Thibault instantly recalled his adventure with the unknown combatant, whose mantle he had clung to, and whom he had so triumphantly disposed of by hitting him on the forehead with a stone. As far as he could make out, this would be the same window from which the giant had descended when he made use of Thibault's two shoulders as a ladder. The surmise of identity was, undoubtedly, founded on a logical conclusion. As a man was now climbing in at the window, a man could very well have been climbing down from it; and if a man did climb down from it—unless, of course, Madam Magloire's acquaintances were many in number, and she had a great variety of tastes—if a man did climb down from it, in all probability, it was the same man who, at this moment was climbing in.

But whoever this nocturnal visitor might be, Madame Suzanne held out her hand to the intruder, who took a heavy jump into the room, which made the floor tremble and set all the furniture shaking. The apparition was certainly not a spirit, but a corporeal body, and moreover one that came under the category of heavy bodies.

"Oh! Take care, my lord," Madame Suzanne's voice was heard to say, "heavily as my husband sleeps, if you make such a noise as that, you will wake him up."

"By the devil and his horns! My fair friend," replied the stranger. "I cannot alight like a bird!" and Thibault recognized the voice as that of the man with whom he had had the altercation a night or two before.

"Although while I was waiting under your window for the happy moment, my heart was so sick with longing that I felt as if wings must grow ere long, to bear me up into this dear wished-for little room."

"And I too, my lord," replied Madame Magloire with a simper, "I too was troubled to leave you outside to freeze in the cold wind, but the guest who was with us this evening only left us half an hour ago."

"And what have you been doing, my dear one, during this last half hour?"

"I was obliged to help Monsieur Magloire, my lord, and to make sure that he would not come and interrupt us."

"You were right as you always are, my heart's love."

"My lord is too kind," replied Suzanne—or, more correctly, tried to reply, for her last words were interrupted as if by some foreign body being placed upon her lips, which prevented her from finishing the sentence; and at the same moment, Thibault heard a sound which was remarkably like that of a kiss. The wretched man was beginning to understand the extent of the disappointment of which he was again the victim. His reflections were interrupted by the voice of the newcomer, who coughed two or three times.

"Suppose we shut the window, my love," said the voice, after this preliminary coughing.

"Oh! My lord, forgive me," said Madame Magloire, "it ought to have been closed before." And so saying she went to the window, which she first shut close, and then closed even more hermetically by drawing the curtains across it. The stranger meanwhile, who made himself thoroughly at home, had drawn an easy chair up to the fire, and sat with his legs stretched out, warming his feet in the most luxurious fashion. Reflecting no doubt, that for a man half frozen, the most immediate necessity is to thaw himself, Madame Suzanne seemed to find no cause of offence in this behavior on the part of her aristocratic lover, but came up to his chair and leant her pretty arms over the back in the most fascinating posture. Thibault had a good view of the group from behind, well thrown up by the light of the fire, and he was overcome with inward rage. The stranger appeared for a while to have no thought beyond that of warming himself; but at last the fire having performed its appointed task, he asked:

"And this stranger, this guest of yours, who was he?"

"Ah! My lord," answered Madame Magloire, "you already know him I think only too well."

"What!" said the favored lover. "Do you mean to say it was that drunken lout of the other night, again?"

"The very same, my lord."

"Well, all I can say is—if ever I get him into my grip again!"

"My lord," responded Suzanne, in a voice as soft as music, "you must not harbor evil designs against your enemies; on the contrary, you must forgive them as we are taught to do by our Holy Religion."

"There is also another religion which teaches that, my dearest love, one of which you are the all-supreme goddess, and I but a humble neophyte … And I am wrong in wishing evil to the scoundrel, for it was owing to the treacherous and cowardly way in which he attacked and did for me, that I had the opportunity I had so long wished for, of being introduced into this house. The lucky blow on my forehead with his stone, made me faint; and because you saw I had fainted, you called your husband; it was on account of your husband finding me without consciousness beneath your window, and believing I had been set upon by thieves, that he had me carried indoors; and lastly, because you were so moved by pity at the thought of what I had suffered for you, that you were willing to let me in here. And so, this good-for-nothing fellow, this contemptible scamp, is after all the source of all good, for all the good of life for me is in your love;

nevertheless if ever he comes within reach of my whip, he will not have a very pleasant time of it."

"It seems then," muttered Thibault, swearing to himself, "that my wish has again turned to the advantage of someone else! Ah! My friend, Black Wolf, I have still something to learn, but, confound it all! I will in future think so well over my wishes before expressing them that the pupil will become master ... but to whom does that voice, that I seem to know, belong?" Thibault continued, trying to recall it. "For the voice is familiar to me, of that I am certain!"

"You would be even more incensed against him, poor wretch, if I were to tell you something."

"And what is that, my love?"

"Well, that good-for-nothing fellow, as you call him, is making love to me."

"Phew!"

"That is so, my lord," said Madame Suzanne, laughing.

"What! That boor, that low rascal! Where is he? Where does he hide himself? By Beelzebub! I'll throw him to my dogs to eat!"

And then, all at once, Thibault recognized his man. "Ah! My lord baron," he muttered, "it's you, is it?"

"Pray do not trouble yourself about it, my lord," said Madame Suzanne, laying her two hands on her lover's shoulders, and obliging him to sit down again. "Your lordship is the only person whom I love, and even were it not so, a man with a lock of red hair right in the middle of his forehead is not the one to whom I should give away my heart." And as the recollection of this lock of hair, which had made her laugh so at dinner, came back to her, she again gave way to her amusement.

A violent feeling of anger towards the bailiff's wife took possession of Thibault.

"Ah! Traitress!" he exclaimed to himself. "What would I not give for your husband, your good, upright husband, to walk in at this moment and surprise you."

Scarcely was the wish uttered, when the door of communication between Suzanne's room and that of Monsieur Magloire was thrown wide open, and in walked her husband with an enormous nightcap on his head, which made him look nearly five feet high, and holding a lighted candle in his hand.

"Ah! Ah!" muttered Thibault. "Well done! It's my turn to laugh now, Madame Magloire."

13

WHERE IT IS DEMONSTRATED THAT A WOMAN NEVER SPEAKS MORE ELOQUENTLY THAN WHEN SHE HOLDS HER TONGUE

A s Thibault was talking to himself he did not catch the few hurried words which Suzanne whispered to the baron; and all he saw was that she appeared to totter, and then fell back into her lover's arms, as if in a dead faint.

The bailiff stopped short as he caught sight of this curious group, lit up by his candle. He was facing Thibault, and the latter endeavored to read in Monsieur Magloire's face what was passing in his mind.

But the bailiff's jovial physiognomy was not made by nature to express any strong emotion, and Thibault could detect nothing in it but a benevolent astonishment on the part of the amiable husband.

The baron, also, evidently detected nothing more, for with a coolness and ease of manner, which produced on Thibault a surprise beyond expression, he turned to the bailiff, and asked:

"Well, friend Magloire, and how do you carry your wine this evening?"

"Why, is it you, my lord?" replied the bailiff opening his fat little eyes.

"Ah! Pray excuse me, and believe me, had I known I was to

have the honor of seeing you here, I should not have allowed myself to appear in such an unsuitable costume."

"Pooh-pooh! Nonsense!"

"Yes, indeed, my lord; you must permit me to go and make a little toilette."

"No ceremony, I pray!" rejoined the baron. "After curfew, one is at least free to receive one's friends in what costume one likes. Besides, my dear friend, there is something which requires more immediate attention."

"What is that, my lord?"

"To restore Madame Magloire to her senses, who, you see, has fainted in my arms."

"Fainted! Suzanne fainted! Ah! My God!" cried the little man, putting down his candle on the chimneypiece. "How ever did such a misfortune happen?"

"Wait, wait, Monsieur Magloire!" said my lord. "We must first get your wife into a more comfortable position in an armchair; nothing annoys women so much as not to be at their ease when they are unfortunate enough to faint."

"You are right, my lord; let us first put her in the armchair ... Oh Suzanne! Poor Suzanne! How can such a thing as this have happened?"

"I pray you at least, my dear fellow, not to think any ill of me at finding me in your house at such a time of night!"

"Far from it, my lord," replied the bailiff. "The friendship with which you honor us, and the virtue of Madame Magloire are sufficient guarantees for me to be glad at any hour to have my house honored by your presence."

"Triple dyed idiot!" murmured the shoe maker. "Unless I ought rather to call him a doubly clever dissembler ... No matter which, however! We have yet to see how my lord is going to get out of it."

"Nevertheless," continued Maître Magloire, dipping a hand-kerchief into some aromatic water, and bathing his wife's temples with it, "nevertheless, I am curious to know how my poor wife can have received such a shock."

"It's a simple affair enough, as I will explain, my dear fellow. I was returning from dining with my friend, de Vivières, and passing through Erneville on my way to Vez, I caught sight of an open window, and a woman inside making signals of distress."

"Ah! My God!"

"That is what I exclaimed, when I realized that the window belonged to your house; and can it be my friend the bailiff's wife, I thought, who is in danger and in need of help?"

"You are good indeed, my lord," said the bailiff quite overcome. "I trust it was nothing of the sort."

"On the contrary, my dear man."

"How! On the contrary?"

"Yes, as you will see."

"You make me shudder, my lord! And do you mean that my wife was in need of help and did not call me?"

"It had been her first thought to call you, but she abstained from doing so, for, and here you see her delicacy of feeling, she was afraid that if you came, your precious life might be endangered."

The bailiff turned pale and gave an exclamation.

"My precious life, as you are good enough to call it, is in danger?"

"Not now, since I am here."

"But tell me, I pray, my lord, what had happened? I would question my wife, but as you see she is not yet able to answer."

"And am I not here to answer in her stead?"

"Answer then, my lord, as you are kind enough to offer to do so; I am listening."

The baron made a gesture of assent, and went on:

"So I ran to her, and seeing her all trembling and alarmed, I asked, 'What is the matter, Madame Magloire, and what is causing you so much alarm?' 'Ah! My lord,' she replied, 'just think what I feel, when I tell you that yesterday and today, my husband has been entertaining a man about whom I have the worst suspicions. Ugh! A man who has introduced himself under the pretense of friendship to my dear Magloire, and actually makes love to me, to me.'"

"She told you that?"

"Word for word, my dear fellow! She cannot hear what we are saying, I hope?"

"How can she, when she is insensible?"

"Well, ask her yourself when she comes to, and if she does not tell you exactly to the letter what I have been telling you, call me a Turk, an infidel and a heretic."

"Ah! These men! These men!" murmured the bailiff.

"Yes, race of vipers!" continued my Lord of Vez. "Do you wish me to go on?"

"Yes, indeed!" said the little man, forgetting the scantiness of his attire in the interest excited in him by the baron's tale.

"'But Madame,' I said to my friend Madame Magloire, 'How could you tell that he had the audacity to love you?'"

"Yes," put in the bailiff. "How did she find it out? I never noticed anything myself."

"You would have been aware of it, my dear friend, if only you had looked under the table; but, fond of your dinner as you are, you were not likely to be looking at the dishes on the table and underneath it at the same time."

"The truth is, my lord, we had the most perfect little supper! Just you think now—cutlets of young wild-boar."

"Very well," said the baron. "Now you are going to tell me about your supper, instead of listening to the end of my tale, a tale which concerns the life and honor of your wife!"

"True, true, my poor Suzanne! My lord, help me to open her hands, that I may slap them on the palms."

The Lord of Vez gave all the assistance in his power to Monsieur Magloire, and by dint of their united efforts they forced open Madame Magloire's hands.

The good man, now easier in his mind, began slapping his

wife's palms with his chubby little hands, all the while giving his attention to the remainder of the baron's interesting and veracious story.

"Where had I got to?" he asked.

"You had got just to where my poor Suzanne, whom one may indeed call 'the chaste Suzanna.'"

"Yes, you may well say that!" interrupted the Lord of Vez.

"Indeed, I do! You had just got to where my poor Suzanne began to be aware."

"Ah, yes—that your guest like Paris of old was wishing to make another Menelaus of you; well, then she rose from table ... You remember that she did so?"

"No ... I was perhaps a little—just a little—overcome."

"Quite so! Well then she rose from table, and said it was time to retire."

"The truth is, that the last hour I heard strike was eleven," said the jovial bailiff.

"Then the party broke up."

"I don't think I left the table," said the bailiff.

"No, but Madame Magloire and your guest did. She told him which was his room, and Perrine showed him to it; after which, kind and faithful wife as she is, Madame Magloire tucked you into bed, and went into her own room."

"Dear little Suzanne!" said the bailiff in a voice of emotion.

"And it was then, when she found herself in her room, and all alone, that she got frightened; she went to the window and opened it; the wind, blowing into the room, put out her candle. You know what it is to have a sudden panic come over you, do you not?"

"Oh! Yes," replied the bailiff naïvely, "I am very timid myself."

"After that she was seized with panic, and not daring to wake you, for fear any harm should come to you, she called to the first horseman she saw go by—and luckily, that horseman was myself."

"It was indeed fortunate, my lord."

"Was it not? ... I ran, I made myself known."

"'Come up, my lord, come up,' she cried. 'Come up quickly —I am sure there is a man in my room.'"

"Dear! Dear!" said the bailiff. "You must indeed have felt terribly frightened."

"Not at all! I thought it was only losing time to stop and ring; I gave my horse to l'Eveillé, I stood up on the saddle, climbed from that to the balcony, and, so that the man who was in the room might not escape, I shut the window. It was just at that moment that Madame Magloire, hearing the sound of your door opening, and overcome by such a succession of painful feelings, fell fainting into my arms."

"Ah! My lord!" said the bailiff. "How frightful all this is that you tell me."

"And be sure, my dear friend, that I have rather softened than added to its terror; anyhow, you will hear what Madame Magloire has to tell you when she comes to."

"See, my lord, she is beginning to move."

"That's right! Burn a feather under her nose."

"A feather?"

"Yes, it is a sovereign antispasmodic; burn a feather under her nose, and she will revive instantly."

"But where shall I find a feather?" asked the bailiff.

"Here! Take this, the feather round my hat." And the lord of Vez broke off a bit of the ostrich feather which ornamented his hat, gave it to Monsieur Magloire, who lighted it at the candle and held it smoking under his wife's nose.

The remedy was a sovereign one, as the baron had said; the effect of it was instantaneous; Madame Magloire sneezed.

"Ah!" cried the bailiff delightedly. "Now she is coming to! My wife! My dear wife! My dear little wife!"

Madame Magloire gave a sigh.

"My lord! My lord!" cried the bailiff. "She is saved! Saved!"

Madame Magloire opened her eyes, looked first at the bailiff and then at the baron, with a bewildered gaze, and then finally fixing them on the bailiff:

"Magloire! Dear Magloire!" she said. "Is it really you? Oh! How glad I am to see you again after the bad dream I have had!"

"Well!" muttered Thibault. "She is a brazen-faced huzzy, if you like! If I do not get all that I want from the ladies I run after, they, at least, afford me some valuable object lessons by the way!"

"Alas! My beautiful Suzanne," said the bailiff. "It is no bad dream you have had, but, as it seems, a hideous reality."

"Ah! I remember now," responded Madame Magloire. Then, as if noticing for the first time that the Lord of Vez was there:

"Ah! My lord," she continued, "I hope you have repeated nothing to my husband of all those foolish things I told you?"

"And why not, dear lady?" asked the baron.

"Because an honest woman knows how to protect herself, and has no need to keep on telling her husband a lot of nonsense like that."

"On the contrary, Madame," replied the baron. "I have told my friend everything."

"Do you mean that you have told him that during the whole of supper time that man was fondling my knee under the table?"

"I told him that, certainly."

"Oh! The wretch!" exclaimed the bailiff.

"And that when I stooped to pick up my table napkin, it was not that, but his hand, that I came across."

"I have hidden nothing from my friend Magloire."

"Oh! The ruffian!" cried the bailiff.

"And that Monsieur Magloire having a passing giddiness which made him shut his eyes while at table, his guest took the opportunity to kiss me against my will?"

"I thought it was right for a husband to know everything."

"Oh! The knave!" cried the bailiff.

"And did you even go so far as to tell him that having come into my room, and the wind having blown out the candle, I fancied I saw the window curtains move, which made me call to you for help, believing that he was hidden behind them?"

"No, I did not tell him that! I was going to when you sneezed."

"Oh! The vile rascal!" roared the bailiff, taking hold of the baron's sword which the latter had laid on a chair, and drawing it out of the scabbard, then, running toward the window which his wife had indicated, "He had better not be behind these curtains, or I will spit him like a woodcock," and with this he gave one or two lunges with the sword against the window hangings.

But all at once the bailiff stayed his hand, and stood as if arrested like a schoolboy caught trespassing out of bounds; his hair rose on end beneath his cotton nightcap, and this conjugal headdress became agitated as by some convulsive movement. The sword dropped from his trembling hand, and fell with a clatter on the floor. He had caught sight of Thibault behind the curtains, and as Hamlet kills Polonius, thinking to slay his father's murderer, so he, believing that he was thrusting at nothing, had nearly killed his crony of the night before, who had already had time enough to prove himself a false friend.

Moreover as he had lifted the curtain with the point of the sword, the bailiff was not the only one who had seen Thibault. His wife and the Lord of Vez had both been participators in the unexpected vision, and both uttered a cry of surprise. In telling their tale so well, they had had no idea that they were so near the truth. The baron, too, had not only seen that there was a man, but had also recognized that the man was Thibault.

"Damn me!" he exclaimed, as he went nearer to him. "If I mistake not, this is my old acquaintance, the man with the boar spear!"

"How! How! Man with the boar spear?" asked the bailiff, his teeth chattering as he spoke. "Anyway I trust he has not his boar spear with him now!" And he ran behind his wife for protection.

"No, no, do not be alarmed," said the Lord of Vez, "even if he has got it with him, I promise you it shall not stay long in his hands. So, master poacher," he went on, addressing himself to Thibault, "you are not content to hunt the game belonging to his Highness the Duke of Orleans, in the forest of Villers-Cotterets, but you must come and make excursions in the open and poach on the territory of my friend Maître Magloire?"

"A poacher! Do you say?" exclaimed the bailiff. "Is not Monsieur Thibault a landowner, the proprietor of farms, living in his country house on the income from his estate of a hundred acres?"

"What, he?" said the baron, bursting into a loud guffaw. "So he made you believe all that stuff, did he? The rascal has got a clever tongue. He! A landowner! That poor starveling! Why, the only property he possesses is what my stable boys wear on their feet—the wooden shoes he gets his living by making."

Madame Suzanne, on hearing Thibault thus classified, made a gesture of scorn and contempt, while Maître Magloire drew back a step, while the color mounted to his face. Not that the good little man was proud, but he hated all kinds of deceit; it was not because he had clinked glasses with a shoe maker that he turned red, but because he had drunk in company with a liar and a traitor.

During this avalanche of abuse Thibault had stood immovable with his arms folded and a smile on his lips. He had no fear but that when his turn came to speak, he would be able to take an easy revenge. And the moment to speak seemed now to have come. In a light, bantering tone of voice—which showed that he was gradually accustoming himself to conversing with people of a superior rank to his own—he then exclaimed;

"By the devil and his horns! As you yourself remarked a little while ago, you can tell tales of other people, my lord, without much compunction, and I fancy if everyone followed your example, I should not be at such a loss what to say, as I choose to appear!"

The lord of Vez, perfectly aware, as was the bailiff's wife, of the menace conveyed in these words, answered by looking Thibault up and down with eyes that were starting with anger.

"Oh!" said Madame Magloire, somewhat imprudently. "You will see, he is going to invent some scandalous tale about me."

"Have no fear, Madame," replied Thibault, who had quite recovered his self-possession, "you have left me nothing to invent on that score."

"Oh! The vile wretch!" she cried. "You see, I was right; he has got some malicious slander to report about me; he is determined to revenge himself because I would not return his sheep's eyes, to punish me because I was not willing to warn my husband that he was paying court to me." During this speech of Madame Suzanne's the lord of Vez had picked up his sword and advanced threateningly towards Thibault. But the bailiff threw himself between them, and held back the baron's arm. It was fortunate for Thibault that he did so, for the latter did not move an inch to avoid the blow, evidently prepared at the last moment to utter some terrible wish which would avert the danger from him; but the bailiff interposing, Thibault had no need to resort to this means of help.

"Gently, my lord!" said the Maître Magloire. "This man is not worthy our anger. I am but a plain citizen myself, but you see, I have only contempt for what he says, and I readily forgive him the way in which he has endeavored to abuse my hospitality."

Madame Magloire now thought that her moment had come for moistening the situation of affairs with her tears, and burst into loud sobs.

"Do not weep, dear wife!" said the bailiff, with his usual kind and simple good nature. "Of what could this man accuse you, even suppose he had something to bring against you! Of having deceived me? Well, I can only say, that made as I am, I feel I still have favors to grant you and thanks to render you, for all the happy days which I owe to you. Do not fear for a moment that this apprehension of an imaginary evil will alter my behavior towards you. I shall always be kind and indulgent to you,

Suzanne, and as I shall never shut my heart against you, so will I never shut my door against my friends. When one is small and of little account it is best to submit quietly and to trust; one need have no fear then but of cowards and evildoers, and I am convinced, I am happy to say, that they are not so plentiful as they are thought to be. And, after all, by my faith! If the bird of misfortune should fly in, by the door or by the window, by Saint Gregory, the patron of drinkers, there shall be such a noise of singing, such a clinking of glasses, that he will soon be obliged to fly out again by the way he came in!"

Before he had ended, Madame Suzanne had thrown herself at his feet, and was kissing his hands. His speech, with its mingling of sadness and philosophy, had made more impression upon her than would have a sermon from the most eloquent of preachers. Even the lord of Vez did not remain unmoved; a tear gathered in the corner of his eye, and he lifted his finger to wipe it away, before holding out his hand to the bailiff, saying as he did so:

"By the horn of Beelzebub! My dear friend, you have an upright mind and a kind heart, and it would be a sin indeed to bring trouble upon you; and if I have ever had a thought of doing you wrong, may God forgive me for it! I can safely swear, whatever happens, that I shall never have such another again."

While this reconciliation was taking place between the three secondary actors in this tale, the situation of the fourth, that is of the principal character in it, was becoming more and more embarrassing.

Thibault's heart was swelling with rage and hatred; himself unaware of the rapid growth of evil within him, he was fast growing, from a selfish and covetous man, into a wicked one. Suddenly, his eyes flashing, he cried aloud: "I do not know what holds me back from putting a terrible end to all this!"

On hearing this exclamation, which had all the character of a menace in it, the baron and Suzanne understood it to mean that some great and unknown and unexpected danger was hanging over everybody's heads. But the baron was not easily intimidated, and he drew his sword for the second time and made a movement towards Thibault. Again the bailiff interposed.

"My lord baron! My lord baron!" said Thibault in a low voice. "This is the second time that you have, in wish at least, passed your sword through my body; twice therefore you have been a murderer in thought! Take care! One can sin in other ways besides sinning in deed."

"Thousand devils!" cried the baron, beside himself with anger. "The rascal is actually reading me a moral lesson! My friend, you were wanting a little while ago to spit him like a woodcock, allow me to give him one light touch, such as the matador gives the bull, and I will answer for it, that he won't get up again in a hurry."

"I beseech you on my knees, as a favor to your humble servant, my lord," replied the bailiff, "to let him go in peace; and deign to remember, that, being my guest, there should no hurt nor harm be done to him in this poor house of mine."

"So be it!" answered the baron. "I shall meet him again. All kinds of bad reports are about concerning him, and poaching is not the only harm reported of him; he has been seen and recognized running the forest along with a pack of wolves—and astonishingly tame wolves at that. It's my opinion that the scoundrel does not always spend his midnights at home, but sits astride a broomstick oftener than becomes a good Catholic; the owner of the mill at Croyolles has made complaint of his wizardries. However, we will not talk of it any more now; I shall have his hut searched, and if everything there is not as it should be, the wizard's hole shall be destroyed, for I will not allow it to remain on his Highness's territory. And now, take yourself off, and that quickly!"

The shoe maker's exasperation had come to a pitch during this menacing tirade from the baron; but, nevertheless, he profited by the passage that was cleared for him, and went out of the room. Thanks to his faculty of being able to see in the dark, he walked straight to the door, opened it, and passed over the threshold of the house, where he had left behind so many fond hopes, now lost forever, slamming the door after him with such violence that the whole house shook. He was obliged to call to mind the useless expenditure of wishes and hair of the preceding evening, to keep himself from asking that the whole house, and all within it, might be devoured by the flames. He walked on for ten minutes before he became conscious that it was pouring with rain—but the rain, frozen as it was, and even because it was so bitterly cold, seemed to do Thibault good. As the good Magloire had artlessly remarked, his head was on fire.

On leaving the bailiffs house, Thibault had taken the first road he came to; he had no wish to go in one direction more than another, all he wanted was space, fresh air, and movement. His desultory walking brought him first of all on to the Value lands; but even then he did not notice where he was until he saw the mill of Croyolles in the distance. He muttered a curse against its fair owner as he passed, rushed on like a madman between Vauciennes and Croyolles, and seeing a dark mass in front of him, plunged into its depths. This dark mass was the forest.

The forest path to the rear of Ham, which leads from Croyolles to Préciamont, was now ahead of him, and into this he turned, guided solely by chance.

14

A VILLAGE WEDDING

He had made but a few steps within the forest, when he found himself surrounded by his wolves. He was pleased to see them again; he slackened his pace; he called to them; and the wolves came crowding round him. Thibault caressed them as a shepherd might his sheep, as a keeper of the hounds his dogs. They were his flock, his hunting pack; a flock with flaming eyes, a pack with looks of fire. Overhead, among the bare branches, the screech owls were hopping and fluttering, making their plaintive calls, while the other owls uttered their melancholy cries in concert. The eyes of these night birds shone like winged coals flying about among the trees, and there was Thibault in the middle of it all, the center of the devilish circle.

Even as the wolves came up to fawn upon him and crouch at his feet, so the owls appeared to be attracted towards him. The tips of their silent wings brushed against his hair; some of them alighted to perch upon his shoulder.

"Ah!" murmured Thibault. "I am not then the enemy of all created things; if men hate me, the animals love me."

He forgot what place the animals, who loved him, held in the chain of created beings. He did not remember that these animals which loved him, were those which hated mankind, and which mankind cursed.

He did not pause to reflect that these animals loved him, because he had become among men, what they were among animals; a creature of the night! A man of prey! With all these animals together, he could not do an atom of good; but, on the other hand, he could do a great deal of harm. Thibault smiled at the thought of the harm he could do.

He was still some distance from home, and he began to feel tired. He knew there was a large hollow oak somewhere near, and he took his bearings and made for it; but he would have missed his way if the wolves, who seemed to guess his thoughts, had not guided him to it.

While flocks of owls hopped along from branch to branch, as if to illuminate the way, the wolves trotted along in front to show it him.

The tree stood about twenty paces back from the road; it was, as I have said, an old oak, numbering not years, but centuries. Trees which live ten, twenty, thirty times the length of a man's life, do not count their age by days and nights, but by seasons. The autumn is their twilight, the winter, their night; the spring is their dawn, the summer their day. Man envies the tree, the butterfly envies man. Forty men could not have encircled the trunk of the old oak with their arms.

The hollow made by time, that daily dislodged one more little piece of wood with the point of its scythe, was as large as an ordinarily sized room; but the entrance to it barely allowed a man to pass through.

Thibault crept inside; there he found a sort of seat cut out of the thickness of the trunk, as soft and comfortable to sit in as an arm chair. Taking his place in it, and bidding good night to his wolves and his screech owls, he closed his eyes and fell asleep, or at least appeared to do so.

The wolves lay down in a circle round the tree; the owls perched in the branches. With these lights spread around its trunk, with these lights scattered about its branches, the oak had the appearance of a tree lit up for some infernal revel.

It was broad daylight when Thibault awoke; the wolves had long ago sought their hiding places, the owls flown back to their ruins. The rain of the night before had ceased, and a ray of sunlight, one of those pale rays which are a harbinger of spring, came gliding through the naked branches of the trees, and having as yet none of the short-lived verdure of the year to shine upon, lit up the dark green of the mistletoe.

From afar came a faint sound of music, gradually it grew nearer, and the notes of two violins and a hautboy could be distinguished.

Thibault thought at first that he must be dreaming. But as it was broad daylight, and he appeared to be in perfect possession of his senses, he was obliged to acknowledge that he was wide awake, the more so, that having well rubbed his eyes, to make quite sure of the fact, the rustic sounds came as distinctly as ever to his ear. They were drawing rapidly nearer; a bird sang, answering the music of man with the music of God; and at the foot of the bush where it sat and made its song, a flower,—only a snowdrop it is true—was shining like a star. The sky above was as blue as on an April day. What was the meaning of this spring-like festival, now, in the heart of winter?

The notes of the bird as it sang in salutation of this bright, unexpected day, the brightness of the flower that shone as if with its radiance to thank the sun for coming to visit it, the sounds of merrymaking which told the lost and unhappy man that his fellow creatures were joining with the rest of nature in their rejoicings under the azure canopy of heaven, all the aroma of joy, all this up springing of happiness, brought no calmer thoughts back to Thibault, but rather increased the anger and bitterness of his feelings.

He would have liked the whole world to be as dark and

gloomy as was his own soul. On first detecting the sounds of the
approaching rural band, he thought of running away from it; but
a power, stronger than his will, as it seemed to him, held him
rooted to the spot; so he hid himself in the hollow of the oak and
waited. Merry voices and lively songs could be heard mingling
with the notes of the violins and hautboy; now and again a gun
went off, or a cracker exploded; and Thibault felt sure that all
these festive sounds must be occasioned by some village
wedding. He was right, for he soon caught sight of a procession
of villagers, all dressed in their best, with long ribands of many
colors floating in the breeze, some from the women's waists,
some from the men's hats or buttonholes. They emerged into
view at the end of the long lane of Ham.

They were headed by the fiddlers; then followed a few peasants, and among them some figures, which by their livery,
Thibault recognized as keepers in the service of the lord of Vez.
Then came Engoulevent, the second huntsman, giving his arm to
an old blind woman, who was decked out with ribands like the
others; then the major-domo of the castle of Vez, as representa-
tive probably of the father of the little huntsman, giving his arm
to the bride.

And the bride herself—Thibault stared at her with wild fixed
eyes; he endeavored, but vainly, to persuade himself that he did
not recognize her—it was impossible not to do so when she came
within a few paces from where he was hiding. The bride was
Agnelette.

Agnelette!

And to crown his humiliation, as if to give a final blow to
his pride, no pale and trembling Agnelette dragged reluctantly
to the altar, casting looks behind her of regret or remembrance,
but an Agnelette as bright and happy as the bird that was
singing, the snowdrop that flowered, the sunlight that was
shining; an Agnelette, full of delighted pride in her wreath of
orange flowers, her tulle veil and muslin dress; an Agnelette, in
short, as fair and smiling as the virgin in the church at Villers-

Cotterets, when dressed in her beautiful white dress at Whit-suntide.

She was, no doubt, indebted for all this finery to the Lady of the castle, the wife of the lord of Vez, who was a true Lady Bountiful in such matters.

But the chief cause of Agnelette's happiness and smiles was not the great love she felt towards the man who was to become her husband, but her contentment at having found what she so ardently desired, that which Thibault had wickedly promised to her without really wishing to give her—someone who would help her to support her blind old grandmother.

The musicians, the bride and bridegroom, the young men and maidens, passed along the road within twenty paces of Thibault, without observing the head with its flaming hair and the eyes with their fiery gleam, looking out from the hollow of the tree. Then, as Thibault had watched them appear through the undergrowth, so he watched them disappear. As the sounds of the violins and hautboy had gradually become louder and louder, so now they became fainter and fainter, until in another quarter of an hour the forest was as silent and deserted as ever, and Thibault was left alone with his singing bird, his flowering snowdrop, his glittering ray of sunlight. But a new fire of hell had been lighted in his heart, the worst of the fires of hell; that which gnaws at the vitals like the sharpest serpent's tooth, and corrodes the blood like the most destructive poison—the fire of jealousy.

On seeing Agnelette again, so fresh and pretty, so innocently happy, and, worse still, seeing her at the moment when she was about to be married to another, Thibault, who had not given a thought to her for the last three month, Thibault, who had never had any intention of keeping the promise which he made her, Thibault now brought himself to believe that he had never ceased to love her.

He persuaded himself that Agnelette was engaged to him by oath, that Engoulevent was carrying off what belonged to him, and he almost leaped from his hiding place to rush after her and reproach her with her infidelity. Agnelette, now no longer his, at once appeared to his eyes as endowed with all the virtues and good qualities, all in short that would make it advantageous to marry her, which, when he had only to speak the word and everything would have been his, he had not even suspected.

After being the victim of so much deception, to lose what he looked upon as his own particular treasure, to which he had imagined that it would not be too late to return at any time, simply because he never dreamed that anyone would wish to take it from him, seemed to him the last stroke of ill fortune. His despair was no less profound and gloomy that it was a mute despair. He bit his fists, he knocked his head against the sides of the tree, and finally began to cry and sob. But they were not those tears and sobs which gradually soften the heart and are often kindly agents in dispersing a bad humor and reviving a better one; no, they were tears and sobs arising rather from anger than from regret, and these tears and sobs had no power to drive the hatred out of Thibault's heart. As some of his tears fell visibly down his face, so it seemed that others fell on his heart within like drops of gall.

He declared that he loved Agnelette; he lamented at having lost her; nevertheless, this furious man, with all his tender love, would gladly have been able to see her fall dead, together with her bridegroom, at the foot of the altar when the priest was about to join them. But happily, God, who was reserving the two children for other trials, did not allow this fatal wish to formulate itself in Thibault's mind. They were like those who, surrounded by storm, hear the noise of the thunder and see the forked flashes of the lightning, and yet remain untouched by the deadly fluid.

Before long the shoe maker began to feel ashamed of his tears and sobs; he forced back the former, and made an effort to swallow the latter.

He came out of his lair, not quite knowing where he was, and rushed off in the direction of his hut, covering a league in a quarter of an hour; this mad race, however, by causing him to perspire, somewhat calmed him down. At last he recognized the surroundings of his home; he went into his hut as a tiger might enter its den, closed the door behind him, and went and crouched down in the darkest corner he could find in his miserable lodging. There, his elbows on his knees, his chin on his hands, he sat and thought. And what thoughts were they which occupied this unhappy, desperate man? Ask of Milton what were Satan's thoughts after his fall.

He went over again all the old questions which had upset his mind from the beginning, which had brought despair upon so many before him, and would bring despair to so many that came after him.

Why should some be born in bondage and others be born to power? Why should there be so much inequality with regard to a thing which takes place in exactly the same way in all classes—namely birth? By what means can this game of nature's, in which chance forever holds the cards against mankind, be made a fairer one?

And is not the only way to accomplish this, to do what the clever gamester does—get the devil to back him up? He had certainly thought so once.

To cheat? He had tried that game himself. And what had he gained by it? Each time he had held a good hand, each time he had felt sure of the game, it was the devil after all who had won.

What benefit had he reaped from this deadly power that had been given him of working evil to others?

None.

Agnelette had been taken from him; the owner of the mill had driven him away; the bailiff's wife had made game of him.

His first wish had caused the death of poor Marcotte, and had not even procured him a haunch of the buck that he had been so ambitious to obtain, and this had been the starting point of all his disappointed longings, for he had been obliged to give the buck to the dogs so as to put them off the scent of the black wolf.

And then this rapid multiplication of devil's hairs was appalling! He recalled the tale of the philosopher who asked for a grain of wheat, multiplied by each of the sixty-four squares of the chess board—the abundant harvests of a thousand years were required to fill the last square. And he—how many wishes yet remained to him?—seven or eight at the outside. The unhappy man dared not look at himself either in the spring which lurked at the foot of one of the trees in the forest, or in the mirror that hung against the wall. He feared to render an exact account to himself of the time still left to him in which to exercise his power; he preferred to remain in the night of uncertainty than to face that terrible dawn which must rise when the night was over.

But still, there must be a way of continuing matters, so that the misfortunes of others should bring him good of some kind. He thought surely that if he had received a scientific education, instead of being a poor shoe maker, scarcely knowing how to read or cypher, he would have found out, by the aid of science, some combinations which would infallibly have procured for him both riches and happiness.

Poor fool! If he had been a man of learning, he would have known the legend of Doctor Faust. To what did the omnipotence conferred on him by Mephistopheles lead Faust, the dreamer, the thinker, the preeminent scholar? To the murder of Valentine! To Margaret's suicide! To the pursuit of Helen of Troy, the pursuit of an empty shadow!

And, moreover, how could Thibault think coherently at all of ways and means while jealousy was raging in his heart, while he continued to picture Agnelette at the altar, giving herself for life to another than himself.

And who was that other? That wretched little Engoulevent, the man who had spied him out when he was perched in the tree, who had found his boar spear in the bush, which had been the cause of the stripes he had received from Marcotte.

Ah! If he had but known! To him and not to Marcotte would he have willed that evil should befall! What was the physical torture he had undergone from the blows of the strap compared to the moral torture he was enduring now!

And if only ambition had not taken such hold upon him, had not borne him on the wings of pride above his sphere, what happiness might have been his, as the clever workman, able to earn as much as six francs a day, with Agnelette for his charming little housekeeper! For he had certainly been the one whom Agnelette had first loved; perhaps, although marrying another man, she still loved him. And as Thibault sat pondering over these things, he became conscious that time was passing, that night was approaching.

However modest might be the fortune of the wedded pair, however limited the desires of the peasants who had followed them, it was quite certain that bride, bridegroom and peasants were all at this hour feasting merrily together.

And he, he was sad and alone. There was no one to prepare a meal for him; and what was there in his house to eat or drink? A little bread! A little water! And solitude! In place of that blessing from heaven which we call a sister, a mistress, a wife.

But, after all, why should not he also dine merrily and abundantly? Could he not go and dine wheresoever he liked? Had he not money in his pocket from the last game he had sold to the host of the Boule-d'Or? And could he not spend on himself as much as the wedded couple and all their guests together? He had only himself to please.

"And, by my faith!" he exclaimed. "I am an idiot indeed to stay here, with my brain racked by jealousy, and my stomach with hunger, when, with the aid of a good dinner and two or three bottles of wine, I can rid myself of both torments before another hour is over. I will be off to get food, and better still, to get drink!"

In order to carry this determination into effect, Thibault took the road to Ferté-Milon, where there was an excellent restaurant, known as the Dauphin d'Or, able it was said to serve up dinners equal to those provided by his head cook for his Highness, the Duke of Orleans.

15

THE LORD OF VAUPARFOND

Thibault, on arriving at the Dauphin d'Or, ordered himself as fine a dinner as he could think of. It would have been quite easy for him to have engaged a private room, but he would not then have enjoyed the personal sense of superiority. He wished the company of ordinary diners to see him eat his pullet, and his eel in its delicate sauce. He wished the other drinkers to envy him his three different wines, drunk out of three different shaped glasses. He wished everybody to hear him give his orders in a haughty voice, to hear the ring of his money.

As he gave his first order, a man in a gray coat, seated in the darkest corner of the room with a half bottle of wine before him, turned round, as if recognizing a voice he knew. And, as it turned out, this was one of Thibault's acquaintances—it is scarcely necessary to add, a tavern acquaintance.

Thibault, since he had given up making shoes by day and, instead, had his wolves about at night, had made many such acquaintances. On seeing that it was Thibault, the other man turned his face away quickly, but not so quickly but that Thibault had time to recognize Auguste François Levasseur, valet to Raoul the Lord of Vauparfond.

"Halloa! François!" Thibault called out. "What are you doing sitting there in the corner, and sulking like a Monk in Lent, instead of taking your dinner openly and cheerfully as I am doing, in full view of everybody?"

François made no reply to this interrogation, but signed to Thibault to hold his tongue.

"I am not to speak? Not to speak?" said Thibault. "And supposing it does not suit me to hold my tongue, supposing I wish to talk, and that I am bored at having to dine alone? And that it pleases me to say; 'Friend François, come here; I invite you to dine with me?!' You will not? No? Very well, then I shall come and fetch you." And Thibault rose from his seat, and followed by all eyes, went up to his friend and gave him a slap on the shoulder vigorous enough to dislocate it.

"Pretend that you have made a mistake, Thibault, or you will lose me my place; do you not see that I am not in livery, but am only wearing my drab greatcoat! I am here as proxy in a love affair for my master, and I am waiting for a letter from a lady to carry back to him."

"That's another matter altogether, and I understand now and am sorry for my indiscretion. I should like, however, to have dined in your company."

"Well, nothing is easier; order your dinner to be served in a separate room, and I will give word to our host, that if another man dressed in gray like me comes in, he is to show him upstairs; he and I are old cronies, and understand one another."

"Good," said Thibault; and he therewith ordered his dinner to be taken up to a room on the first floor, which looked out upon the street.

François seated himself so as to be able to see the person he was expecting, while some distance off, as he came down the hill of Ferté-Milon. The dinner which Thibault had ordered was quite sufficient for the two; all that he did was to send for another bottle or so of wine. Thibault had only taken two lessons from Maître Magloire, but he had been an apt pupil, and they had done their work; moreover Thibault had something which he wished to forget, and he counted on the wine to accomplish this for him. It was good fortune, he felt, to have met a friend with whom he could talk, for, in the state of mind and heart in which he was, talking was as good a help towards oblivion as drinking.

Accordingly, he was no sooner seated, and the door shut, and his hat stuck well down on to his head so that François might not notice the change in the color of his hair, than he burst at once into conversation, boldly taking the bull by the horns.

"And now, friend François," he said, "you are going to explain to me some of your words which I did not quite understand."

"I am not surprised at that," replied François, leaning back in his chair with an air of conceited impertinence, "we attendants on fashionable lords learn to speak court language, which everyone of course does not understand."

"Perhaps not, but if you explain it to your friends, they may possibly understand."

"Quite so! Ask what you like and I will answer."

"I look to your doing so the more, that I will undertake to supply you with what will help to loosen your tongue. First, let me ask, why do you call yourself a gray coat? I thought gray coat another name for a jackass."

"Jackass yourself, friend Thibault," said François, laughing at the shoe maker's ignorance. "No, a gray coat is a liveried servant, who puts on a gray overall to hide his livery, while he stands sentinel behind a pillar, or mounts guard inside a doorway."

"So you mean that at this moment then, my good François, you are on sentry go? And who is coming to relieve you?"

"Champagne, who is in the Comtesse de Mont-Gobert's service."

"I see; I understand exactly. Your master, the Lord of Vaupar-fond, is in love with the Comtesse de Mont-Gobert, and you are now awaiting a letter which Champagne is to bring from the lady."

"Optimé! As the tutor to Monsieur Raoul's young brother says."

"My Lord Raoul is a lucky fellow!"

"Yes indeed," said François, drawing himself up.

"And what a beautiful creature the countess is!"

"You know her then?"

"I have seen her out hunting with his Highness the Duke of Orleans and Madame de Montesson."

Thibault in speaking had said out hunting.

"My friend, let me tell you that in society we do not say hunting and shooting, but huntin' and shootin'."

"Oh!" said Thibault. "I am not so particular to a letter as all that. To the health of my Lord Raoul!"

As François put down his glass on the table, he uttered an exclamation; he had that moment caught sight of Champagne.

They threw open the window and called to this third comer, and Champagne, with all the ready intuition of the well-bred servant, understood at once, and went upstairs. He was dressed, like François, in a long gray coat, and had brought a letter with him.

"Well," asked François, as he caught sight of the letter in his hand, "and is there to be a meeting tonight?"

"Yes," answered Champagne, with evident delight.

"That's all right," said François cheerfully.

Thibault was surprised at these expressions of apparent sympathy on the part of the servants with their master's happiness.

"Is it your master's good luck that you are so pleased about?" he asked of François.

"Oh, dear me no!" replied the latter. "But when my master is engaged, I am at liberty!"

"And do you make use of your liberty?"

"One may be a valet, and yet have one's own share of good

luck, and also know how to spend the time more or less profitably," answered François, bridling as he spoke.

"And you, Champagne?"

"Oh, I," replied the last comer, holding his wine up to the light, "yes, I too hope to make good use of it."

"Well, then, here's to all your love affairs! Since everybody seems to have one or more on hand," said Thibault.

"The same to yours!" replied the two other men in chorus.

"As to myself," said the shoe maker, a look of hatred to his fellow creatures passing over his face, "I am the only person who loves nobody, and whom nobody loves."

His companion looked at him with a certain surprised curiosity.

"Ah! Ah!" said François. "Is the report that is whispered abroad about you in the countryside a true tale then?"

"Report about me?"

"Yes, about you," put in Champagne.

"Oh, then they say the same thing about me at Mont-Gobert as they do at Vauparfond?"

Champagne nodded his head.

"Well, and what is it they do say?"

"That you are a werewolf," said François.

Thibault laughed aloud. "Tell me, now, have I a tail?" he said. "Have I a wolf's claws, have I a wolf's snout?"

"We only repeat what other people say," rejoined Champagne, "we do not say that it is so."

"Well, anyhow, you must acknowledge," said Thibault, "that werewolves have excellent wine."

"By my faith, yes!" exclaimed both the valets.

"To the health of the devil who provides it, gentlemen."

The two men who were holding their glasses in their hand, put both glasses down on the table.

"What is that for?" asked Thibault.

"You must find someone else to drink that health with you," said François. "I won't, that's flat!"

"Nor I," added Champagne.

"Well and good then! I will drink all three glasses myself," and he immediately proceeded to do so.

"Friend Thibault," said the baron's valet, "it is time we separated."

"So soon?" said Thibault.

"My master is awaiting me, and no doubt with some impatience ... the letter, Champagne?"

"Here it is."

"Let us take farewell then of your friend Thibault, and be off to our business and our pleasures, and leave him to his pleasures and business." And so saying, François winked at his friend, who responded with a similar sign of understanding between them.

"We must not separate," said Thibault, "without drinking a stirrup cup together."

"But not in those glasses," said François, pointing to the three from which Thibault had drunk to the enemy of mankind.

"You are very particular, gentlemen; better call the sacristan and have them washed in holy water."

"Not quite that, but rather than refuse the polite invitation of a friend, we will call for the waiter, and have fresh glasses brought."

"These three, then," said Thibault, who was beginning to feel the effects of the wine he had drunk, "are fit for nothing more than to be thrown out of window? To the devil with you!" he exclaimed as he took up one of them and sent it flying. As the glass went through the air it left a track of light behind it, which blazed and went out like a flash of lightning. Thibault took up the two remaining glasses and threw them in turn, and each time the same thing happened, but the third flash was followed by a loud peal of thunder.

Thibault shut the window, and was thinking, as he turned to his seat again, how he should explain this strange occurrence to his companions; but his two companions had disappeared.

"Cowards!" he muttered. Then he looked for a glass, but found none left. "Hum! That's awkward," he said. "I must drink out of the bottle, that's all!"

And suiting the action to the word, Thibault finished up his dinner by draining the bottle, which did not help to steady his brain, already somewhat shaky.

At nine o'clock, Thibault called the innkeeper, paid his account, and departed.

He was in an angry disposition of enmity against all the world; the thoughts from which he had hoped to escape possessed him more and more. Agnelette was being taken farther and farther from him as the time went by; everyone, wife or mistress, had someone to love them. This day which had been one of hatred and despair to him, had been one full of the promise of joy and happiness for everybody else; the lord of Vauparfond, the two wretched valets, François and Champagne, each of them had a bright star of hope to follow; while he, he alone, went stumbling along in the darkness. Decidedly there was a curse upon him.

"But," he went on thinking to himself, "if so, the pleasures of the damned belong to me, and I have a right to claim them."

As these thoughts went surging through his brain, as he walked along cursing aloud, shaking his fist at the sky, he was on the way to his hut and had nearly reached it, when he heard a horse coming up behind him at a gallop.

"Ah!" said Thibault. "Here comes the Lord of Vauparfond, hastening to the meeting with his love. I should laugh, my fine Sir Raoul, if my Lord of Mont-Gobert managed just to catch you! You would not get off quite so easily as if it were Maître Magloire; there would be swords out, and blows given and received!"

Thus engaged in thinking what would happen if the Comte de Mont-Gobert were to surprise his rival, Thibault, who was walking in the road, evidently did not get out of the way quickly enough, for the horseman, seeing a peasant of some kind barring his passage, brought his whip down upon him in a violent blow, calling out at the same time:

"Get out of the way, you beggar, if you don't wish to be trampled under the horse's feet!"

Thibault, still half drunk, was conscious of a crowd of mingled sensations, of the lashing of the whip, the collision with the horse, and the rolling through cold water and mud, while the horseman passed on.

He rose to his knees, furious with anger, and shaking his fist at the retreating figure:

"Would the devil," he exclaimed. "I might just for once have my turn at being one of you great lords, might just for twenty-four hours take your place, Monsieur Raoul de Vauparfond, instead of being only Thibault, the shoe maker, so that I might know what it was to have a fine horse to ride, instead of tramping on foot; might be able to whip the peasants I met on the road, and have the opportunity of paying court to these beautiful women, who deceive their husbands, as the Comtesse de Mont-Gobert does!"

The words were hardly out of his mouth, when the baron's horse shied, throwing the rider over its head.

16

MY LADY'S LADY

Thibault was delighted at seeing what had happened to the young baron, whose hand, anything but light, had so shortly before made use of his whip on Thibault's shoulders, which still smarted with the blow. The latter now ran at full speed to see how far Monsieur Raoul de Vauparfond was injured; he found a body lying insensible, stretched across the road, with the horse standing and snorting beside it.

But Thibault could hardly believe his senses on perceiving that the figure lying in the road was not the same as had, but five minutes previously, ridden past him and given him the lash with the whip. In the first place, this figure was not in the dress of a gentleman, but clothed like a peasant, and, what was more, the clothes he had on seemed to Thibault to be the same as he himself had been wearing only a moment before.

His surprise increased more and more and amounted almost to stupefaction on further recognizing, in the inert, unconscious figure, not only his own clothes, but his own face. His astonishment naturally led him to turn his eyes from this second Thibault to his own person, when he became aware that an equally remarkable change had come over his costume. Instead of shoes and gaiters, his legs were now encased in an elegant pair of hunting boots, reaching to the knee, as soft and smooth as a pair of silk stockings, with a roll over the instep, and finished off with a pair of fine silver spurs. The knee breeches were no longer of corduroy, but of the most beautiful buckskin, fastened with little gold buckles. His long coarse olive-colored coat was replaced by a handsome green hunting coat, with gold lace facings, thrown open to display a waistcoat of fine white jean, while over the artistically pleated shirt hung the soft wavy folds of a cambric cravat. Not a single article of dress about him but had been transformed, even to his old lantern-shaped hat, which was now a three-cornered one, trimmed with gold lace to match the coat. The stick also, such as workmen carry partly for walking and partly for self-defense, and which he had been holding in his hand a minute before, had now given place to a light whip, with which he gave a cut through the air, listening with a sense of aristocratic pleasure to the whistling sound it made. And finally, his slender figure was drawn in at the waist by a belt, from which hung a hunting knife, half-sword, half-dagger.

Thibault was pleased beyond measure at finding himself clothed in such a delightful costume, and with a feeling of vanity, natural under the circumstances, he was overcome with the desire to ascertain without delay how the dress suited his face. But where could he go to look at himself, out there in the midst of pitch darkness? Then, looking about him, he saw that he was only a stone's throw from his own hut.

"Ah! To be sure!" he said. "Nothing easier, for I have my glass there."

And he made haste towards his hut, intending, like Narcissus, to enjoy his own beauty in peace and all to himself. But the door of the hut was locked, and Thibault felt vainly for the key. All he could find in his pockets was a well-filled purse, a sweetmeat box containing scented lozenges, and a little mother-of-pearl and gold penknife. What could he have done then with his door key? Then suddenly a bright thought occurred to him—

possibly the key was in the pocket of that other Thibault who was lying out there in the road. He went back and felt in the breeches pocket, where he discovered the key at once, in company with a few sous. Holding the rough clumsy thing in the tips of his fingers, he returned to open the door. The inside of the hut was even darker than the night outside, and Thibault groped about to find the steel, the tinder and flint, and the matches, and then proceeded to try and light the candle, which consisted of an end stuck into an empty bottle. In a second or two this was accomplished, but in the course of the operation Thibault was obliged to take hold of the candle with his fingers.

"Pah!" he said. "What pigs these peasants are! I wonder how they can live in this dirty sort of way!"

However, the candle was alight, which was the chief matter, and Thibault now took down his mirror, and bringing it to the light, looked at himself in it. His eye had scarcely caught sight of the reflected image, then he uttered a cry of astonishment, it was no longer himself that he saw, or rather, although it was still Thibault in spirit, it was no longer Thibault in body. His spirit had entered into the body of a handsome young man of twenty-five or twenty-six years of age, with blue eyes, pink fresh cheeks, red lips, and white teeth; in short, it had entered into the body of Baron Raoul de Vauparfond. Then Thibault recalled the wish that he had uttered in his moment of anger after the blow from the whip and his collision with the horse. His wish had been that for four and twenty hours he might be the Baron de Vauparfond, and the Baron de Vauparfond be Thibault, which now explained to him what had at first seemed inexplicable, why the uncon-scious man now lying in the road was dressed in his clothes and had his face.

"But I must not forget one thing," he said, "that is, that although I seem to be here, I am not really here, but lying out there, so I must be careful to see that during the twenty-four hours, during which I shall be imprudent enough to be away from myself, no irreparable harm comes to me. Come now,

Monsieur de Vauparfond, do not be so fastidious; carry the poor man in, and lay him gently on his bed here." And, although with his aristocratic instincts Monsieur de Vauparfond found the task very repugnant to him, Thibault, nevertheless, courageously took up his own body in his arms and carried himself from the road to the bed. Having thus placed the body in safety, he blew out the light, for fear that any harm should come to this other self before he came to; then, carefully locking the door, he hid the key in the hollow of a tree, where he was in the habit of leaving it when not wishing to take it with him.

The next thing to do was to get hold of the horse's bridle and mount into the saddle. Once there, Thibault had a preliminary moment of some uneasiness, for, having travelled more on foot than on horseback, he was not an accomplished rider, and he naturally feared that he might not be able to keep his seat when the horse began to move. But it seemed, that, while inheriting Raoul's body, he also inherited his physical qualities, for the horse, being an intelligent beast, and perfectly conscious of the momentary want of assurance on the part of his rider, made an effort to throw him, whereupon Thibault instinctively gathered up the reins, pressed his knees against the horse's sides, dug his spurs into them, and gave the animal two or three cuts of the whip, which brought it to order on the spot.

Thibault, perfectly unknown to himself, was a past master in horsemanship. This little affair with the horse enabled Thibault more fully to realize his duality. As far as the body was concerned, he was Baron Raoul de Vauparfond from top to toe; but as far as the spirit was concerned, he was still Thibault. It was, therefore, certain that the spirit of the young lord who had lent him his body was now sleeping in the form of the unconscious Thibault which he had left behind in the hut.

The division of substance and spirit between himself and the baron, however, left him with a very vague idea of what he was going, or would have, to do. That he was going to Mont-Gobert in answer to the countess's letter, so much he knew. But what was in the letter? At what hour was he expected? How was he to gain admission to the castle? Not one of these questions could he answer, and it only remained for him to discover what to do, step by step, as he proceeded. Suddenly it flashed across him that probably the countess's letter was somewhere on his person. He felt about his dress, and, sure enough, inside the side pocket of his coat was something, which by its shape, seemed to be the article he wanted. He stopped his horse, and putting his hand into his pocket, drew out a little scented leather case lined with white satin. In one side of the case were several letters, in the other only one; no doubt the latter would tell him what he wanted to know, if he could once get to read it. He was now only a short distance from the village of Fleury, and he galloped on hoping that he might find a house still lighted up. But villagers go to bed early, in those days even earlier than they do now, and Thibault went from one end of the street to the other without seeing a single light. At last, thinking he heard some kind of movement in the stables of an inn, he called. A stable boy sallied out with a lantern, and Thibault, forgetting for the moment that he was a lord, said: "Friend, could you show me a light for a moment? You would be doing me a service."

"And that's what you go and call a chap out of bed for?" answered the stable boy rudely. "Well, you are a nice sort of young'un, you are!" And turning his back on Thibault he was just going to reenter the stable, when Thibault, perceiving that he had gone on a wrong tack, now raised his voice, calling out:

"Look here, sirrah, bring your lantern here and give me a light, or I'll lay my whip across your back!"

"Ah! Pardon, my lord!" said the stable boy. "I did not see who it was I was speaking to." And he immediately stood on tiptoe holding the lantern up as Thibault directed him:

Thibault unfolded the letter and read:

My Dear Raoul,

The goddess Venus has certainly taken us under her protection. A grand hunt of some kind is to take place tomorrow out in the direction of Thury; I know no particulars about it, all I do know is, that he is going away this evening. You, therefore, start at nine o'clock, so as to be here at half-past ten. Come in by the way you know; someone whom you know will be awaiting you, and will bring you, you know where. Last time you came, I don't mean to upbraid you, but it did seem to me you stayed a long time in the corridors.

Jane.

"Devil take it!" muttered Thibault.

"I beg your pardon, my lord?" said the stable boy.

"Nothing, you lout, except that I do not require you any longer and you can go."

"A good journey to you, my lord!" said the stable boy, bowing to the ground, and he went back to his stable.

"Devil take it!" repeated Thibault. "The letter gives me precious little information, except that we are under the protection of the Goddess Venus, that he goes away this evening, that the Comtesse de Mont-Gobert expects me at half-past ten, and that her Christian name is Jane. As for the rest, I am to go in by the way I know, I shall be awaited by someone I know, and taken where I know." Thibault scratched his ear, which is what everybody does, in every country of the world, when plunged into awkward circumstances. He longed to go and wake up the Lord of Vauparfond's spirit, which was just now sleeping in Thibault's body on Thibault's bed; but, apart from the loss of time which this would involve, it might also cause considerable inconvenience, for the baron's spirit, on seeing its own body so near to it, might be taken with the desire of reentering it. This would give rise to a struggle in which Thibault could not well defend himself without doing serious harm to his own person; some other way out of the difficulty must therefore be found. He had heard a great deal about the wonderful sagacity of animals, and had himself, during his life in the country, had occasion more than once to admire their instinct, and he now determined to trust to that of his horse. Riding back into the main road, he turned the horse in the direction of Mont-Gobert, and let it have its head. The horse immediately started off at a gallop; it had evidently understood. Thibault troubled himself no further, it was now the horse's affair to bring him safely to his destination.

On reaching the corner of the park wall the animal stopped, not apparently because it was in doubt as to which road to take, but something seemed to make it uneasy, and it pricked its ears. At the same time, Thibault also fancied that he caught sight of two shadows; but they must have been only shadows, for although he stood up in his stirrups and looked all around him, he could see absolutely nothing. They were probably poachers he thought, who had reasons like himself for wishing to get inside the park. There being no longer anything to bar his passage, he had only, as before, to let the horse go its own way, and he accordingly did so.

The horse followed the walls of the park at a quick trot, carefully choosing the soft edge of the road, and not uttering a single neigh; the intelligent animal seemed as if it knew that it must make no sound or at least as little sound as possible.

In this way, they went along the whole of one side of the park, and on reaching the corner, the horse turned as the wall turned, and stopped before a small breach in the same. "It's through here, evidently," said Thibault, "that we have to go."

The horse answered by sniffing at the breach, and scraping the ground with its foot; Thibault gave the animal the rein, and it managed to climb up and through the breach, over the loose stones which rolled away beneath its hoof. Horse and rider were now within the park. One of the three difficulties had been successfully overcome: Thibault had got in by the way he knew; it now remained to find the person whom he knew, and he thought it wisest to leave this also to his horse. The horse went on for another five minutes, and then stopped at a short distance from the castle, before the door of one of those little huts of rough logs and bark and clay, which are built up in parks, as painters introduce buildings into their landscapes, solely for the sake of ornament.

On hearing the horse's hoofs, someone partly opened the door, and the horse stopped in front of it.

A pretty girl came out, and asked in a low voice, "Is it you, Monsieur Raoul?"

"Yes, my child, it is I," answered Thibault, dismounting.

"Madame was terribly afraid that drunken fool of a Champagne might not have given you the letter."

"She need not have been afraid; Champagne brought it me with the most exemplary punctuality."

"Leave your horse then and come."

"But who will look after it?"

"Why Cramoisi, of course, the man who always does."

"Ah, yes, to be sure," said Thibault, as if these details were familiar to him, "Cramoisi will look after it."

"Come, come," said the maid, "we must make haste or Madame will complain again that we loiter in the corridors." And as she spoke these words, which recalled a phrase in the letter which had been written to Raoul, she laughed, and showed a row of pearly white teeth, and Thibault felt that he should like to loiter in the park, before waiting to get into the corridors.

Then the maid suddenly stood still a moment with her head bent, listening.

"What is it?" asked Thibault.

"I thought I heard the sound of a branch creaking under somebody's foot."

"Very likely," said Thibault, "no doubt Cramoisi's foot."

"All the more reason that you should be careful what you do ... at all events out here."

"I don't understand."

"Do you not know that Cramoisi is the man I am engaged to?"

"Ah! To be sure! But when I am alone with you, my dear Rose, I always forget that."

"I am called Rose now, am I! I never knew such a forgetful man as you are, Monsieur Raoul."

"I call you Rose, my pretty one, because the rose is the queen of flowers, as you are the queen of waiting-maids."

"In good truth, my lord," said the maid, "I have always found you a lively, witty gentleman, but you surpass yourself this evening."

Thibault drew himself up, flattered by this remark—really a letter addressed to the baron, but which it had fallen to the shoe maker to unseal.

"Let us hope your mistress will think the same!" he said.

"As to that," said the waiting maid, "any man can make one of these ladies of fashion think him the cleverest and wittiest in the world, simply by holding his tongue."

"Thank you," he said. "I will remember what you say."

"Hush!" said the woman to Thibault. "There is Madame behind the dressing room curtains; follow me now staidly." For they had now to cross an open space that lay between the wooded part of the park and the flight of steps leading up to the Castle.

Thibault began walking towards the latter.

"Now, now," said the maid, catching hold of him by the arm, "what are you doing, you foolish man?"

"What am I doing? Well, I confess Suzette, I don't know in the least what I am doing!"

"Suzette! So that's my name now, is it? I think Monsieur does me the honor of calling me in turn by the name of all his mistresses. But come, this way! You are not dreaming I suppose of going through the great reception rooms. That would give a fine opportunity to my lord the count, truly!"

And the maid hurried Thibault towards a little door, to the right of which was a spiral staircase.

Halfway up, Thibault put his arm round his companion's waist, which was as slender and supple as a snake.

"I think we must be in the corridors, now, eh?" he asked, trying to kiss the young woman's pretty cheek.

"No, not yet," she answered; "but never mind that."

"By my faith," he said, "if my name this evening were Thibault instead of Raoul, I would carry you up with me to the garrets, instead of stopping on the first floor!"

At that moment a door was heard grating on its hinges.

"Quick, quick, Monsieur!" said the maid. "Madame is growing impatient."

And drawing Thibault after her, she ran up the remaining stairs to the corridor, opened a door, pushed Thibault into a room, and shut the door after him, firmly believing that it was Baron Raoul de Vauparfond or, as she herself called him, the most forgetful man in the world, whom she had thus secured.

17

THE BARON DE MONT-GOBERT

Thibault found himself in the countess's room. If the magnificence of Bailiff Magloire's furniture rescued from the lumber room of his Highness the Duke of Orleans, had astonished Thibault, the daintiness, the harmony, the taste of the countess's room filled him with intoxicating delight. The rough child of the forest had never seen anything like it, even in dreams; for one cannot even dream of things of which we have no idea.

Double curtains were drawn across the two windows, the one set of white silk trimmed with lace, the other of pale China blue satin, embroidered with silver flowers. The bed and the toilet table were draped to match the windows, and were nearly smothered in clouds of Valenciennes lace.

The walls were hung with very light rose-colored silk, over which thick folds of Indian muslin, delicate as woven air, undulated like waves of mist at the slightest breath of air from the door. The ceiling was composed of a medallion painted by Boucher, and representing the toilet of Venus; she was handing her cupids the various articles of a woman's apparel, and these were now all distributed, with the exception of the goddess's girdle.

The central medallion was surrounded by a series of panels, on which were painted supposed views of Cnidos, Paphos, and Amathus. All the furniture—chairs, armchairs, settees, sociables —was covered with China satin similar to that of the curtains; over the groundwork of the carpet, of the color of pale green water, were scattered bouquets of blue cornflowers, pink poppies, and white daisies. The tables were of rosewood; the corner pieces of Indian lacquer; and the whole room was softly lighted by pink wax candles held in two candelabra. A vague and indescribably delicate perfume pervaded the air, one could not say from what sweet essence, for it was scarcely even a perfume, but rather an emanation, the same kind of odorous exhalation whereby Aeneas, in the Aeneid, recognized the presence of his mother.

Thibault pushed into the room by the waiting-maid, made one step forward, and then stopped. He had taken everything in at a glance, inhaled everything at a breath. For a second there passed before his mind's eye like a vision—Agnelette's little cottage, Madame Polet's dining room, the bed-chamber of the bailiff's wife; but they disappeared as quickly to give place to this delicious paradise of love into which he had been transported as by magic. He could scarcely believe that what he looked upon was real. Were there really men and women in the world, so blessed by fortune as to live in such surroundings as these? Had he not been carried to some wizard's castle, to some fairy's palace? And those who enjoyed such favor as this, what special good had they done? What special evil had they done, who were deprived of these advantages? Why, instead of wishing to be the baron for four and twenty hours, had he not wished to be the countess's lapdog all his life? How would he bear to be Thibault again after having seen all this? He had just reached this point in his reflections, when the dressing room door opened and the countess herself appeared, a fit bird for such a nest, a fit flower for such a sweet-scented garden.

Her hair, fastened only by four diamond pins, hung down

loosely to one side, while the rest was gathered into one large curl that hung over the other shoulder and fell into her bosom. The graceful lines of her lithe and well-formed figure, no longer hidden by puffings of dress, were clearly indicated beneath her loose pink silk gown, richly covered with lace; so fine and transparent was the silk of her stockings, that it was more like pearl-white flesh than any texture, and her tiny feet were shod in little slippers made of cloth of silver, with red heels. But not an atom of jewelry—no bracelets on the arms, no rings on the fingers; just one row of pearls round the throat, that was all—but what pearls! Worth a king's ransom!

As this radiant apparition came towards him, Thibault fell on his knees; he bowed himself, feeling crushed at the sight of this luxury, of this beauty, which to him seemed inseparable.

"Yes, yes, you may well kneel—kneel lower, lower yet—kiss my feet, kiss the carpet, kiss the floor, but I shall not any the more forgive you … you are a monster!"

"In truth, Madame, if I compare myself with you, I am even worse than that!"

"Ah! Yes, pretend that you mistake my words and think I am only speaking of your outward appearance, when you know I am speaking of your behavior … and, indeed, if your perfidious soul were imaged in your face, you would verily and indeed be a monster of ugliness. But yet it is not so, for Monsieur, for all his wickedness and infamous doings, still remains the handsomest gentleman in all the country round. But, come now, Monsieur, ought you not to be ashamed of yourself?"

"Because I am the handsomest gentleman in the neighborhood?" asked Thibault, detecting by the tone of the lady's voice that his crime was not an irremediable one.

"No, Monsieur, but for having the blackest soul and the falsest heart ever hidden beneath such a gay and golden exterior. Now, get up, and come and give an account of yourself to me."

And the countess so speaking held out a hand to Thibault which offered pardon at the same time that it demanded a kiss.

Thibault took the soft, sweet hand in his own and kissed it; never had his lips touched anything so like satin. The countess now seated herself on the settee and made a sign to Raoul to sit down beside her.

"Let me know something of your doings, since you were last here," said the countess to him.

"First tell me, dear countess," replied Thibault, "when I last was here."

"Do you mean you have forgotten? One does not generally acknowledge things of that kind, unless seeking for a cause of quarrel."

"On the contrary, dear friend, it is because the recollection of that last visit is so present with me, that I think it must have been only yesterday we were together, and I try in vain to recall what I have done, and I assure you I have committed no other crime since yesterday but that of loving you."

"That's not a bad speech; but you will not get yourself out of disgrace by paying compliments."

"Dear countess," said Thibault, "supposing we put off explanations to another time."

"No, you must answer me now; it is five days since I last saw you; what have you been doing all that time?"

"I am waiting for you to tell me, countess. How can you expect me, conscious as I am of my innocence, to accuse myself?"

"Very well then! I will not begin by saying anything about your loitering in the corridors."

"Oh, pray, let us speak of it! How can you think, countess, that knowing you, the diamond of diamonds, was waiting for me, I should stop to pick up an imitation pearl?"

"Ah! But I know how fickle men are, and Lisette is such a pretty girl!"

"Not so, dear Jane, but you must understand that she being our confidante, and knowing all our secrets, I cannot treat her quite like a servant."

"How agreeable it must be to be able to say to oneself 'I am deceiving the Comtesse de Mont-Gobert and I am the rival of Monsieur Cramoisi!'"

"Very well then, there shall be no more loitering in the corridors, no more kisses for poor Lisette, supposing of course there ever have been any!"

"Well, after all, there is no great harm in that."

"Do you mean that I have done something even worse?"

"Where had you been the other night, when you were met on the road between Erneville and Villers-Cotterets?"

"Someone met me on the road?"

"Yes, on the Erneville Road; where were you coming from?"

"I was coming home from fishing."

"Fishing! What fishing?"

"They had been drawing the Berval ponds."

"Oh! We know all about that; you are such a fine fisher, are you not, Monsieur? And what sort of an eel were you bringing back in your net, returning from your fishing at two o'clock in the morning!"

"I had been dining with my friend, the baron, at Vez."

"At Vez? Ha! I fancy you went there mainly to console the beautiful recluse, whom the jealous baron keeps shut up there a regular prisoner, so they say. But even that I can forgive you."

"What, is there a blacker crime still," said Thibault, who was beginning to feel quite reassured, seeing how quickly the pardon followed on the accusation; however serious it appeared at first.

"Yes, at the ball given by his Highness the Duke of Orleans."

"What ball?"

"Why, the one yesterday! It's not so very along ago, is it?"

"Oh, yesterday's ball? I was admiring you."

"Indeed; but I was not there."

"Is it necessary for you to be present, Jane, for me to admire you; cannot one admire you in remembrance as truly as in person? And if, when absent, you triumph by comparison, the victory is only so much the greater."

"I daresay, and it was in order to carry out the comparison to its utmost limits that you danced four times with Madame de Bonneuil; they are very pretty, are they not, those dark women who cover themselves with rouge, and have eyebrows like the Chinese mannequins on my screens and moustaches like a grenadier."

"Do you know what we talked about during those four dances?"

"It is true then, that you danced four times with her?"

"It is true, no doubt, since you say so."

"Is that a proper sort of answer?"

"What other could I give? Could anyone contradict what was said by so pretty a mouth? Not I certainly, who would still bless it, even though it were pronouncing my sentence of death."

And, as if to await this sentence, Thibault fell on his knees before the countess, but at that moment, the door opened, and Lisette rushed in full of alarm.

"Ah! Monsieur, Monsieur," she cried "save yourself! Here comes my master the count!"

"The count!" exclaimed the countess.

"Yes, the count in person, and his huntsman Lestocq, with him."

"Impossible!"

"I assure you, Madame, Cramoisi saw them as plain as I see you; the poor fellow was quite pale with fright."

"Ah! Then the meet at Thury was all a pretense, a trap to catch me?"

"Who can tell, Madame? Alas! Alas! Men are such deceiving creatures!"

"What is to be done?" asked the countess.

"Wait for the count and kill him," said Thibault resolutely, furious at again seeing his good fortune escaping from him, at losing what above all things it had been his ambition to possess.

"Kill him! Kill the count? Are you mad, Raoul? No, no, you must fly, you must save yourself. Lisette! Lisette! Take the baron through my dressing room." And in spite of his resistance, Lisette by dint of pushing got him safely away. Only just in time! Steps were heard coming up the wide main staircase. The countess, with a last word of love to the supposed Raoul, glided quickly into her bedroom, while Thibault followed Lisette. She led him rapidly along the corridor, where Cramoisi was keeping guard at the other end; then into a room, and through this into another, and finally into a smaller one which led into a little tower; here, the fugitives came again on to a staircase corresponding with the one by which they had gone up, but when they reached the bottom they found the door locked. Lisette, with Thibault still following, went back up a few steps into a sort of office in which was a window looking over the garden; this she opened. It was only a few feet from the ground, and Thibault jumped out, landing safely below.

"You know where your horse is," called Lisette "jump on its back, and do not stop till you get to Vauparfond."

Thibault would have liked to thank her for all her kindly warnings, but she was some six feet above him and he had no time to lose. A stride or two brought him to the clump of trees under which stood the little building which served as stable for his horse. But was the horse still there? He heard a neigh which reassured him: only the neigh sounded he thought more like a cry of pain. Thibault went in, put out his hand, felt the horse, gathered up the reins, and leaped on to its back without touching the stirrups; Thibault, as we have already said, had suddenly become a consummate horseman. But the horse no sooner felt the weight of the rider on its back than the poor beast began to totter on its legs. Thibault dug his spurs in savagely, and the horse made a frantic effort to stand. But in another instant, uttering one of those pitiful neighs which Thibault had heard when he approached the stable, it rolled helplessly over on its side. Thibault quickly disengaged his leg from under the animal, which, as the poor thing struggled to rise, he had no difficulty in doing, and he found himself again on his feet. Then it became clear to him, that in order to prevent his escape, Monsieur le Comte de Mont-Gobert had hamstrung his horse.

Thibault uttered an oath: "If I ever meet you, Monsieur Comte de Mont-Gobert," he said, "I swear that I will hamstring you, as you have hamstrung this poor beast!"

Then he rushed out of the little building, and remembering the way he had come, turned in the direction of the breach in the wall, and walking quickly towards it, found it, climbed over the stones, and was again outside the park. But his further passage was barred, for there in front of him was the figure of a man, who stood waiting, with a drawn sword in his hand. Thibault recognized the Comte de Mont-Gobert, the Comte de Mont-Gobert thought he recognized Raoul de Vauparfond.

"Draw, baron!" said the count; further explanation was unnecessary.

Thibault, on his side, equally enraged at having the prey, on which he had already set tooth and claw, snatched away from him, was as ready to fight as the count. He drew, not his sword, but his hunting knife, and the two men crossed weapons.

Thibault, who was something of an adept at quarter staff, had no idea of fencing; what was his surprise therefore, when he found, that he knew by instinct how to handle his weapon, and could parry and thrust according to all the rules of the art. He parried the first two or three of the count's blows with admirable skill.

"Ah, I heard, I remember," muttered the count between his clenched teeth, "that at the last match you rivalled Saint-Georges himself at the foils."

Thibault had no conception who Saint-Georges might be, but he was conscious of a strength and elasticity of wrist, thanks to which he felt he might have rivalled the devil himself.

So far, he had only been on the defensive; but the count having aimed one or two unsuccessful lunges at him, he saw his opportunity, struck out, and sent his knife clean through his adversary's shoulder.

The count dropped his sword, tottered, and falling on to one knee, cried "Help, Lestocq!"

Thibault ought then to have sheathed his knife and fled; but, unfortunately, he remembered the oath he had taken as regards the count, when he had found that his horse had been hamstrung. He slipped the sharp blade of his weapon under the bent knee and drew it towards him; the count uttered a cry; but as Thibault rose from his stooping posture, he too felt a sharp pain between his shoulder blades, followed by a sensation as of extreme cold over the chest, and finally the point of a weapon appeared above his right breast. Then he saw a cloud of blood, and knew no more. Lestocq, called to his master's aid as the latter fell, had run to the spot, and, as Thibault rose from hamstringing the count, had seized that moment to dig his hunting knife into his back.

18

DEATH AND RESURRECTION

The cold morning air brought Thibault back to consciousness; he tried to rise, but the extremity of his pain held him bound. He was lying on his back, with no remembrance of what had happened, seeing only the low gray sky above him. He made another effort, and turning managed to lift himself on his elbow. As he looked around him, he began to recall the events of the previous night; he recognized the breach in the wall; and then there came back to him the memory of the love meeting with the countess and the desperate duel with the count. The ground near him was red with blood, but the count was no longer there; no doubt, Lestocq, who had given him this fine blow that was nailing him to the spot, had helped his master indoors; Thibault they had left there, to die like a dog, as far as they cared. He had it on the tip of his tongue to hurl after them all the maledictory wishes wherewith one would like to assail one's cruelest enemy. But since Thibault had been no longer Thibault, and indeed during the remainder of the time that he would still be Baron Raoul, or at least so in outward appearance, his demoniacal power had been and would continue in abeyance.

He had until nine o'clock that evening; but would he live till then? This question gave rise in Thibault to a very uneasy state of mind. If he were to die before that hour, which of them would die, he or the baron? It seemed to him as likely to be one as the other. What, however, disturbed and angered him most was his consciousness that the misfortune which had befallen him was again owing to his own fault. He remembered now that before he had expressed the wish to be the baron for four and twenty hours, he had said some such words as these:

"I should laugh, Raoul, if the Comte de Mont-Gobert were to take you by surprise; you would not get off so easily as if he were the Bailiff Magloire; there would be swords drawn, and blows given and received."

At last, with a terrible effort, and suffering the while excruciating pain, Thibault succeeded in dragging himself on to one knee. He could then make out people walking along a road not far off on their way to market, and he tried to call to them, but the blood filled his mouth and nearly choked him. So, he put his hat on the point of his knife and signaled to them like a shipwrecked mariner, but his strength again failing, he once more fell back unconscious. In a little while, however, he again awoke to sensation; he appeared to be swaying from side to side as if in a boat. He opened his eyes; the peasants, it seemed, had seen him, and although not knowing who he was, had had compassion on this handsome young man lying covered with blood, and had concocted a sort of handbarrow out of some branches, on which they were now carrying him to Villers-Cotterets. But by the time they reached Puiseux, the wounded man felt that he could no longer bear the movement, and begged them to put him down in the first peasant's hut they came to, and to send a doctor to him there. The carriers took him to the house of the village priest, and left him there, Thibault before they parted, distributing gold among them from Raoul's purse, accompanied by many thanks for all their kind offices. The priest was away saying mass, but on returning and finding the wounded man, he uttered loud cries of lamentation.

Had he been Raoul himself, Thibault could not have found a better hospital. The priest had at one time been Curé of Vauparfond, and while there had been engaged to give Raoul his first schooling. Like all country priests, he knew, or thought he knew, something about doctoring; so he examined his old pupil's wound. The knife had passed under the shoulder blade, through the right lung, and out between the second and third ribs.

He did not for a moment disguise to himself the seriousness of the wound, but he said nothing until the doctor had been to see it. The latter arrived and after his examination, he turned and shook his head.

"Are you going to bleed him?" asked the priest.

"What would be the use?" asked the doctor. "If it had been done at once after the wound was given, it might perhaps have helped to save him, but it would be dangerous now to disturb the blood in any way."

"Is there any chance for him?" asked the priest, who was thinking that the less there was for the doctor to do, the more there would be for the priest.

"If his wound runs the ordinary course," said the doctor, lowering his voice, "he will probably not last out the day."

"You give him up then?"

"A doctor never gives up a patient, or at least if he does so, he still trusts to the possibility of nature mercifully interfering on the patient's behalf; a clot may form and stop the hemorrhage; a cough may disturb the clot, and the patient bleed to death."

"You think then that it is my duty to prepare the poor young man for death," asked the curate.

"I think," answered the doctor, shrugging his shoulders, "you would do better to leave him alone; in the first place because he is, at present, in a drowsy condition and cannot hear what you say; later on, because he will be delirious, and unable to understand you." But the doctor was mistaken; the wounded man, drowsy as he was, overheard this conversation, more reassuring as regards the salvation of his soul than the recovery of his body.

How many things people say in the presence of sick persons, believing that they cannot hear, while all the while, they are taking in every word! In the present case, this extra acuteness of hearing may perhaps have been due to the fact that it was Thibault's soul which was awake in Raoul's body; if the soul belonging to it had been in this body, it would probably have succumbed more entirely to the effects of the wound.

The doctor now dressed the wound in the back, but left the front wound uncovered, merely directing that a piece of linen soaked in iced water should be kept over it. Then, having poured some drops of a sedative into a glass of water, and telling the priest to give this to the patient whenever he asked for drink, the doctor departed, saying that he would come again the following morning, but that he much feared he should take his journey for nothing.

Thibault would have liked to put in a word of his own, and to say himself what he thought about his condition, but his spirit was as if imprisoned in this dying body, and, against his will, was forced to submit to lying thus within its cell. But he could still hear the priest, who not only spoke to him, but endeavored by shaking him to arouse him from his lethargy. Thibault found this very fatiguing, and it was lucky for the priest that the wounded man, just now, had no superhuman power, for he inwardly sent the good man to the devil, many times over.

Before long, it seemed to him that some sort of hot burning pan was being inserted under the soles of his feet, his loins, his head; his blood began to circulate, then to boil, like water over a fire. His ideas became confused, his clenched jaws opened; his tongue which had been bound became loosened; some disconnected words escaped him.

"Ah, ah!" he thought to himself. "This no doubt is what the good doctor spoke about as delirium." and, for the while at least, this was his last lucid idea.

His whole life—and his life had really only existed since his first acquaintance with the black wolf—passed before him. He saw himself following, and failing to hit the buck; saw himself tied to the oak tree, and the blows of the strap falling on him; saw himself and the black wolf drawing up their compact; saw himself trying to pass the devil's ring over Agnelette's finger; saw himself trying to pull out the red hairs, which now covered a third of his head. Then he saw himself on his way to pay court to the pretty Madame Polet of the mill, meeting Landry, and getting rid of his rival; pursued by the farm servants, and followed by his wolves. He saw himself making the acquaintance of Madame Magloire, hunting for her, eating his share of the game, hiding behind the curtains, discovered by Maître Magloire, flouted by the Baron of Vez, turned out by all three. Again he saw the hollow tree, with his wolves couching around it and the owls perched on its branches, and heard the sounds of the approaching violins and hautboy and saw himself looking, as Agnelette and the happy wedding party went by. He saw himself the victim of angry jealousy, endeavoring to fight against it by the help of drink, and across his troubled brain came the recollection of François, of Champagne, and the innkeeper; he heard the galloping of Baron Raoul's horse, and he felt himself knocked down and rolling in the muddy road. Then he ceased to see himself as Thibault; in his stead arose the figure of the handsome young rider whose form he had taken for a while. Once more he was kissing Lisette, once more his lips were touching the countess's hand; then he was wanting to escape, but he found himself at a crossroad where three ways only met, and each of these was guarded by one of his victims: the first, by the specter of a drowned man, that was Marcotte; the second, by a young man dying of fever on a hospital bed, that was Landry; the third, by a wounded man, dragging himself along on one knee, and trying in vain to stand up on his mutilated leg, that was the Comte de Mont-Gobert.

He fancied that as all these things passed before him, he told the history of them one by one, and that the priest, as he listened to this strange confession, looked more like a dying man, was paler and more trembling than the man whose confession he was listening to; that he wanted to give him absolution, but that he, Thibault, pushed him away, shaking his head, and that he cried out with a terrible laugh: "I want no absolution! I am damned! Damned! Damned!"

And in the midst of all this hallucination, this delirious madness, the spirit of Thibault could hear the priest's clock striking the hours, and as they struck he counted them. Only this clock seemed to have grown to gigantic proportions and the face of it was the blue vault of heaven, and the numbers on it were flames; and the clock was called eternity, and the monstrous pendulum, as it swung backwards and forwards called out in turn at every beat: "Never! Forever!" And so he lay and heard the long hours of the day pass one by one; and then at last the clock struck nine. At half past nine, he, Thibault, would have been Raoul, and Raoul would have been Thibault, for just four and twenty hours. As the last stroke of the hour died away, Thibault felt the fever passing from him, it was succeeded by a sensation of coldness, which almost amounted to shivering. He opened his eyes, all trembling with cold, and saw the priest at the foot of the bed saying the prayers for the dying, and the hands of the actual clock pointing to a quarter past nine.

His senses had become so acute, that, imperceptible as was their double movement, he could yet see both the larger and smaller one slowly creeping along; they were gradually nearing the critical hour; half past nine! Although the face of the clock was in darkness, it seemed illuminated by some inward light. As the minute hand approached the number six, a spasm becoming every instant more and more violent shook the dying man; his feet were like ice, and the numbness slowly, but steadily, mounted from the feet to the knees, from the knees to the thighs, from the thighs to the lower part of the body. The sweat was running down his forehead, but he had no strength to wipe it away, nor even to ask to have it done. It was a sweat of agony which he knew every moment might be the sweat of death. All kinds of strange shapes, which had nothing of the human about them, floated before his eyes; the light faded away; wings as of bats seemed to lift his body and carry it into some twilight region, which was neither life nor death, but seemed a part of both. Then the twilight itself grew darker and darker; his eyes closed, and like a blind man stumbling in the dark, his heavy wings seemed to flap against strange and unknown things.

After that he sank away into unfathomable depths, into bottomless abysses, but still he heard the sound of a bell.

The bell rang once, and scarcely had it ceased to vibrate when the dying man uttered a cry. The priest rose and went to the side of the bed; with that cry Baron Raoul had breathed his last: it was exactly one second after the half hour after nine.

❧ 19 ❧

THE DEAD AND THE LIVING

A t the same moment that the trembling soul of the young baron passed away, Thibault, awaking as if from an agitated sleep full of terrible dreams, sat up in his bed. He was surrounded by fire, every corner of his hut was in flames; at first he thought it was a continuation of his nightmare, but then he heard cries of, "Death to the wizard! Death to the sorcerer! Death to the werewolf!"

And he understood that some terrible attack was being made upon him.

The flames came nearer, they reached the bed, he felt their heat upon him; a few seconds more and he would be burned alive in the midst of the flaming pile.

Thibault leaped from his bed, seized his boar spear, and dashed out of the back door of his hut. No sooner did his enemies see him rush through the fire and emerge from the smoke than their cries of "death to him!" "Death!" were redoubled.

One or two shots were fired at him; Thibault heard the bullets whizz past; those who shot at him wore the livery of the Grand Master, and Thibault recalled the menace of the lord of Vez, uttered against him a few days before.

He was then beyond the pale of the law; he could be smoked out of his hole like a fox; he could be shot down like a buck. Luckily for Thibault, not one of the bullets struck him, and as the circle of fire made by the burning hut was not a large one, he was soon safely beyond it, and once again in shelter of the vast and gloomy forest, where, had it not been for the cries of the menials who were burning down his house, the silence would have been as complete as the darkness.

He sat down at the foot of a tree and buried his head in his hands. The events of the last forty-eight hours had succeeded each other with such rapidity, that there was no lack of matter to serve as subjects of reflection to the shoe maker.

The twenty-four hours, during which he had lived another existence than his own, seemed to him like a dream, so much so, that he would not have dared to take his oath that all this recent affair between the baron, and Countess Jane, and the Comte de Mont-Gobert had really taken place. The church clock of Oigny struck ten, and he lifted his head. Ten o'clock! And only half-an-hour before he had been still in the body of Baron Raoul, as he lay dying in the house of the Curé of Puiseux.

"Ah!" he exclaimed. "I must find out for certain what has happened! It is not quite three miles to Puiseux and I shall be there in half-an-hour; I should like to ascertain if the baron is really dead."

A melancholy howl made answer to his words; he looked round; his faithful bodyguards were back again; he had his pack about him once more.

"Come, wolves! Come, my only friends!" he cried. "Let us be off!" And he started with them across the forest in the direction of Puiseux.

The huntsmen of the Lord of Vez, who were poking up the remaining embers of the ruined hut, saw a man pass, as in a vision, running at the head of a dozen or more wolves. They crossed themselves, and became more convinced than ever that Thibault was a wizard. And anybody else who had seen

Thibault, flying along as swiftly as his swiftest wolf, and covering the ground between Oigny and Puiseux in less than a quarter of an hour, would certainly have thought so too.

He stopped at the entrance to the village, and turning to his wolves, he said:

"Friend wolves, I have no further need of you tonight, and indeed, I wish to be alone. Amuse yourselves with the stables in the neighborhood, I give you leave to do just what you like; and if you chance to come across one of those two-footed animals, called men, forget, friend wolves, that they claim to be made in the image of their Creator, and never fear to satisfy your appetite." Whereupon the wolves rushed off in different directions, uttering howls of joy, while Thibault went on into the village.

The Curé's house adjoined the church, and Thibault made a circuit so as to avoid passing in front of the cross. When he reached the presbytery, he looked in through one of the windows, and there he saw a bed with a lighted wax candle beside it; and over the bed itself was spread a sheet, and beneath the sheet could be seen the outlines of a figure lying rigid in death. There appeared to be no one in the house; the priest had no doubt gone to give notice of the death to the village authorities.

Thibault went inside, and called the priest, but no one answered. He walked up to the bed, there could be no mistake about the body under the sheet being that of a dead man; he lifted the sheet, there could be no mistaking that the dead body was that of Raoul de Vauparfond. On his face lay the still, unearthly beauty which is born of eternity. His features, which in life had been somewhat too feminine for those of a man, had now assumed the somber grandeur of death. At the first glance you might have thought he only slept; but on gazing longer you recognized in that immovable calm something more profound than sleep. The presence of one who carries a sickle for scepter, and wears a shroud for mantle was unmistakable, and you knew King Death was there.

Thibault had left the door open, and he heard the sound of light footsteps approaching; at the back of the alcove hung a serge curtain, which masked a door by which he could retreat, if necessary, and he now went and placed himself behind it. A woman dressed in black, and covered with a black veil, paused in some hesitation at the door. The head of another woman passed in front of hers and looked carefully round the room.

"I think it is safe for Madame to go in; I see no one about, and besides, I will keep watch."

The woman in black went in, walked slowly towards the bed, stopped a moment to wipe the perspiration from her forehead, then, without further hesitation, lifted the sheet which Thibault had thrown back over the face of the dead man; Thibault then saw that it was the countess.

"Alas!" she said. "What they told me was true!"

Then she fell on her knees, praying and sobbing. Her prayer being ended, she rose again, kissed the pale forehead of the dead, and the blue marks of the wound through which the soul had fled.

"O my well beloved, my Raoul," she murmured. "Who will tell me the name of your murderer? Who will help me to avenge your death?" As the countess finished speaking, she gave a cry and started back; she seemed to hear a voice that answered, "I will!" and something had shaken the green serge curtain.

The countess however was no chicken-hearted woman; she took the candle that was burning at the head of the bed and went and looked behind the curtain; but no creature was to be seen, a closed door was all that met her eye.

She put back the candle, took a pair of gold scissors from a little pocket case, cut off a curl of the dead man's hair, placed the curl in a black velvet sachet which hung over her heart, gave one last kiss to her dead lover, laid the sheet over his face, and left the house. Just as she was crossing the threshold, she met the priest, and drawing back, drew her veil more closely over her face.

"Who are you?" asked the priest.

"I am Grief," she answered, and the priest made way for her to pass.

The countess and her attendant had come on foot, and were returning in the same manner, for the distance between Puiseux and Mont-Gobert was not much more than half-a-mile. When about half way along their road, a man, who had been hiding behind a willow tree, stepped forward and barred their further passage.

Lisette screamed, but the countess, without the least sign of fear, went up to the man, and asked: "Who are you?"

"The man who answered 'I will' just now, when you were asking who would denounce the murderer to you."

"And you can help me to revenge myself on him?"

"Whenever you like."

"At once?"

"We cannot talk here very well."

"Where can we find a better place?"

"In your own room for one."

"We must not enter the castle together."

"No; but I can go through the breach in the park wall: Mademoiselle Lisette can wait for me in the hut where Monsieur Raoul used to leave his horse, she can take me up the winding stair and into your room. If you should be in your dressing room, I will wait for you, as Monsieur Raoul waited the night before last."

The two women shuddered from head to foot.

"Who are you to know all these details?" asked the countess.

"I will tell you when the time comes for me to tell you."

The countess hesitated a moment, then, recovering her resolution, she said:

"Very well then; come through the breach; Lisette will wait for you in the stable."

"Oh! Madame," cried the maid, "I shall never dare to go and bring that man to you!"

"I will go myself then," said the countess.

"Well said!" put in Thibault. "There spoke a woman worth calling one!" And so saying he slid down into a kind of ravine beside the road, and disappeared. Lisette very nearly fainted.

"Lean on me, Mademoiselle," said the countess, "and let us walk on; I am anxious to hear what this man has to say to me."

The two women entered the castle by way of the farm; no one had seen them go out, and no one saw them return. On reaching her room, the countess waited for Lisette to bring up the stranger. Ten minutes had elapsed when the maid hurried in with a pale face.

"Ah! Madame," she said, "there was no need for me to go to fetch him."

"What do you mean?" asked the countess.

"Because he knew his way up as well as I did! And oh! Madame! If you knew what he said to me! That man is the devil, Madame, I feel sure!"

"Show him in," said the countess.

"I am here!" said Thibault.

"You can leave us now, my girl," said the countess to Lisette. The latter quitted the room and the countess remained alone with Thibault.

Thibault's appearance was not one to inspire confidence. He gave the impression of a man who had once and for all made up his mind, but it was also easy to see that it was for no good purpose; a Satanic smile played about his mouth, and there was a demonical light in his eyes. He had made no attempt to hide his red hairs, but had left them defiantly uncovered, and they hung over his forehead like a plume of flame. But still the countess looked him full in the face without changing color.

"My maid says that you know the way to my room; have you ever been here before?"

"Yes, Madame, once."

"And when was that?"

"The day before yesterday."

"At what time?"

"From half-past ten till half-past twelve at night."

The countess looked steadily at him and said:

"That is not true."

"Would you like me to tell you what took place?"

"During the time you mention?"

"During the time I mention."

"Say on," replied the countess, laconically.

Thibault was equally laconic.

"Monsieur Raoul came in by that door," he said, pointing to the one leading into the corridor, "and Lisette left him here alone. You entered the room by that one," he continued, indicating the dressing room door, "and you found him on his knees. Your hair was unbound, only fastened back by three diamond pins, you wore a pink silk dressing gown, trimmed with lace, pink silk stockings, cloth-of-silver slippers and a chain of pearls round your neck."

"You describe my dress exactly," said the countess. "Continue."

"You tried to pick a quarrel with Monsieur Raoul, first because he loitered in the corridors to kiss your waiting-maid; secondly, because someone had met him late at night on the road between Erneville and Villers-Cotterets; thirdly, because, at the ball given at the castle, at which you yourself were not present, he danced four times with Madame de Bonneuil."

"Continue."

"In answer to your accusations, your lover made excuses for himself, some good, some bad; you, however, were satisfied with them for you were just forgiving him when Lisette rushed in full of alarm calling to Monsieur Raoul to escape, as your husband had just returned."

"Lisette was right, you can be nothing less than the devil," said the countess with a sinister laugh, "and I think we shall be able to do business together ... Finish your account."

"Then you and your maid together pushed Monsieur Raoul, who resisted, into the dressing room; Lisette forced him along the corridors and through two or three rooms; they then went down a winding staircase, in the wing of the castle opposite to the one by which they had gone up. On arriving at the foot of the staircase, the fugitives found the door locked; then they ran into a kind of office where Lisette opened the window, which was about seven or eight feet above the ground.

Monsieur Raoul leaped down out of this window, ran to the stable, found his horse still there, but hamstrung; then he swore that if he met the count at any time he would hamstring him as the count had hamstrung his horse, for he thought it a cowardly act to injure a poor beast so unnecessarily. Then he went on foot to the breach, climbed it, and found the count awaiting him outside the park, with his sword drawn. The baron had his hunting knife with him; he drew it, and the duel began."

"Was the count alone?"

"Wait ... the count appeared to be alone; after the fourth or fifth pass the count was wounded in the shoulder, and sank on one knee, crying: 'help, Lestocq!' Then the baron remembered his oath, and hamstrung the count as he had hamstrung the horse; but as the baron rose, Lestocq drove his knife into his back; it passed under the shoulder blade and out through the chest. I need not tell you where ... you kissed the wound yourself."

"And after that?"

"The count and his huntsman returned to the castle, leaving the baron lying helpless; when the latter came to, he made signs to some passing peasants, who put him on a litter, and bore him away, with the intention of taking him to Villers-Cotterets; but he was in such pain, that they could not carry him farther than Puiseux; there they laid him on the bed where you found him, and on which he breathed his last a second after the half hour after nine in the evening."

The countess rose, and without speaking, went to her jewel case and took out the pearls she had worn two nights before. She handed them to Thibault.

"What are they for?" he asked.

"Take them," said the countess. "They are worth fifty thousand livres."

"Are you still anxious for revenge?"

"Yes," replied the countess.

"Revenge will cost more than that."

"How much will it cost?"

"Wait for me tomorrow night," said Thibault, "and I will tell you."

"Where shall I await you?" asked the countess.

"Here," said Thibault, with the leer of a wild animal.

"I will await you here," said the countess.

"Till tomorrow then."

"Till tomorrow."

Thibault went out. The countess went and replaced the pearls in her dressing case; lifted up a false bottom, and drew from underneath it a small bottle containing an opal-colored liquid, and a little dagger with a jeweled handle and case, and a blade inlaid with gold. She hid both beneath her pillow, knelt at her prie-dieu, and, her prayer finished, threw herself dressed on to her bed.

20

TRUE TO TRYST

On quitting the countess's room, Thibault had left the castle by the way which he had described to her, and soon found himself safe beyond its walls and outside the park. And now, for the first time in his life, Thibault had really nowhere to go. His hut was burnt, he was without a friend, and like Cain, he was a wanderer on the face of the earth. He turned to the unfailing shelter of the forest, and there made his way to the lower end of Chavigny; as the day was breaking he came across a solitary house, and asked if he could buy some bread. The woman belonging to it, her husband being away, gave him some, but refused to receive payment for it; his appearance frightened her. Having now food sufficient for the day, Thibault returned to the forest, with the intention of spending his time till evening in a part which he knew between Fleury and Longpont, where the trees were especially thick and tall.

As he was looking for a resting place behind a rock, his eye was attracted by a shining object lying at the bottom of a slope, and his curiosity led him to climb down and see what it was. The shining object was the silver badge belonging to a huntsman's shoulder belt; the shoulder belt was slung round the neck of a dead body, or rather of a skeleton, for the flesh had been entirely eaten off the bones, which were as clean as if prepared for an anatomist's study or a painter's studio. The skeleton looked as if it had only lain there since the preceding night.

"Ah! Ah!" said Thibault. "This is probably the work of my friends, the wolves; they evidently profited by the permission which I gave them."

Curious to know if possible who the victim was, he examined it more closely; his curiosity was soon satisfied, for the badge, which the wolves had no doubt rejected as less easily digestible than the rest, was lying on the chest of the skeleton, like a ticket on a bale of goods.

J. B. LESTOCQ,
Head Keeper to the Comte de Mont-Gobert.

"Well done!" laughed Thibault. "Here is one at least who did not live long to enjoy the result of his murderous act."

Then, contracting his brow, he muttered to himself, in a low voice, and this time without laughing:

"Is there perhaps, after all, what people call a Providence?"

Lestocq's death was not difficult to account for. He had probably been executing some order for his master that night, and on the road between Mont-Gobert and Longpont, had been attacked by wolves. He had defended himself with the same knife with which he had wounded the baron, for Thibault found the knife a few paces off, at a spot where the ground showed traces of a severe struggle; at last, being disarmed, the ferocious beasts had dragged him into the hollow, and there devoured him.

Thibault was becoming so indifferent to everything that he felt neither pleasure nor regret, neither satisfaction nor remorse, at Lestocq's death; all he thought was, that it simplified matters for the countess, as she would now only have her husband upon whom she need revenge herself.

Then he went and found a place where the rocks afforded him the best shelter from the wind, and prepared to spend his day there in peace. Towards midday, he heard the horn of the Lord of Vez, and the cry of his hounds; the mighty huntsman was after game, but the chase did not pass near enough to Thibault to disturb him.

At last the night came. At nine o'clock Thibault rose and set out for the castle of Mont-Gobert. He found the breach, followed the path he knew, and came to the little hut where Lisette had been awaiting him on the night when he had come in the guise of Raoul. The poor girl was there this evening, but alarmed and trembling.

Thibault wished to carry out the old traditions and tried to kiss her, but she sprang back with visible signs of fear.

"Do not touch me," she said, "or I shall call out."

"Oh, indeed! My pretty one," said Thibault. "You were not so sour tempered the other day with Baron Raoul."

"Maybe not," said the girl, "but a great many things have happened since the other day."

"And many more to happen still," said Thibault in a lively tone.

"I think," said the waiting-maid in a mournful voice, "that the climax is already reached." Then, as she went on in front. "If you wish to come," she added, "follow me."

Thibault followed her; Lisette, without the slightest effort at concealment, walked straight across the open space that lay between the trees and the castle.

"You are courageous today," said Thibault, "and supposing someone were to see us."

"There is no fear now," she answered. "The eyes that could have seen us are all closed."

Although he did not understand what the young girl meant by these words, the tone in which they were spoken made Thibault shiver.

He continued to follow her in silence as they went up the winding stairs to the first floor. As Lisette laid her hand on the key of the door, Thibault suddenly stopped her. Something in the silence and solitude of the castle filled him with fear; it seemed as if a curse might have fallen on the place.

"Where are we going?" said Thibault, scarcely knowing himself what he said.

"You know well enough, surely."

"Into the countess's room?"

"Into the countess's room."

"She is waiting for me?"

"She is waiting for you."

And Lisette opened the door. "Go in," she said.

Thibault went in, and Lisette shut the door behind him and waited outside.

It was the same exquisite room, lighted in the same manner, filled with the same sweet scent. Thibault looked round for the countess, he expected to see her appear at the dressing room door, but the door remained closed. Not a sound was to be heard in the room, except the ticking of the Sèvres clock, and the beating of Thibault's heart. He began to look about him with a feeling of shuddering fear for which he could not account; then his eyes fell on the bed; the countess was lying asleep upon it. In her hair were the same diamond pins, round her neck the same pearls; she was dressed in the same pink silk dressing gown, and had on the same little slippers of cloth of silver which she had worn to receive Baron Raoul.

Thibault went up to her; the countess did not stir.

"You are sleeping, fair countess?" he said, leaning over to look at her.

But all at once, he started upright, staring before him, his hair standing on end, the sweat breaking out on his forehead. The terrible truth was beginning to dawn upon him; was the countess sleeping the sleep of this world or of eternity?

He fetched a light from the mantelpiece, and with trembling hand, held it to the face of the mysterious sleeper. It was pale as ivory, with the delicate veins traced over the temples, and the lips still red. A drop of pink burning wax fell on this still face of sleep; it did not awake the countess.

"Ah!" cried Thibault. "What is this?" and he put down the candle, which his shaking hand could no longer hold, on the night table.

The countess lay with her arms stretched out close to her sides; she appeared to be clasping something in either hand. With some effort, Thibault was able to open the left one; within it he found the little bottle, which she had taken from her dressing case the night before. He opened the other hand; within it lay a piece of paper on which were written these few words: "True to tryst,"—yes, true and faithful unto death, for the countess was dead!

All Thibault's illusions were fading one after the other, like the dreams of the night which gradually fade away, as the sleeper becomes more and more thoroughly awake. There was a difference, however, for other men find their dead alive again in their dreams; but with Thibault, his dead did not arise and walk, but remained lying forever in their last sleep.

He wiped his forehead, went to the door leading into the corridor, and opened it, to find Lisette on her knees, praying.

"Is the countess dead then?" asked Thibault.

"The countess is dead, and the count is dead."

"From the effect of the wounds given him by Baron Raoul?"

"No, from the blow with the dagger given him by the countess."

"Ah!" said Thibault, grimacing hideously, in his effort to force a laugh in the midst of this grim drama. "All this tale you hint at is new to me."

Then Lisette told him the tale in full. It was a plain tale, but a terrible one.

The countess had remained in bed part of the day, listening to the village bells of Puiseux, which were tolling as the baron's body was being borne from thence to Vauparfond, where he was to be laid in the family grave. Towards four o'clock the bells ceased; then the countess rose, took the dagger from under her pillow, hid it in her breast, and went towards her husband's room. She found the valet in attendance in good spirits; the doctor had just left, having examined the wound, and declared the count's life out of danger.

"Madame will agree that it is a thing to rejoice at!" said the valet.

"Yes, to rejoice at indeed."

And the countess went on into her husband's room. Five minutes later she left it again.

"The count is sleeping," she said. "Do not go in until he calls."

The valet bowed and sat down in the anteroom to be in readiness at the first call from his master. The countess went back to her room.

"Undress me, Lisette," she said to her waiting maid, "and give me the clothes that I had on the last time he came."

The maid obeyed; we have already seen how every detail of toilet was arranged exactly as it had been on that fatal night. Then the countess wrote a few words on a piece of paper, which she folded and kept in her right hand. After that, she lay down on her bed.

"Will Madame not take anything," asked the maid.

The countess opened her left hand, and showed her a little bottle she was holding inside it.

"Yes, Lisette," she said. "I am going to take what is in this bottle."

"What, nothing but that!" said Lisette.

"It will be enough, Lisette; for after I have taken it, I shall have need of nothing more."

And as she spoke, she put the bottle to her mouth and drank the contents at a draught. Then she said:

"You saw that man, Lisette, who waited for us in the road; I have a meeting with him this evening, here in my room, at half past nine. You know where to go and wait for him, and you will bring him here. I do not wish that anyone should be able to say that I was not true to my word, even after I am dead."

Thibault had nothing to say; the agreement made between them had been kept. Only the countess had accomplished her revenge herself, singlehanded, as everyone understood, when the valet feeling uneasy about his master, and going softly into his room to look at him, found him lying on his back with a dagger in his heart; and then hurrying to tell Madame what had happened, found the countess dead also.

The news of this double death soon spread through the castle, and all the servants had fled, saying that the exterminating angel was in the castle; the waiting-maid alone remained to carry out her dead mistress's wishes.

Thibault had nothing more to do at the castle, so he left the countess on her bed, with Lisette near her, and went down stairs. As Lisette had said, there was no fear now of meeting either master or servants; the servants had run away, the master and mistress were dead. Thibault once more made for the breach in the wall. The sky was dark, and if it had not been January, you might have imagined a thunder storm was brewing; there was barely light enough to see the footpath, as he went along. Once or twice Thibault paused; he fancied he had detected the sound of the dry branches cracking under someone's footsteps keeping pace with his, both to right and left.

Having come to the breach, Thibault distinctly heard a voice say: "that's the man!" and at the same moment, two gendarmes, concealed on the farther side of the wall, seized Thibault by the collar, while two others came up behind.

It appeared that Cramoisi, jealous with regard to Lisette, had been prowling about at nights on the watch, and had, only the evening before, noticed a strange man come in and go out of the park along the more secluded paths, and he had reported the fact to the head of the police.

When the recent serious events that had taken place at the castle became generally known, orders were given to send four men and take up any suspicious looking person seen prowling about. Two of the men, with Cramoisi for guide, had ambushed on the farther side of the breach, and the two others had dogged Thibault through the park. Then as we have seen, at the signal given by Cramoisi, they had all four fallen upon him as he issued from the breach.

There was a long and obstinate struggle; Thibault was not a man that even four others could overcome without difficulty; but he had no weapon by him, and his resistance was therefore useless. The gendarmes had been more bent on securing him, on account of having recognized that it was Thibault, and Thibault was beginning to earn a very bad name, so many misfortunes having become associated with it; so Thibault was knocked down, and finally bound and led off between two mounted men. The other two gendarmes walked one in front, and one behind. Thibault had merely struggled out of a natural feeling of self-defense and pride, for his power to inflict evil was, as we know, unlimited, and he had but to wish his assailants dead, and they would have fallen lifeless at his feet.

But he thought there was time enough for that; as long as there still remained a wish to him, he could escape from man's justice, even though he were at the foot of the scaffold.

So, Thibault, securely bound, his hands tied, and fetters upon his feet, walked along between his four gendarmes, apparently in a state of resignation. One of the gendarmes held the end of the rope with which he was bound, and the four men made jokes and laughed at him, asking the wizard Thibault, why, being possessed of such power, he had allowed himself to be taken. And Thibault replied to their scoffings with the well-known Proverb: "He laughs best who laughs last," and the gendarmes expressed a wish that they might be the ones to do so.

On leaving Puiseux behind, they came to the forest. The weather was growing more and more threatening; the dark clouds hung so low that the trees looked as if they were holding up a huge black veil, and it was impossible to see four steps ahead. But he, Thibault saw; saw lights swiftly passing, and crossing one another, in the darkness on either side. Closer and closer drew the lights, and pattering footfalls were heard among the dry leaves. The horses became restive, shied, and snorted, sniffing the air and trembling beneath their riders, while the coarse laughter of the men themselves died down. It was Thibault's turn to laugh now.

"What are you laughing at?" asked one of the gendarmes.

"I am laughing at your having left off laughing," said Thibault.

The lights drew nearer, and the footfalls became more distinct, at the sound of Thibault's voice. Then a more ominous sound was heard, a sound of teeth striking together, as jaws opened and shut.

"Yes, yes, my friends," said Thibault, "you have tasted human flesh, and you found it good."

He was answered by a low growl of approbation, half like a dog's, and half like a hyena's.

"Quite so," said Thibault. "I understand; after having made a meal of a keeper, you would not mind tasting a gendarme."

The gendarmes themselves were beginning to shudder with fear. "To whom are you talking?" they asked him.

"To those who can answer me," said Thibault; and he gave a howl. Twenty or more howls responded, some from close at hand, some from farther off.

"H'm!" said one of the gendarmes. "What are these beasts that are following us? This good-for-nothing seems to under-stand their language?"

"What!" said the shoe maker. "You take Thibault the wolf master prisoner, you carry him through the forest at night, and then you ask what are the lights and the howls that follow him! ... Do you hear, friends?" cried Thibault. "These gentlemen are asking who you are. Answer them, all of you together, that they may have no further doubt on the matter."

The wolves, obedient to their master's voice, gave one

prolonged, unanimous howl. The horses panted and shivered, and one or two of them reared. The gendarmes endeavored to calm their animals, patting and gentling them.

"That is nothing," said Thibault. "Wait till you see each horse with two wolves hanging on to its hindquarters and another at its throat."

The wolves now came in between the horses' legs, and began caressing Thibault; one of them stood up, and put its front paws on Thibault's chest, as if asking for orders.

"Presently, presently," said Thibault, "there is plenty of time; do not be selfish, give your comrades time to come up."

The men could no longer control their horses, which were rearing and shying, and although going at a foot's pace, were streaming with sweat.

"Do you not think," said Thibault, "you would do best now to come to terms with me? That is, if you were to let me free on condition that you all sleep in your beds tonight."

"Go at a walking pace," said one of the gendarmes. "As long as we do that, we have nothing to fear."

Another one drew his sword. A second or two later there was a howl of pain; one of the wolves had seized hold of this gendarme's boot, and the latter had pierced him through with his weapon.

"I call that a very imprudent thing to do," said Thibault; "the wolves eat each other, whatever the proverb may say, and once having tasted blood, I do not know that even I shall have the power to hold them back."

The wolves threw themselves in a body on their wounded comrade, and in five minutes there was nothing left of its carcass but the bare bones. The gendarmes had profited by this respite to get on ahead, but without releasing Thibault, whom they obliged to run alongside of them; what he had foreseen, however, happened. There was a sudden sound as of an approaching hurricane—the whole pack was in pursuit, following them up at full gallop. The horses, having once started trotting, refused to go at a walking pace again, and frightened by the stamping, the smell, and the howls, now set off galloping, in spite of their riders' efforts to hold them in. The man who had hold of the rope, now requiring both hands to master his horse, let go of Thibault; and the wolves leaped on to the horses, clinging desperately to the cruppers and withers and throats of the terrified animals. No sooner had the latter felt the sharp teeth of their assailants, then they scattered, rushing in every direction.

"Hurrah, wolves! Hurrah!" cried Thibault. But the fierce animals had no need of encouragement, and soon each horse had six or seven more wolves in pursuit of him.

Horses and wolves disappeared, someone way some the other, and the men's cries of distress, the agonized neighings of the horses, and the furious howls of the wolves became gradually fainter and fainter as they travelled farther away.

Thibault was left free once more, and alone. His hands however were still bound, and his feet fettered. First, he tried to undo the cord with his teeth, but this he found impossible. Then he tried to wrench his bonds apart by the power of his muscles, but that too was unavailing; the only result of his efforts was to make the cord cut into his flesh.

It was his turn to bellow with pain and anger. At last, tired of trying to wrest his hands free, he lifted them, bound as they were, to heaven, and cried:

"Oh! Black wolf! Friend, let these cords that bind me be loosened; thou knowest well that it is only to do evil that I wish for my hands to be free."

And at the same moment his fetters were broken and fell to the ground, and Thibault beat his hands together with another roar, this time of joy.

21

THE GENIUS OF EVIL

The next evening, about nine o'clock, a man might be seen walking along the Puits-Sarrasin road and making for the Osiéres forest path.

It was Thibault, on his way to pay a last visit to the hut, and to see if any remains of it had been left by the fire. A heap of smoking cinders alone marked the place where it had stood; and as Thibault came in sight of it, he saw the wolves, as if he had appointed them to meet him there, forming an immense circle round the ruins, and looking upon them with an expression of mournful anger. They seemed to understand that by destroying this poor hut, made of earth and branches, the one who, by the compact with the black wolf, had been given them for master, had been made a victim. As Thibault entered the circle, all the wolves gave simultaneously a long and sinister sounding howl, as if to make him understand that they were ready to help in avenging him.

Thibault went and sat down on the spot where the hearth had stood; it was recognizable from a few blackened stones still remaining, which were otherwise uninjured, and by a higher heap of cinders just at that spot.

He stayed there some minutes, absorbed in his unhappy

thoughts. But he was not reflecting that the ruin which he saw around him was the consequence and the punishment of his jealous and covetous desires, which had gone on gathering strength. He felt neither repentance nor regret. That which dominated all other feeling in him was his satisfaction at the thought of being henceforth able to render to his fellow creatures evil for evil, his pride in having, thanks to his terrible auxiliaries, the power to fight against those who persecuted him.

And as the wolves continued their melancholy howling: "Yes, my friends," said Thibault, "yes, your howls answer to the cry of my heart ... My fellow creatures have destroyed my hut, they have cast to the winds the ashes of the tools wherewith I earned my daily bread; their hatred pursues me as it pursues you, I expect from them neither mercy nor pity. We are their enemies as they are ours; and I will have neither mercy nor compassion on them. Come then, let us go from this hut to the castle, and carry thither the desolation which they have brought home to me."

And then the master of the wolves, like a chief of banditti followed by his desperadoes, set off with his pack in quest of pillage and carnage.

This time it was neither red deer, nor fallow deer, nor any timid game of which they were in pursuit. Sheltered by the darkness of the night Thibault first directed his course to the Château of Vez, for there was lodged his chief enemy. The baron had three farms belonging to the estate, stables filled with horses, and others filled with cows, and the park was full of sheep. All these places were attacked the first night, and on the morrow two horses, four cows, and ten sheep were found killed.

The baron was doubtful at first if this could be the work of the beasts against which he waged so fierce a warfare; there seemed something partaking rather of intelligence and revenge in it than of the mere unreasoning attacks of a pack of wild animals. Still it seemed manifest that the wolves must have been the aggressors, judging by the marks of teeth on the carcasses and the footprints left on the ground. Next night the baron set watchers to lie in wait, but Thibault and his wolves were at work on the farther side of the forest. This time it was the stables and parks of Soucy and of Vivierès which were decimated, and the following night those of Boursonnes and Yvors. The work of annihilation, once begun, must be carried out with desperate determination, and the master never left his wolves now; he slept with them in their dens, and lived in the midst of them, stimulating their thirst for blood.

Many a woodman, many a heath-gatherer, came face to face in the thickets with the menacing white teeth of a wolf, and was either carried off and eaten, or just saved his life by the aid of his courage and his billhook. Guided by a human intelligence, the wolves had become organized and disciplined, and were far more formidable than a band of discontented soldiery let loose in a conquered country.

The terror of them became general; no one dared go beyond the towns and villages unarmed; horses and cattle were all fed inside the stables, and the men themselves, their work done, waited for one another, so as not to go about singly. The Bishop of Soissons ordered public prayer to be made, asking God to send a thaw, for the unusual ferocity of the wolves was attributed to the great quantity of snow that had fallen. But the report also went about that the wolves were incited to their work, and led about by a man; that this man was more indefatigable, crueler and more insatiable than the wolves themselves; that in imitation of his companions he ate raw flesh and quenched his thirst in blood. And the people went further and said that this man was Thibault.

The Bishop pronounced sentence of excommunication against the former shoe maker. The Lord of Vez, however, had little faith in the thunders of the Church being of much effect, unless supported by some well-conducted hunting. He was somewhat cast down at so much blood being spilt, and his pride was sorely hurt that his, the Grand Master's, own cattle should have suffered so heavily from the very wolves he was especially appointed to destroy.

At the same time, he could not but feel a secret delight, at the thought of the triumphant view-halloos in store for him, and of the fame which he could not fail to win among all sportsmen of repute. His passion for the chase, excited by the way in which his adversaries the wolves had so openly entered upon the struggle, became absolutely overpowering; he allowed neither respite nor repose; he took no sleep himself and ate his meals in the saddle. All night long he scoured the country in company with l'Eveillé and Engoulevent, who, in consideration of his marriage had been raised to the rank of pricker; and the dawn had no sooner appeared before he was again in the saddle, ready to start and chase the wolf until it was too dark to distinguish the hounds. But alas! All his knowledge of the art of Venery, all his courage, all his perseverance, were lost labor. He occasionally brought down some wretched cub, some miserable beast eaten with mange, some imprudent glutton which had so gorged itself with carnage that its breath would not hold out after an hour or two's run; but the larger, well-grown wolves, with their thick dark coats, their muscles like steel springs and their long slender feet—not one of these lost a hair in the war that was being made upon them. Thanks to Thibault they met their enemies in arms on nearly equal ground.

As the Baron of Vez remained forever with his dogs, so did Thibault with his wolves; after a night of sack and pillage, he kept the pack awake on the watch to help the one that the baron had started. This wolf again, following Thibault's instructions, had recourse at first to stratagem. It doubled, crossed its tracks, waded in the streams, leaped up into the bending trees so as to make it more difficult still for huntsmen and hounds to follow the scent, and finally when it felt its powers failing, it adopted bolder measures and went straight ahead. Then the other wolves and their master intervened; at the least sign of hesitation on the part of the hounds, they managed so cleverly to put them on the wrong scent, that it required an experienced eye to detect that the dogs were not all following up the same track, and nothing less than the baron's profound knowledge could decide which was the right one. Even he sometimes was mistaken.

Again, the wolves in their turn followed the huntsmen; it was a pack hunting a pack; only the one hunted in silence, which made it far the more formidable of the two. Did a tired hound fall behind, or another get separated from the main body, it was seized and killed in an instant, and Engoulevent, whom we have had occasion to mention several times before and who had taken poor Marcotte's place, having hastened one day to the help of one of his hounds that was uttering cries of distress, was himself attacked and only owed his life to the swiftness of his horse.

It was not long before the baron's pack was decimated; his best hounds were nearly dead with fatigue, and his more second-rate ones had perished by the wolves' teeth. The stable was in no better condition than the kennel; Bayard was foundered, Tancred had sprained a tendon leaping over a ditch, and a strained fetlock had placed Valourous on the list of invalids. Sultan, luckier than his three companions had fallen honorably on the field of battle, having succumbed to a sixteen hours' run under the weight of his gigantic master, who never for a moment lost courage notwithstanding the fact that the dead bodies of his finest and most faithful servitors lay heaped around him.

The baron, following the example of the noble-hearted Romans who exhausted the resources of military art against the Carthaginians who were forever reappearing as enemies, the baron, I repeat, changed his tactics and tried what battues could accomplish. He called on all available men among the peasants, and beat up the game throughout the forest with such a formidable number of men, that not so much as a hare was left in its form near any spot which they had passed.

But Thibault made it his business to find out beforehand where these battues were going to take place, and if he ascertained that the beaters were on the side of the forest towards Viviers or Soucy, he and his wolves made an excursion to Boursonnes or Yvors; and if the baron and his men were busy near Haramont or Longpré, the people of Corcy and Vertefeuille were made painfully aware of Thibault and his wolves.

In vain the Lord of Vez drew his cordon at night round the suspected enclosures, so as to begin the attack with daylight; never once did his men succeed in starting a wolf, for not once did Thibault make a mistake in his calculations. If by chance he had not been well informed, and was uncertain in what direction the baron and his men were going, he called all his wolves together, sending express couriers after them as the night set in; he then led them unobserved down the wooded lane leading to Lessart-l'Abbesse, which at that time ran between the forest of Compiègne and the forest of Villers-Cotterets, and so was able to pass from one to the other. This state of things went on for several months.

Both the baron and Thibault carried out the task each had set before himself, with equally passionate energy; the latter, like his adversary, seemed to have required some supernatural power, whereby he was able to resist fatigue and excitement; and this was the more remarkable seeing that during the short intervals of respite accorded by the Lord of Vez, the wolf leader was by no means at peace in himself.

It was not that the terrible deeds in which he was an active agent, and at which he presided, filled him exactly with horror, for he thought them justifiable; he threw the responsibility of them, he said, on to those who had forced him to commit them; but there were moments of failing spirit, for which he could not account, when he went about in the midst of his ferocious companions, feeling gloomy, morose and heavy hearted.

Again the image of Agnelette would rise before him, seeming to him like the personification of his own past life, honest and laborious, peaceful and innocent. And more than that, he felt he loved her more than he had ever thought it possible for him to love anybody. At times he would weep at the thought of all his lost happiness, at others he was seized with a wild fit of jealousy against the one to whom she now belonged—she, who at one time, might if he had liked, have been his.

One day, the baron in order to prepare some fresh means of destruction, had been forced for the while to leave the wolves in peace. Thibault, who was in one of the moods we have just described, wandered forth from the den where he lived in company with the wolves. It was a splendid summer's night, and he began to rove about the woodlands, where the moon was lighting up the trunks of the trees, dreaming of the time when he trod the mossy carpet underfoot free from trouble and anxiety, until at last the only happiness which was now left him, forgetfulness of the present, stole over his senses. Lost in this sweet dream of his earlier life, he was all of a sudden aroused by a cry of distress from somewhere near at hand. He was now so accustomed to such sounds, that, ordinarily, he would have paid no attention to it, but his heart was for the moment softened by the recollection of Agnelette, and he felt more disposed than usual to pity; as it happened also he was near the place where he had first seen the gentle child, and this helped to awaken his kinder nature.

He ran to the spot whence the cry had come, and as he leaped from the underwood into the deep forest lane near Ham, he saw a woman struggling with an immense wolf which had thrown her on the ground. Thibault could not have said why he was so agitated at this sight, nor why his heart beat more violently than usual; he rushed forward and seizing the animal by the throat hurled it away from its victim, and then lifting the woman in his arms, he carried her to the side of the lane and laid her on the slope. Here a ray of moonlight, breaking through the clouds, fell on the face of the woman he had saved, and Thibault saw that it was Agnelette.

Near to the spot was the spring in which Thibault had once gazed at himself, and had seen the first red hair; he ran to it, took up water in his hands, and threw it into the woman's face. Agnelette opened her eyes, gave a cry of terror, and tried to rise and flee.

"What!" cried the wolf leader, as if he were still Thibault the shoe maker. "You do not know me again, Agnelette?"

"Ah! Yes indeed, I know you, Thibault; and it is because I know who you are," cried the young woman, "that I am afraid!" Then throwing herself on her knees, and clasping her hands: "Oh do not kill me, Thibault!" she cried. "Do not kill me! It would be such dreadful trouble for the poor old grandmother! Thibault, do not kill me!"

The wolf leader stood overcome with consternation; up to this hour he had not fully realized the hideous renown which he had gained; but the terror which the sight of him inspired in the woman who had loved him and whom he still loved, filled him with a horror of himself.

"I'll kill you, Agnelette!" he said. "Just when I have snatched you from death! Oh! How you must hate and despise me for such a thought to enter your head."

"I do not hate you, Thibault," said the young woman. "But I hear such things about you, that I feel afraid of you."

"And do they say nothing of the infidelity which has led Thibault to commit such crimes?"

"I do not understand you," said Agnelette looking at Thibault with her large eyes, blue as the heavens.

"What!" exclaimed Thibault. "You do not understand that I loved you—that I adored you Agnelette, and that the loss of you sent me out of my mind?"

"If you loved me, if you adored me, Thibault, what prevented you from marrying me?"

"The spirit of evil," muttered Thibault.

"I too loved you," continued the young woman, "and I suffered cruelly waiting for you."

Thibault heaved a sigh. "You loved me, Agnelette?" he asked.

"Yes," replied the young woman with her soft voice and

gentle eyes.

"But now, all is over," said Thibault, "and you love me no more."

"Thibault," answered Agnelette, "I no longer love you, because it is no longer right to love you; but one cannot always forget one's first love as one would wish."

"Agnelette!" cried Thibault, trembling all over. "Be careful what you say!"

"Why should I be careful what I say, since it is the truth," said the girl with an innocent shake of the head. "The day you told me that you wished to make me your wife, I believed you, Thibault; for why should I think that you would lie to me when I had just done you a service? Then, later I met you, but I did not go in search of you; you came to me, you spoke words of love to me, you were the first to refer to the promise that you had made me. And it was not my fault either, Thibault, that I was afraid of that ring which you wore, which was large enough for you and yet, oh, it was horrible! Not big enough for one of my fingers."

"Would you like me not to wear this ring anymore?" said Thibault. "Would you like me to throw it away?" And he began trying to pull it off his finger, but as it had been too small to go on Agnelette's finger, so now it was too small to be taken off Thibault's. In vain he struggled with it, and tried to move it with his teeth; the ring seemed rivetted to his finger for all eternity.

Thibault saw that it was no use trying to get rid of it; it was a token of compact between himself and the black wolf, and with a sigh he let his arms fall hopelessly to his sides.

"That day," went on Agnelette, "I ran away; I know that I was wrong to do so, but I was no longer mistress of myself after seeing that ring and more still." She lifted her eyes as she spoke, looking timidly up at Thibault's hair. Thibault was bareheaded, and, by the light of the moon Agnelette could see that it was no longer a single hair that shone red as the flames of hell, but that half the hair on Thibault's head was now of this devil's color.

"Oh!" she exclaimed, drawing back. "Thibault! Thibault!

What has happened to you since I last saw you?"

"Agnelette!" cried Thibault throwing himself down with his face to the ground, and holding his head between his hands. "I could not tell any human creature, not even a priest what has happened to me since then; but to Agnelette, all I can say is: Agnelette! Agnelette! Have pity on me, for I have been most unhappy!"

Agnelette went up to him and took his hands in hers.

"You did love me then? You did love me?" he cried.

"What can I do, Thibault!" said the girl with the same sweetness and innocence as before. "I took you at your word, and every time I heard someone knocking at our hut door, I thought it was you come to say to my old grandmother, 'Mother, I love Agnelette, Agnelette loves me; will you give her to me for my wife?'"

"Then when I went and opened the door, and found that it was not you, I used to go into a corner and cry."

"And now, Agnelette, now?"

"Now," she answered. "Now, Thibault, it may seem strange, but in spite of all the terrible tales that are told about you, I have not been really frightened; I was sure that you could not wish any harm to me, and I was walking boldly through the forest, when that dreadful beast from which you saved me, suddenly sprang upon me."

"But how is it that you are near your old home? Do you not live with your husband?"

"We lived together for a while at Vez, but there was no room there for my grandmother; and so I said to my husband, 'my grandmother must be thought of first; I must go back to her; when you wish to see me you will come.'"

"And he consented to that arrangement?"

"Not at first, but I pointed out to him that my grandmother is seventy years of age; that if she were only to live another two or three years, God grant it may be more! It would only be two or three years of some extra trouble for us, whereas, in all probability we had long years of life before us. Then he understood that it was right to give to those that had least."

But all the while that Agnelette was giving this explanation, Thibault could think of nothing but that the love she once had for him was not yet dead.

"So," said Thibault, "you loved me? And so, Agnelette you could love me again ...?"

"That is impossible now because I belong to another."

"Agnelette, Agnelette! Only say that you love me!"

"No, Thibault, if I loved you, I should do everything in the world to hide it from you."

"And why?" cried Thibault. "Why? You do not know my power. I know that I have only a wish or two left, but with your help, by combining these wishes together, I could make you as rich as a queen ... We could leave the country, leave France, Europe; there are large countries, of which you do not even know the names, Agnelette, called America and India. They are paradises, with blue skies, tall trees, and birds of every kind. Agnelette, say that you will come with me; nobody will know that we have gone off together, nobody will know where we are, nobody will know that we love one another, nobody will know even that we are alive."

"Fly with you, Thibault!" said Agnelette, looking at the wolf leader as if she had but half understood what he said. "Do you forget that I no longer belong to myself? Do you not know that I am married?"

"What does that matter," said Thibault, "if it is I whom you love, and if we can live happily together!"

"Oh! Thibault! Thibault! What are you saying!"

"Listen," went on Thibault, "I am going to speak to you in the name of this world and the next. Do you wish to save me, Agnelette, body and soul? If so, do not resist my pleading, have pity on me, come with me; let us go somewhere together, where we shall no longer hear these howlings, or breathe this atmosphere of reeking flesh; and, if it scares you to think of being a rich, grand lady, somewhere then where I can again be Thibault the workman, Thibault, poor but beloved, and, therefore, Thibault happy in his hard work, some place where Agnelette will have no other husband but me."

"Ah! Thibault! I was ready to become your wife, and you scorned me!"

"Do not remember my sins, Agnelette, which have been so cruelly punished."

"Thibault, another has done what you were not willing to do. He took the poor young girl; he burdened himself with the poor old blind woman; he gave a name to the one and bread to the other; he had no ambition beyond that of gaining my love; he desired no dowry beyond my marriage vow; can you think of asking me to return evil for good? Do you dare to suggest that I should leave the one who has given me such proof of his love for the one who has given me proof only of his indifference?"

"But what matter still, Agnelette, since you do not love him and since you do love me?"

"Thibault, do not turn and twist my words to make them appear to say what they do not. I said that I still preserved my friendship for you, I never said that I did not love my husband. I should like to see you happy, my friend; above all I should like to see you abjure your evil ways and repent of your sins; and last of all, I wish that God may have mercy upon you, and that you may be delivered from that spirit of evil, of which you spoke just now. For this I pray night and morning on my knees; but even that I may be able to pray for you, I must keep myself pure; if the voice that supplicates for mercy is to rise to God's throne, it must be an innocent one; above all, I must scrupulously keep the oath which I swore at His altar."

On hearing these decisive words from Agnelette, Thibault again became fierce and morose. "Do you not know, Agnelette, that it is very imprudent of you to speak to me here like that?"

"And why, Thibault?" asked the young woman.

"We are alone here together; it is dark, and not a man of the open would dare to come into the forest at this hour; and know, the king is not more master in his kingdom than I am here?"

"I do not understand you, Thibault?"

"I mean that having prayed, implored, and conjured, I can now threaten."

"You, threaten?"

"What I mean is," continued Thibault, paying no heed to Agnelette's words, "that every word you speak does not excite my love for you more than it rouses my hatred towards him; in short, I mean that it is imprudent of the lamb to irritate the wolf when the lamb is in the power of the wolf."

"I told you, Thibault, before, that I started to walk through the forest without any feeling of fear at meeting you. As I was coming to, I felt a momentary terror, remembering involuntarily what I had heard said about you; but at this moment, Thibault, you will try in vain to make me turn pale."

Thibault flung both hands up to his head.

"Do not talk like that," he said. "You cannot think what the devil is whispering to me, and what an effort I have to make to resist his voice."

"You may kill me if you like," replied Agnelette, "but I will not be guilty of the cowardice which you ask of me; you may kill me, but I shall remain faithful to my husband; you may kill me, but I shall pray to God to help him as I die."

"Do not speak his name, Agnelette; do not make me think about that man."

"You can threaten me as much as you like, Thibault, for I am in your hands; but, happily, he is far from you, and you have no power over him."

"And who told you that, Agnelette? Do you not know that, thanks to the diabolical power I possess and which I can hardly fight against, I am able to strike as well far as near?"

"And if I should become a widow, Thibault, do you imagine that I should be vile enough to accept your hand when it was stained with the blood of the one whose name I bear?"

"Agnelette," said Thibault falling on his knees. "Agnelette, save me from committing a further crime."

"It is you, not I, who will be responsible for the crime. I can give you my life, Thibault, but not my honor."

"Oh," roared Thibault, "love flies from the heart when hatred enters; take care, Agnelette! Take heed to your husband! The devil is in me, and he will soon speak through my mouth. Instead of the consolation which I had hoped from your love, and which your love refuses, I will have vengeance. Stay my hand, Agnelette, there is yet time, stay it from cursing, from destroying; if not, understand that it is not I, but you, who strike him dead! Agnelette, you know now ... Agnelette, you do not stop me from speaking? Let it be so then, and let the curse fall on all three of us, you and him and me! Agnelette, I wish your husband to die, and he will die!"

Agnelette uttered a terrible cry; then, as if her reason reasserted itself, protesting against this murder at a distance which seemed impossible to her, she exclaimed:

"No, no; you only say that to terrify me, but my prayers will prevail against your maledictions."

"Go then, and learn how heaven answers your prayers. Only, if you wish to see your husband again alive, Agnelette, you had better make haste, or you will but stumble against his dead body."

Overcome by the tone of conviction with which these last words were pronounced, and yielding to an irresistible feeling of terror, Agnelette, without responding to Thibault, who stood on the further side of the lane with his hand held out and pointing towards Préciamont, set off running in the direction which it seemed to indicate, and soon disappeared into the night as she turned out of sight at the corner of the road. As she passed from his view, Thibault uttered a howl, which might have been taken for the howling of a whole pack of wolves, and plunging into the thicket, "Ah! Now," he cried aloud to himself, "I am indeed a lost and accursed soul!"

THIBAULT'S LAST WISH

U rged in her flight by a hideous terror, and anxious to reach the village where she had left her husband with all speed possible, Agnelette, for the very reason that she was running so hastily, was forced by her failing breath, to pause at intervals along the way.

During these short spaces of rest, she endeavored to reason with herself, trying to convince herself of the folly of attaching importance to words which could have no power in themselves, and which were dictated by jealousy and hatred, words which had by now been scattered to the winds; but notwithstanding all her mental arguments, she had no sooner regained her breath than she started off again at the same precipitate pace, for she felt she should know no peace until she had seen her husband again. Best part of her way led through the forest, and near the wildest and most solitary enclosures, but she gave no thought to the wolves, which were the terror of every town and village within ten miles round. Only one fear possessed her, that of coming across her husband's dead body. More than once, as her foot struck against a stone or a branch, her heart stopped beating, and she felt as if her last breath had been drawn, while a sharp cold seemed to enter her very vitals, her hair stood on end, and her face grew wet with perspiration.

At last, at the end of the long path she had been traversing, arched over by the trees, she saw ahead of her, a vista of open country lying bathed in the soft silver light of the moon. As she emerged from the gloom into the light, a man, who had been concealed behind a bush in the hollow lying between the forest and the open country, sprang in front of her and took her in his arms.

"Ah! Ah!" he said, laughing. "And where are you off to, Madame, at this hour of the night, and at this pace too?" Agnelette recognized her husband.

"Etienne! Dear, dear Etienne," cried the young woman, throwing her arms round his neck. "How thankful I am to see you again, and to find you alive and well! Oh, my God, I thank Thee!"

"What, did you think, you poor little Agnelette," said Engoulevent, "that Thibault and his wolves had been making their dinner of me?"

"Ah! Do not even speak of Thibault, Etienne! Let us fly, dear one, fly to where there are houses!"

The young huntsman laughed again. "Well, now then, you will make all the gossips of Préciamont and Vez declare that a husband is of no use at all, not even to restore his wife's courage."

"You are right, Etienne; but although I have just had the courage to come through these great dreadful woods, now that I have you with me and should feel reassured, I tremble with fear, and yet I know not why."

"What has happened to you? Come, tell me all about it," said Etienne, giving his wife a kiss. Then Agnelette told him how she had been attacked by the wolf, how Thibault had rescued her from its claws, and what had passed between them afterwards. Engoulevent listened with the greatest attention.

"Listen," he said to Agnelette. "I am going to take you home and shut you up carefully with my grandmother, so that no harm may come to you; and then I shall ride over and tell my lord of Vez where Thibault has taken up his quarters."

"Oh! No, no!" cried Agnelette. "You would have to ride through the forest, and there is no knowing what danger you might run."

"I will make a détour," said Etienne. "I can go round by Croyolles and Value instead of crossing the forest."

Agnelette sighed and shook her head, but made no further resistance; she knew that Engoulevent would not give in on this matter, and she reserved her strength wherewith to renew her entreaties when she was once indoors.

And in truth, the young huntsman only considered that he was doing his duty, for a great battue had been arranged for the next day in a part of the forest on the further side from that on which Agnelette had met Thibault. Etienne, therefore, was bound to go without delay and report to his master the where-abouts of the wolf leader. There was not too much of the night left for the work of rearranging for the morrow's battue.

As they drew near Préciamont, Agnelette, who had not spoken for a while, decided that she had, during her silence, amassed a sufficient number of reasons to justify her in begin-ning her solicitations afresh, which she did with even more earnestness than she had put into her former arguments. She reminded Etienne that Thibault, even though he might be a werewolf, had, so far from hurting her, actually saved her life; and that after all, he had not abused his power when he had her in it, but had allowed her to leave him and rejoin her husband. And after that, to betray where he was to his mortal enemy, the Lord of Vez, was not performing a duty, but committing an act of treachery; and Thibault, who would certainly get wind of this treachery, would never under similar circumstances show mercy to any one again. Agnelette became quite eloquent as she pleaded Thibault's cause. But, when marrying Engoulevent, she had made no more secret of her former engagement to the shoe

maker than she had of this last interview with him, and however
perfect a confidence he had in his wife, Engoulevent was nevertheless not unsusceptible to jealousy. More than that, there
existed an old grudge between the two men, ever since the day
when Engoulevent had spied out Thibault in his tree, and his
boar spear in a neighboring bush. So he stood his ground, and
though listening to Agnelette, continued to walk briskly towards
Préciamont. And so arguing together, and each insisting that he
or she was in the right, they came to within a stone's throw of
the first forest fences. To protect themselves as far as possible
from Thibault's sudden and unexpected assaults, the peasants
had instituted patrol parties, who mounted guard at night as in
times of war. Etienne and Agnelette were so preoccupied with
their discussion, that they did not hear the call of "Who goes
there!" from the sentinel behind the hedge, and went walking on
in the direction of the village.

The sentinel, seeing something moving in the darkness which
to his prepossessed imagination appeared to be a monstrous
form of some kind, and hearing no answer to his challenge, he
prepared to shoot. Looking up at that moment, the young
huntsman suddenly caught sight of the sentinel, as the moonlight shone on the barrel of his gun. Calling out "Friend," he
threw himself in front of Agnelette, flinging his arms round her,
so as to make a shield of his body. But at the same instant the
gun went off, and the unfortunate Etienne, giving one last sigh,
fell forward without a groan against the wife he was clasping in
his arms. The bullet had pierced his heart. When the people of
Préciamont, on hearing the gun shot, came running up to the
spot, they found Engoulevent dead, and Agnelette lying unconscious beside her husband.

They carried her to her grandmother's, but she only came to
her senses to fall into a state of despair which bordered on delirium, and which at last became almost madness. She accused
herself of her husband's death, called him by name, begged the
invisible spirits, which seemed to haunt her, even in the short

intervals of slumber which her excited state of brain made possible, to have mercy upon him. She called Thibault's name, and addressed such heartbroken supplications to him that those about her were moved to tears. By degrees, in spite of the incoherence of her words, the real facts became evident, and it grew to be generally understood that the wolf leader was in some way accountable for the unhappy accident which had caused poor Etienne's death. The common enemy was therefore accused of having cast a spell over the two unfortunate young creatures, and the animosity felt towards the former shoe maker became intensified.

In vain doctors were sent for from Villers-Cotterets and Ferté-Milon, Agnelette became worse and worse; her strength was rapidly failing; her voice, after the first few days, grew feebler, her breath shorter, although her delirium was as violent as ever, and everything, even the silence on the doctors' part, led to the belief that poor Agnelette would soon follow her husband to the grave. The voice of the old blind woman alone seemed to have any power to allay the fever. When she heard her grandmother speaking, she grew calmer, the haggard staring eyes grew softer and suffused with tears; she would pass her hand over her forehead as if to drive away some haunting thought, and a sorrowful wandering smile would pass across her lips.

One evening, towards night, her slumber seemed to be more agitated and distressed than usual. The hut, feebly lit by a little copper lamp, was in semi-darkness; the grandmother sat by the hearth, with that immobility of countenance under which peasants and savages hide their strongest feelings. At the foot of the bed on which Agnelette lay, so worn and white that, had it not been for the regular rise and fall of her bosom with its troubled breathing, you might have taken her for dead, knelt one of the women, whom the baron was paying to attend upon the widow of his young huntsman, engaged in telling her beads; the other was silently spinning with her distaff. All at once, the sick woman, who for some minutes past had been shivering at intervals, seemed to be fighting against some horrible dream, and gave a piercing cry of anguish. At that moment the door burst open, a man seemingly encircled by flames, rushed into the room, leapt to Agnelette's bed, clasped the dying woman in his arms, pressed his lips upon her forehead, uttering cries of sorrow, then, rushing to another door which gave on to the open country, opened it and disappeared. The apparition had come and gone so quickly that it seemed almost like a hallucination, and as if Agnelette were endeavoring to repulse some invisible object as she cried out, "Take him away! Take him away!" But the two watchers had seen the man and had recognized Thibault, and there was a clamoring outside, in the midst of which the name of Thibault could be distinguished. Soon the clamor came nearer to Agnelette's hut, and those who were uttering the cries ere long appeared on the threshold; they were in pursuit of the wolf leader. Thibault had been seen prowling in the neighborhood of the hut, and the villagers, warned of this by their sentinels, had armed themselves with pitchforks and sticks preparatory to giving him chase.

Thibault, hearing of the hopeless condition in which Agnelette was, had not been able to resist his longing to see her once again, and at the risk of what might happen to him, he had passed through the village, trusting to the rapidity of his movements, had opened the door of the hut and rushed in to see the dying woman.

The two women showed the peasants the door by which Thibault had escaped, and like a pack that has recovered the scent they started afresh on his track with renewed cries and threats. Thibault, it need hardly be said, escaped from them and disappeared in the forest.

Agnelette's condition, after the terrible shock given her by Thibault's presence and embrace, became so alarming that before the night was over the priest was sent for; she had evidently now but a few hours longer to live and suffer. Towards midnight the priest arrived, followed by the sacristan carrying the cross, and the choir boys bearing the holy water.

These went and knelt at the foot of the bed, while the priest took his place at the head beside Agnelette. And now, some mysterious power seemed to reanimate the dying woman. For a long time she spoke in a low voice with the priest, and as the poor child had no need of long prayers for herself, it was certain that she must be praying for another. And who was that other? God, the priest, and Agnelette alone knew.

❧ 23 ❧

THE ANNIVERSARY

A s soon as Thibault ceased to hear the furious cries of his pursuers behind him, he slackened his pace, and the usual silence again reigning throughout the forest, he paused and sat down on a heap of stones. He was in such a troubled state of mind that he did not recognize where he was, until he began to notice that some of the stones were blackened, as if they had been licked by flames; they were the stones of his own former hearth.

Chance had led him to the spot where a few months previously his hut had stood.

The shoe maker evidently felt the bitterness of the comparison between that peaceful past and this terrible present, for large tears rolled down his cheeks and fell upon the cinders at his feet. He heard midnight strike from the Oigny church clock, then one after the other from the other neighboring village towers. At this moment the priest was listening to Agnelette's dying prayers.

"Cursed be the day!" cried Thibault. "When I first wished for anything beyond what God chooses to put within the reach of a poor workman! Cursed be the day when the black wolf gave me the power to do evil, for the ill that I have done, instead of adding to my happiness, has destroyed it forever!"

A loud laugh was heard behind Thibault's back.

He turned; there was the black wolf himself, creeping noiselessly along, like a dog coming to rejoin its master. The wolf would have been invisible in the gloom but for the flames shot forth from his eyes, which illuminated the darkness; he went round the hearth and sat down facing the shoe maker.

"What is this!" he said. "Master Thibault not satisfied? It seems that Master Thibault is difficult to please."

"How can I feel satisfied," said Thibault. "I, who since I first met you, have known nothing but vain aspirations and endless regrets? I wished for riches, and here I am in despair at having lost the humble roof of bracken under shelter of which I could sleep in peace without anxiety as to the morrow, without troubling myself about the rain or the wind beating against the branches of the giant oaks.

"I wished for position, and here I am, stoned and hunted down by the lowest peasants, whom formerly I despised. I asked for love, and the only woman who loved me and whom I loved became the wife of another, and she is at this moment cursing me as she lies dying, while I, notwithstanding all the power you have given me, can do nothing to help her!"

"Leave off loving anybody but yourself, Thibault."

"Oh! Yes, laugh at me, do!"

"I am not laughing at you. But did you not cast envious eyes on other people's property before you had set eyes on me?"

"Yes, for a wretched buck, of which there are hundreds just as good browsing in the forest!"

"You thought your wishes were going to stop at the buck, Thibault; but wishes lead on to one another, as the night to the day, and the day to night. When you wished for the buck, you also wished for the silver dish on which it would be served; the silver dish led you on to wish for the servant who carries it and for the carver who cuts up its contents. Ambition is like the vault of heaven; it appears to be bounded by the horizon, but it covers the whole earth. You disdained Agnelette's innocence, and went after Madame Poulet's mill; if you had gained the mill, you would immediately have wanted the house of the Bailiff Magloire; and his house would have had no further attraction for you when once you had seen the Castle of Mont-Gobert.

"You are one in your envious disposition with the fallen angel, your master and mine; only, as you were not clever enough to reap the benefit that might have accrued to you from your power of inflicting evil, it would perhaps have been more to your interest to continue to lead an honest life."

"Yes, indeed," replied the shoe maker. "I feel the truth of the proverb, 'Evil to him who evil wishes'" But, he continued, "can I not become an honest man again?"

The wolf gave a mocking chuckle. "My good fellow, the devil can drag a man to hell," he said, "by a single hair. Have you ever counted how many of yours now belong to him?"

"No."

"I cannot tell you that exactly either, but I know how many you have which are still your own. You have one left! You see it is long past the time for repentance."

"But if a man is lost when but one of his hairs belongs to the devil," said Thibault, "why cannot God likewise save a man in virtue of a single hair?"

"Well, try if that is so!"

"And, besides, when I concluded that unhappy bargain with you, I did not understand that it was to be a compact of this kind."

"Oh, yes! I know all about the bad faith of you men! Was it no compact then to consent to give me your hairs, you stupid fool? Since men invented baptism, we do not know how to get hold of them, and so, in return for any concessions we make them, we are bound to insist on their relinquishing to us some part of their body on which we can lay hands. You gave us the hairs of your head; they are firmly rooted, as you have proved yourself and will not come away in our grasp … No, no, Thibault, you have belonged to us ever since, standing on the threshold of the door that was once there, you cherished within your thoughts of deceit and violence."

"And so," cried Thibault passionately, rising and stamping his foot, "and so I am lost as regards the next world without having enjoyed the pleasures of this!"

"You can yet enjoy these."

"And how, I pray."

"By boldly following the path that you have struck by chance, and resolutely determining on a course of conduct which you have adopted as yet only in a halfhearted way; in short, by frankly owning yourself to be one of us."

"And how am I to do this?"

"Take my place."

"And what then?"

"You will then acquire my power, and you will have nothing left to wish for."

"If your power is so great, if it can give you all the riches that I long for, why do you give it up?"

"Do not trouble yourself about me. The master for whom I shall have won a retainer will liberally reward me."

"And if I take your place, shall I also have to take your form?"

"Yes, in the nighttime; by day you will be a man again."

"The nights are long, dark, full of snares; I may be brought down by a bullet from a keeper, or be caught in a trap, and then goodbye riches, goodbye position and pleasure."

"Not so; for this skin that covers me is impenetrable by iron, lead or steel. As long as it protects your body, you will be not only invulnerable, but immortal; once a year, like all werewolves, you will become a wolf again for four and twenty hours, and during that interval, you will be in danger of death like any other animal. I had just reached that dangerous time a year ago today, when we first met."

"Ah!" said Thibault. "That explains why you feared my Lord baron's dogs."

"When we have dealings with men, we are forbidden to speak anything but the truth, and the whole truth; it is for them to accept or refuse."

"You have boasted to me of the power that I should acquire; tell me, now, in what that power will consist?"

"It will be such that even the most powerful king will not be able to withstand it, since his power is limited by the human and the possible."

"Shall I be rich?"

"So rich, that you will come in time to despise riches, since, by the mere force of your will, you will obtain not only what men can only acquire with gold and silver, but also all that superior beings get by their conjurations."

"Shall I be able to revenge myself on my enemies?"

"You will have unlimited power over everything which is connected with evil."

"If I love a woman, will there again be a possibility of my losing her?"

"As you will have dominion over all your fellow creatures, you will be able to do with them what you like."

"There will be no power to enable them to escape from the trammels of my will?"

"Nothing, except death, which is stronger than all."

"And I shall only run the risk of death myself on one day out of the three hundred and sixty-five?"

"On one day only; during the remaining days nothing can harm you, neither iron, lead, nor steel, neither water, nor fire."

"And there is no deceit, no trap to catch me, in your words?"

"None, on my honor as a wolf!"

"Good," said Thibault. "Then let it be so; a wolf for four and twenty hours, for the rest of the time the monarch of creation! What am I to do? I am ready."

"Pick a holly leaf, tear it in three pieces with your teeth, and throw it away from you, as far as you can."

Thibault did as he was commanded.

Having torn the leaf in three pieces, he scattered them on the air, and although the night till then had been a peaceful one, there was immediately heard a loud peal of thunder, while a tempestuous whirlwind arose, which caught up the fragments and carried them whirling away with it.

"And now, brother Thibault," said the wolf, "take my place, and good luck be with you! As was my case just a year ago, so you will have to become a wolf for four and twenty hours; you must endeavor to come out of the ordeal as happily as I did, thanks to you, and then you will see realized all that I have promised you. Meanwhile, I will pray the lord of the cloven hoof that he will protect you from the teeth of the baron's hounds, for, by the devil himself, I take a genuine interest in you, friend Thibault."

And then it seemed to Thibault that he saw the black wolf grow larger and taller, that it stood up on its hind legs and finally walked away in the form of a man, who made a sign to him with his hand as he disappeared.

We say it seemed to him, for Thibault's ideas, for a second or two, became very indistinct. A feeling of torpor passed over him, paralyzing his power of thought. When he came to himself, he was alone. His limbs were imprisoned in a new and unusual form; he had, in short, become in every respect the counterpart of the black wolf that a few minutes before had been speaking to him. One single white hair on his head alone shone in contrast to the remainder of the somber colored fur; this one white hair of the wolf was the one black hair which had remained to the man.

Thibault had scarcely had time to recover himself when he fancied he heard a rustling among the bushes, and the sound of a low, muffled bark ... He thought of the baron and his hounds, and trembled. Thus metamorphosed into the black wolf, he decided that he would not do what his predecessor had done, and wait till the dogs were upon him. It was probably a blood-hound he had heard, and he would get away before the hounds were uncoupled.

He made off, striking straight ahead, as is the manner of wolves, and it was a profound satisfaction to him to find that in his new form he had tenfold his former strength and elasticity of limb.

"By the devil and his horns!" the voice of the Lord of Vez was now heard to say to his new huntsman a few paces off. "You hold the leash too slack, my lad; you have let the bloodhound give tongue, and we shall never head the wolf back now."

"I was in fault, I do not deny it, my lord; but as I saw it go by last evening only a few yards from this spot, I never guessed that it would take up its quarters for the night in this part of the wood and that it was so close to us as all that."

"Are you sure it is the same one that has got away from us so often?"

"May the bread I eat in your service choke me, my lord, if it is not the same black wolf that we were chasing last year when poor Marcotte was drowned."

"I should like finely to put the dogs on its track," said the baron, with a sigh.

"My lord has but to give the order, and we will do so, but he will allow me to observe that we have still two good hours of darkness before us, time enough for every horse we have to break its legs."

"That may be, but if we wait for the day, l'Eveillé, the fellow will have had time to get ten leagues away."

"Ten leagues at least," said l'Eveillé, shaking his head.

"I have got this cursed black wolf on my brain," added the baron. "And I have such a longing to have its skin, that I feel sure I shall catch an illness if I do not get hold of it."

"Well then, my lord, let us have the dogs out without a moment's loss of time."

"You are right, l'Eveillé; go and fetch the hounds."

L'Eveillé went back to his horse, that he had tied to a tree outside the wood, and went off at a gallop, and in ten minutes' time, which seemed like ten centuries to the baron, he was back with the whole hunting train. The hounds were immediately uncoupled.

"Gently, gently, my lads!" said the Lord of Vez. "You forget you are not handling your old well-trained dogs; if you get excited with these raw recruits, they'll merely kick up a devil of a row, and be no more good than so many turnspits; let 'em get warmed up by degrees."

And, indeed, the dogs were no sooner loose, than two or three got at once on to the scent of the werewolf, and began to give cry, whereupon the others joined them. The whole pack started off on Thibault's track, at first quietly following up the scent, and only giving cry at long intervals, then more excitedly and of more accord, until they had so thoroughly imbibed the odor of the wolf ahead of them, and the scent had become so strong, that they tore along, baying furiously, and with unparalleled eagerness in the direction of the Yvors coppice.

"Well begun, is half done!" cried the baron. "You look after the relays, l'Eveillé; I want them ready whenever needed! I will encourage the dogs ... And you be on the alert, you others," he added, addressing himself to the younger keepers. "We have more than one defeat to avenge, and if I lose this view halloo through the fault of anyone among you, by the devil and his horns! He shall be the dogs' quarry in place of the wolf!"

After pronouncing these words of encouragement, the baron put his horse to the gallop, and although it was still pitch dark and the ground was rough, he kept the animal going at top speed so as to come up with the hounds, which could be heard giving tongue in the low lands about Bourg-Fontaine.

HUNTING DOWN THE WEREWOLF

T hibault had got well ahead of the dogs, thanks to the precaution he had taken of making good his escape at the first note of the bloodhound. For some time he heard no further sound of pursuit; but, all at once, like distant thunder, the baying of the hounds reached his ears, and he began to feel some anxiety. He had been trotting, but he now went on at greater speed, and did not pause till he had put a few more leagues between himself and his enemies. Then he stood still and took his bearings; he found himself on the heights at Montaigu. He bent his head and listened—the dogs still seemed a long way off, somewhere near the Tillet coppice.

It required a wolf's ear to distinguish them so far off. Thibault went down the hill again, as if to meet the dogs; then, leaving Erneville to the left, he leaped into the little stream which rises there, waded down its course as far as Grimancourt, dashed into the woods of Lessart-l'Abbesse, and finally gained the forest of Compiègne. He was somewhat reassured to find that, in spite of his three hours' hard running, the steel like muscles of his wolf legs were not in the least fatigued. He hesitated, however, to trust himself in a forest which was not so familiar to him as that of Villers-Cotterets.

After another dash of a mile or so, he decided that by doubling boldly he would be most likely to put the dogs off the scent. He crossed at a gallop all the stretch of plain between Pierrefond and Mont-Gobert, took to the woods at the Champ Meutard, came out again at Vauvaudrand, regained the stream by the Sancères timber floatage, and once more found himself in the forest near Long-Pont. Unfortunately for him, just as he reached the end of the Route du Pendu, he came across another pack of twenty dogs, which Monsieur de Montbreton's huntsman was bringing up as a relay, for the baron had sent his neighbor news of the chase.

Instantly the hounds were uncoupled by the huntsman as he caught sight of the wolf, for seeing that the latter kept its distance, he feared it would get too far ahead if he waited for the others to come up before loosing his dogs. And now began the struggle between the werewolf and the dogs in very earnest. It was a wild chase, which the horses, in spite of their skilled riders, had great difficulty in following, a chase over plains, through woods, across heaths, pursued at a headlong pace. As the hunt flew by, it appeared and disappeared like a flash of lightning across a cloud, leaving behind a whirlwind of dust, and a sound of horns and cries which echo had hardly time to repeat. It rushed over hill and dale, through torrents and bogs, and over precipices, as if horses and dogs had been winged like Hippogriffs and Chimeras. The baron had come up with his huntsmen, riding at their head, and almost riding on the tails of his dogs, his eye flashing, his nostrils dilated, exciting the pack with wild shouts and furious blasts, digging his spurs into his horse's sides whenever an obstacle of any kind caused it to hesitate for a single instant. The black wolf, on his side, still held on at the same rapid pace; although sorely shaken at hearing the fresh pack in full pursuit only a short way behind him, just as he had got back to the forest, he had not lost an inch of ground. As he retained to the full all his human consciousness, it seemed to him impossible, as he still ran on, that he should not escape in safety from this ordeal; he felt that it was not possible for him to die before he had taken vengeance for all the agony that others made him suffer, before he had known those pleasures that had been promised him, above all—for at this critical moment his thoughts kept on running on this—before he had gained Agnelette's love. At moments he was possessed by terror, at others by anger. He thought at times that he would turn and face this yelling pack of dogs, and, forgetting his present form, scatter them with stones and blows. Then, an instant after, feeling mad with rage, deafened by the death knell the hounds were ringing in his ears, he fled, he leaped, he flew with the legs of a deer, with the wings of an eagle. But his efforts were in vain; he might run, leap, almost fly, the sounds of death still clung to him, and if for a moment they became more distant, it was only to hear them a moment after nearer and more threatening still. But still the instinct of self-preservation did not fail him; and still his strength was undiminished; only, if by ill luck, he were to come across other relays, he felt that it might give way. So he determined to take a bold course so as to out distance the dogs, and to get back to his lairs, where he knew his ground and hoped to evade the dogs. He therefore doubled for the second time. He first ran back to Puiseux, then skirted past Viviers, regained the forest of Compiègne, made a dash into the forest of Largue, returned and crossed the Aisne at Attichy, and finally got back to the forest of Villers-Cotterets at the low lands of Argent. He trusted in this way to baffle the strategical plans of the Lord of Vez, who had, no doubt, posted his dogs at various likely points.

Once back in his old quarters Thibault breathed more freely. He was now on the banks of the Ourcq between Norroy and Trouennes, where the river runs at the foot of deep rocks on either side; he leaped up on to a sharp pointed crag overhanging the water, and from this high vantage ground he sprang into the waves below, then swam to a crevice at the base of the rock from which he had leapt, which was situated rather below the ordinary level of the water, and here, at the back of this cave, he waited. He had gained at least three miles upon the dogs; and yet, scarcely another ten minutes had elapsed, when the whole pack arrived and stormed the crest of the rock. Those who were leading, mad with excitement, did not see the gulf in front of them, or else, like their quarry they thought they would leap safely into it, for they plunged, and Thibault was splashed, far back as he was hidden, by the water that was scattered in every direction as they fell into it one by one. Less fortunate, however, and less vigorous than he was, they were unable to fight against the current, and after vainly battling with it, they were borne along out of sight before they had even got scent of the were-wolf's retreat. Overhead he could hear the tramping of the horses' feet, the baying of the dogs that were still left, the cries of men, and above all these sounds, dominating the other voices, that of the baron as he cursed and swore. When the last dog had fallen into the water, and been carried away like the others, he saw, thanks to a bend in the river, that the huntsmen were going down it, and persuaded that the baron, whom he recognized at the head of his hunting train, would only do this with the intention of coming up it again, he determined not to wait for this, and left his hiding place. Now swimming, now leaping with agility from one rock to the other, at times wading through the water, he went up the river to the end of the Crêne coppice. Certain that he had now made a considerable advance on his enemies, he resolved to get to one of the villages near and run in and out among the houses, feeling sure that they would not think of coming after him there. He thought of Préciamont; if any village was well known to him, it was that; and then, at Préciamont, he would be near Agnelette. He felt that this neighborhood would put fresh vigor into him, and would bring him good fortune, and that the gentle image of the innocent girl would have some influence on his fate. So he started off in that direction. It was now six o'clock in the evening; the hunt had lasted nearly fifteen hours, and wolf, dogs and huntsmen had covered fifty leagues at least. When, at last, after circling round by Manereux and Oigny, the black wolf reached the borders of the heath by the lane of Ham, the sun was already beginning to sink, and shedding a dazzling light over the flowery plain; the little white and pink flowers scented the breeze that played caressingly around them; the grasshopper was singing in its little house of moss, and the lark was soaring up towards heaven, saluting the eve with its song, as twelve hours before it had saluted the morn. The peaceful beauty of nature had a strange effect on Thibault. It seemed enigmatical to him that nature could be so smiling and beautiful, while anguish such as his was devouring his soul. He saw the flowers, and heard the insects and the birds, and he compared the quiet joy of this innocent world with the horrible pangs he was enduring, and asked himself, whether after all, notwithstanding all the new promises that had been made him by the devil's envoy, he had acted any more wisely in making this second compact than he had in making the first. He began to doubt whether he might not find himself deceived in the one as he had been in the other.

As he went along a little footpath nearly hidden under the golden broom, he suddenly remembered that it was by this very path that he had taken Agnelette home on the first day of their acquaintance; the day, when inspired by his good angel, he had asked her to be his wife. The thought that, thanks to this new compact, he might be able to recover Agnelette's love, revived his spirits, which had been saddened and depressed by the sight of the universal happiness around him. He heard the church bells at Préciamont ringing in the valley below; its solemn, monotonous tones recalled the thought of his fellow men to the black wolf, and of all he had to fear from them. So he ran boldly on, across the fields, to the village, where he hoped to find a refuge in some empty building. As he was skirting the little stone wall of the village cemetery, he heard a sound of voices, approaching along the road he was in. He could not fail to meet whoever they might be who were coming towards him, if he himself went on; it was not safe to turn back, as he would have to cross some rising ground whence he might easily be seen; so there was nothing left for it but to jump over the wall of the cemetery, and with a bound he was on the other side. This grave-yard as usual adjoined the church; it was uncared for, and over-grown with tall grass, while brambles and thorns grew rankly in places.

The wolf made for the thickest of these bramble bushes; he found a sort of ruined vault, whence he could look out without being seen, and he crept under the branches and hid himself inside. A few yards away from him was a newly dug grave; within the church could be heard the chanting of the priests, the more distinctly that the vault must at one time have communi-cated by a passage with the crypt. Presently the chanting ceased, and the black wolf, who did not feel quite at ease in the neigh-borhood of a church, and thought that the road must now be clear, decided that it was time to start off again and to find a safer retreat than the one he had fled to in his haste.

But he had scarcely got his nose outside the bramble bush when the gate of the cemetery opened, and he quickly retreated again to his hole, in great trepidation as to who might now be approaching. The first person he saw was a child dressed in a white alb and carrying a vessel of holy water; he was followed by a man in a surplice, bearing a silver cross, and after the latter came a priest, chanting the psalms for the dead.

Behind these were four peasants carrying a bier covered with a white pall over which were scattered green branches and flow-ers, and beneath the sheet could be seen the outline of a coffin; a few villagers from Préciamont wound up this little procession. Although there was nothing unusual in such a sight as this, seeing that he was in a cemetery, and that the newly dug grave must have prepared him for it, Thibault, nevertheless, felt strangely moved as he looked on. Although the slightest movement might betray his presence and bring destruction upon him, he anxiously watched every detail of the ceremony.

The priest having blessed the newly made grave, the peasants laid down their burden on an adjoining hillock. It is the custom in our country when a young girl, or young married woman, dies in the fullness of her youth and beauty, to carry her to the graveyard in an open coffin, with only a pall over her, so that her friends may bid her a last farewell, her relations give her a last kiss. Then the coffin is nailed down, and all is over. An old woman, led by some kind hand, for she was apparently blind, went up to the coffin to give the dead one a last kiss; the peasants lifted the pall from the still face, and there lay Agnelette.

A low groan escaped from Thibault's agonized breast, and mingled with the tears and sobs of those present. Agnelette, as she lay there so pale in death, wrapped in an ineffable calm, appeared more beautiful than when in life, beneath her wreath of forget-me-nots and daisies. As Thibault looked upon the poor dead girl, his heart seemed suddenly to melt within him. It was he, as he had truly realized, who had really killed her, and he experienced a genuine and overpowering sorrow, the more poignant since for the first time for many long months he forgot to think of himself, and thought only of the dead woman, now lost to him forever.

As he heard the blows of the hammer knocking the nails into the coffin, as he heard the earth and stones being shoveled into the grave and falling with a dull thud on to the body of the only woman he had ever loved, a feeling of giddiness came over him. The hard stones he thought must be bruising Agnelette's tender flesh, so fresh and sweet but a few days ago, and only yesterday still throbbing with life, and he made a movement as if to rush out on the assailants and snatch away the body, which dead, must surely belong to him, since, living, it had belonged to another.

But the grief of the man overcame this instinct of the wild

beast at bay; a shudder passed through the body hidden beneath its wolf skin; tears fell from the fierce blood-red eyes, and the unhappy man cried out: "O God! Take my life, I give it gladly, if only by my death I may give back life to her whom I have killed!"

The words were followed by such an appalling howl, that all who were in the cemetery fled, and the place was left utterly deserted. Almost at the same moment, the hounds, having recovered the scent, came leaping in over the wall, followed by the baron, streaming with sweat as he rode his horse, which was covered with foam and blood.

The dogs made straight for the bramble bush, and began worrying something hidden there.

"Halloo! Halloo!! Halloo!!!" cried the Lord of Vez, in a voice of thunder, as he leapt from his horse, not caring if there was anyone or not to look after it, and drawing out his hunting knife, he dashed towards the vault, forcing his way through the hounds. He found them fighting over a fresh and bleeding wolf skin, but the body had disappeared.

There was no mistake as to its being the skin of the werewolf that they had been hunting, for with the exception of one white hair, it was entirely black. What had become of the body? No one ever knew. Only as from this time forth Thibault was never seen again, it was generally believed that the former sabot maker and no other was the werewolf.

Furthermore, as the skin had been found without the body, and, as, from the spot where it was found a peasant reported to have heard someone speak the words: "O God! Take my life! I give it gladly, if only by my death I may give back life to her whom I have killed," the priest declared openly that Thibault, by reason of his sacrifice and repentance, had been saved!

And what added to the consistency of belief in this tradition was, that every year on the anniversary of Agnelette's death, up to the time when the Monasteries were all abolished at the Revolution, a monk from the Abbey of the Premonstratensians at Bourg-Fontaine, which stands half a league from Préciamont, was seen to come and pray beside her grave.

SUCH IS the history of the black wolf, as it was told to me by old Mocquet, my father's keeper.

ABOUT THE AUTHOR

Alexandre Dumas, also known as Alexandre Dumas père, was born July 24, 1802, in Villers-Cotterêts, France.

Born Dumas Davy de la Pailleterie, he adopted the Dumas family name from his grandmother, a Dominican slave. Despite encountering societal prejudice because he was one-quarter black, Dumas managed to break into French literary circles and became one of the most respected and successful authors of French literature.

He began writing plays after working as a scribe for the Duke of Orleans (later named King Louis Philippe) during the 1830 revolution. Dumas was a prolific writer, best known for novels such as *The Three Musketeers*, *The Man in the Iron Mask*, and *The Count of Monte Cristo*. His work has been translated into more than 100 languages and adapted into a multitude of films.

After suffering a stroke, he died on December 5, 1870, in Puys, France, and was buried in the family vault. In 2002, he was exhumed and reinterred in the hallowed Pantheon in Paris, among other French luminaries.

IF YOU LIKED ...

IF YOU LIKED THE WOLF LEADER, YOU MIGHT ALSO ENJOY:

The Complete War of the Worlds
by H.G. Wells

The War in the Air
by H.G. Wells

The Detective Stories of Edgar Allan Poe
by Edgar Allan Poe

This book was produced as part of the Publishing MA program for Western Colorado University's Graduate Program in Creative Writing.

OTHER WORDFIRE PRESS TITLES

Cold Black Hearts
by Jeffery J. Mariotte

Zomnibus
by Kevin J. Anderson

Residue
by Steve Diamond

Our list of other WordFire Press authors and titles is always growing. To find out more and to see our selection of titles, visit us at:
wordfirepress.com